Realm of Eternal
Blossoms

GUMIHO KISS

CLAIRE KOHLER

First published by Scattered Light Books 2025

This book is a work of fiction. Names, characters, places, and incidents are either the product of the author's imagination or are used fictitiously.

Paperback and ebook cover by MiblArt

Hardback cover by Blue Raven Book Covers

Editing by Amber Lambda

ISBN: 979-8-9855674-4-1

For all the Kdrama fans who wanted the silent bodyguard to get the girl. You're welcome.

Author's Note

While this is a work of fiction, it is also a love letter to Korean culture. I always wish to be respectful of the Korean community and did a tremendous amount of research to portray the early Joseon dynasty in an accurate light (excluding some creative liberties, like making Chin Sun more defiant than she likely would have been in real life). However, writing about a culture different from my own means I have implicit biases despite my best efforts. It is my earnest desire not to misrepresent the culture that inspired this story and instead showcase its beauty to my audience. If this story in any way does not do that, you have my sincere apology, and I humbly ask for your understanding as I continue to grow in my knowledge of Korean history, customs, and perspectives.

This story also contains other elements that may be upsetting to readers. Within these pages, you will read about violence, death, classism, fire, and betrayal. Please proceed with this in mind.

Jurchen
Ming Dynasty
Hamgyŏng
P'yŏngan
Joseon
The Realm of Eternal Blossoms
P'unghae
East Sea
Gangwŏn
Hanseong
Gyeonggi
Sokju
Yellow
Sea
Chungcheong
Gyeongsang
Jeolla

Joseon Social Classes

Yangban - Ruling nobility. Class of scholar-officials. Exempt from taxes and military conscription. Legally required to have at least one family member within three generations accepted as an official to maintain yangban status, but bribery and corruption has made this a moot technicality.

Jungin - Middle class. Also exempt from taxes and military conscription. Consists of educated specialists, such as interpreters, scribes, astronomers, musicians, and jurists. Also includes illegitimate children of yangban. Thought of as nobles by the sangmin and cheonmin. The smallest class.

Sangmin - Commoner class. Includes fishermen, merchants, farmers, and craftsmen. The vast majority of Joseon is part of this class.

Cheonmin - Lowest class in Joseon social hierarchy. Includes entertainers, butchers, blacksmiths, gravediggers, executioners, hunters, and slaves. Considered unclean by the higher classes because of the nature of their occupations.

Status is hereditary, making social advancement impossible.

Prologue

The best stories were the ones that made Hyun Soo a little frightened. Most of them involved goblin trickery or vengeful ghosts, but his favorite was about a great dragon. That was the one he begged his grandmother to tell him so many times he could recite it by heart.

This is how it went.

Long ago, back when the land of Jeoseung was young, all the magical races lived there in harmony. Gumiho, imugi, grim reapers, haetae, and even goblins. It was a realm of plenty, without hardship or strife, save for one thing: mortality.

Though some of the races were longer lived than others, all had to face this same truth, that their lives weren't fated to last forever. To compensate for their sad fate, some hid away in their caves and valleys, doing all they could to preserve the time that was given to them. But others were more daring.

Jeoseung was not the only land they could traverse, for a magical gate existed that allowed one to pass into a second land known as the Realm of Eternal Blossoms. It was populated by fearful creatures who called themselves humans. And they were quick to kill that which they feared.

But the human realm wasn't all bad. If a monster was cautious and didn't allow his true nature to be discovered, he could enjoy luxuries unheard of in Jeoseung. For the shapeshifting races, the goblins and gumiho, hiding their true selves was fairly easy. The grim reapers, who walked between realms without needing a gate, could vanish before they suffered harm. These three—goblin, gumiho, reaper— found great enjoyment straddling both worlds, and often brought back treasures for their kinsmen to partake in.

Wars in the human realm were common, but the residents of Jeoseung knew better than to engage in their neighbors' violence. Peace, equality, and kindness were all the magical races had ever known, and they had no intention of changing that.

Until the night immortality fell from the heavens.

It came in the form of a brilliant white star, which plummeted to the ground one spring evening. A kind-hearted imugi happened to witness its descent and drew closer to investigate. As soon as he touched the mysterious star, he was infused with power. It bestowed on him great beauty, strength, and agelessness, transforming him from a mere serpent into a mighty dragon.

He was ecstatic with his good fortune and wished to share it with all of Jeoseung. He rallied the other imugi first, but as soon as one touched the star and accepted its blessings, some of the star's brilliance began to fade. Fearful of what might happen if the star were to burn out, the great dragon hid it away, encouraging the other imugi to search the world for stars of their own instead.

To make up for his selfishness, the dragon freely offered his wisdom to those who needed it, helping the creatures of

Jeoseung flourish. The only caveat he gave was that his words must always be used for good rather than evil.

One day, a crafty goblin came to him disguised as a nine-tailed fox, asking how one might obtain justice for a wrong committed against him. The dragon told the goblin to seek recompense for that which had been done, but the goblin explained woefully that his entire family had died and there was nothing that could replace what he'd lost. The dragon was filled with fury on the goblin's behalf and demanded to know who was responsible. The goblin named the grim reapers, whose job it was to watch over the magical races, claiming they'd misused their authority to fill their own pockets, and his family had subsequently perished. The dragon, fooled by the deception, demanded that the grim reapers answer for their crime.

But the grim reapers denied all wrongdoing, incensed that a gumiho would tell such wicked lies. They fell upon their fox brothers, who fought back with all the ferocity they were shown. Thousands were slain on both sides, their blood spreading over the world.

The dragon watched from his cave, growing more and more sorrowful as the years passed and the war continued. Eventually, his remorse grew so overwhelming, he took his own life, leaving the star unguarded for the first time in centuries.

Which was what the goblins, waiting patiently in the shadows, had been waiting for.

As soon as the dragon was dead, they swarmed into his cave, searching tirelessly until they unearthed their prize. With the star now in their possession, the most powerful among them declared himself king of Jeoseung and demanded that the other races submit to his rule.

The haetae and imugi, desperate to have peace again,

accepted the goblin king's decree. But the gumiho and grim reapers were outraged, finally recognizing their true enemy had never been each other. The two races banded together against their oppressors, and with their combined might, they overthrew the goblins and banished them to the land of humans.

To keep the goblins from ever returning, they sealed the magical gate between realms, making it impossible for anyone but a grim reaper to pass safely in between. Thus, peace was restored, but it came at a terrible price. The magical races who spent too long in the Realm of Eternal Blossoms eventually forgot their commitment to honor and virtue, slowly transforming into the evil beings humans are right to fear.

"What about the star? What happened to it?" young Hyun Soo always asked.

But his halmeoni never gave him an answer.

Chapter 1

The Fox

Early Joseon dynasty

Night belonged to thieves, killers, and foxes. Gwishin, being all three, glided through the darkness with almost silent footsteps, leaping from rooftop to rooftop like her ghostly namesake.

She had to be cautious. Police officers patrolled the streets of Sokju during curfew, and the city's new magistrate, Hong Shik, had recently increased the security around his office even further. Thieves and mercenaries were more common around here than rats, but they weren't what Hong truly feared. The guards he'd hired were well-trained, some even reputedly former assassins. Such skilled men didn't come at a low price, nor were they necessary for the average criminal.

But Gwishin was no average criminal.

Some part of Chin Sun wondered if she should stay in tonight, lie low for a while. She'd almost been caught the last time she'd donned her face cloth and black hanbok, and with reports of Wokou pirates from the East lurking around the outlying villages, tensions in Sokju were higher than ever. If she waited a few weeks, Hong would relax a bit, and she would be free to roam the night again without fear.

Yet the promised reward was too tempting to ignore. If the intelligence she'd gathered was accurate, an illicit deal was going to take place in Hong's office this very evening. A rumor was circulating that the pirates had infiltrated Sokju —and Hong was in league with them.

If that slug proved himself a traitor tonight . . .

The world shifted, colors merging even as her surroundings became more precise. The price one must pay for the eyes of a fox.

Contrary to her neighbors' superstitions, Chin Sun could tap into her gumiho abilities at will and didn't need to first transform into the nine-tailed monster parents warned their children of.

Humans believed gumiho were wholly evil, consumed by lust and malice. Chin Sun didn't know how other gumiho lived, having never met any magical beings besides herself, but she suspected the stories about them were more fiction than fact. She certainly didn't lurk around cemeteries or eat human livers, nor was she hundreds of years old. As far as she could tell, her body aged just like a human's, and her diet was much the same.

She *was* keen on mice and berries while in nine-tailed fox form, but opportunities to shift had become rarer as she'd grown older and taken on more responsibilities. She only dared discard her human facade in the safety of the forest, where mist and shadow were her closest friends. So far, none of the townsfolk seemed to suspect their masked guardian was more than human, and she intended to keep it that way.

Chin Sun paused when the police bureau came into view. Great stone walls surrounded the outer courtyard, which connected to a covered terrace directly above the entrance. A large wooden plaque hung below the platform's eaves, identifying the compound as Sokju's police head-quarters. Four square flags jutted out from the terrace like spears, banners fluttering in the light breeze.

She counted the guards at the entrance, noting their stiff postures. Two at ground level and three on the upper level. Assassins or not, they were definitely more intimidating than the ones she'd slipped past last month. One guard glanced toward her, and she drew back from the roof's curved edge.

Her heart pounded. Had he seen her?

When no cries of alarm followed, she sneaked to the back of the building and dropped to the ground. Five guards should be easy enough to disarm, but she needed to witness Hong's treachery before she gave away her position.

The light emanating from the magistrate's office was a good sign, but she couldn't hear anything from this far away. She had to get closer.

She reached for the bow slung across her back, then changed her mind. She tossed a stray rock down the alley behind her, the sound quiet enough that only the closest guard noticed. He whistled to the man nearest him, then marched toward the alley alone.

Chin Sun tucked herself into the recess of a doorway, waiting until he'd passed by to strike. With a sharp blow to the back of his head, he was out cold, as useless as a dead fish.

She huffed. She'd thought he'd be more interesting than tha—

Chin Sun whipped around, meeting the second guard's hwando with her own. His narrow eyes assessed her, but her black mask and robes were indistinguishable from the garb of Sokju's criminal underbelly. He would find no markers, no clues to her true identity. She had too much at stake for carelessness.

She pushed forward, her strength more than enough to match her assailant's. He grunted under the strain but didn't fold.

A third guard appeared in the alley, swiping his sword at her.

Chin Sun jumped back, glancing between her opponents. She needed to incapacitate them quickly; otherwise, they'd sound the alarm and the meeting she'd been waiting weeks for would be over.

They must have had the same thought she did, for they turned and darted back toward the compound. Too slow. Chin Sun swept forward, bringing her blade down upon one's head, then the other's.

The guards collapsed to the ground, and Chin Sun dragged their bodies into the alley with the first, safely out of sight. She vaulted over the left compound wall and pressed her back against the interior wall. Footsteps rumbled nearby in a steady rhythm. More guards on patrol.

She waited until they'd crossed the outer courtyard to the entrance, then scurried through the inner courtyard to the main pavilion where the magistrate conducted his business dealings.

Voices whispered within, one of them unmistakably Hong's. The foreign language they spoke was enough to answer Chin Sun's question of the man's loyalty. Unlike most women in Joseon, she'd had the privilege to study multiple languages from an early age, and the hushed conversation was too monotone to belong to the Ming. The whispers tickling Chin Sun's ears were Japanese.

So, he *was* in league with pirates. . . . Reports of attacks on the coast had been frequent lately, but Hong had always sworn he would protect the citizens of Sokju, no matter the cost.

Another lie. Chin Sun scolded herself for the way her heart deflated. She shouldn't be surprised Hong was just as corrupt as the officials who'd come before him. She would deal with him the same way she'd dealt with the rest.

And then what? Where did it end? Hong Shik was Sokju's fifth magistrate in the past four years. Every time she found enough proof to put one behind bars, a worse one sprang up in his place.

She just needed to convince Kim Min Joon to stop skulking about in corners and take the position. He would—

She broke off. She could hardly expect her old friend to step out of the shadows when she was doing the very same thing. Kim Min Joon may have been the son of a prominent yangban and a great candidate for magistrate, but he didn't want to be in the spotlight any more than she did. He preferred being out on the streets among the people he was serving, not stuck behind a desk doing paperwork, even if it did afford more prestige than his current job as a police inspector.

"There he is," called a voice from above.

Chin Sun ducked as an arrow whistled through the air, missing her by a hairsbreadth before it plunged into the ground. More followed in quick succession, raining down like fire from the heavens.

What? Where were they? She swung around, honing in on four men perched on the pavilion roof behind her.

Before they could nock their arrows a second time, Chin Sun darted behind the magistrate's office, adrenaline pouring through her veins.

"After him!"

She took a deep breath as feet rattled against rooftop tiles and a series of dull thuds hit her ears. One, two, three, four.

Chin Sun unsheathed her blade, but when she stepped out of hiding, ten faces sneered back at her, arrows at the ready. Where had they come from? She'd never fought so many at once before.

"Surrender, and your death will be quick," shouted the leader.

Gwishin withdrew, fleeing south toward the market. More arrows flew by, but she didn't stop. She had to keep going while she still could.

She cried out as pain erupted in her upper arm. One of the arrows was lodged in her flesh, creating a thin trickle of blood. She stumbled to a stop, then sped back up again as the guards drew nearer.

Just a little farther. She crouched behind a stall full of brassware, heart racing as the guards ran past.

Murmurs filled her ears, followed by a few shouts and more pounding feet. Too many to just be the magistrate's guards. The night patrolmen must be searching for her now, too.

Chin Sun's home lay in the center of Sokju, as was customary for yangban and jungin families. Yangban were the highest class in Joseon society and, apart from the royal family, the most powerful. Jungin, on the other hand, were considered middle class and, while privileged, didn't enjoy the same benefits as their highborn neighbors.

Since Sokju's government offices were also in the heart of the city, Chin Sun knew better than to return straight home after a night out as Gwishin. Instead, she normally disappeared into the forest at the city's outskirts before circling back home.

But tonight, she wasn't sure that was an option. The pain in her arm was making her dizzy, and she couldn't afford to pass out. She had to get home, and fast.

She hurried back the way she'd come, then cut through some side streets until she reached a familiar stone wall surrounding a group of raised pavilions with lanterns hanging from their eaves. Home.

Would everyone still be asleep?

Chin Sun threw herself over the wall and slunk through the courtyard until she reached her quarters, chest heaving. She went to her secret stash of medical supplies behind the folding screen at the back of her room, then shoved a piece of cloth in her mouth. After slicing off the arrowhead, she yanked at the shaft, the cloth muffling her pained moan.

The shaft came free, but blood streamed onto her clothes. Chin Sun took off her black robe and white underjacket, exposing the wound. She grabbed a handful of dried orchid root powder and pressed it into her injury to stop the bleeding, then began wrapping the area. Now that her adrenaline was wearing off, the burning in her arm was growing more intense.

Sharp knocks at the gate interrupted her, followed by a cacophony of voices and footsteps. Uncle's voice rose above the din, but she couldn't make out his words.

Had they found her? Chin Sun's fear was slick, pulsating, seeping through her pores and filling her nostrils. She ripped the gauze with her teeth and tied it off before stuffing all her incriminating evidence behind the painted screen. She put a fresh sokjeogori underjacket over her shoulders, wincing as the fabric touched her arm.

When the voices outside died away, Chin Sun sighed in relief and crawled onto her sleeping mat. She'd made it, barely. How much longer could she keep this up? At the rate she was going, they were going to find her out soon.

She'd deal with that when it got here. For now, she needed to sleep so she could recover. Her healing rate was faster than a human's, but her body could only take so much.

"Chin Sun-ah, are you awake?" called a nasally voice.

Chin Sun jerked into an upright position. A silhouette hesitated outside the hanji doors, one she recognized like the thrumming of her own heart. "Cousin, what is it?"

A young woman burst into the room, clothed only in her silk undergarments. She threw herself to the floor, trembling all over. "Unni, one of the servants said Gwishin was spotted just outside the house. Father is taking care of it."

"Oh, he is? Good. You need not worry, then. Uncle will keep us safe," Chin Sun replied, more breathless than she would have liked.

Her younger cousin was easily excited, and something as unusual as a sighting of the infamous vigilante would probably keep her awake for several hours.

Sang Mi frowned, then glanced at the door. "I wonder why Gwishin would come here. . . ." She shook her head. "It's late. I apologize for waking you. I just wanted to let you know."

The chagrin in Sang Mi's eyes was genuine, but Chin Sun knew her cousin would do the same thing again within a few days. Sang Mi lacked restraint, even at sixteen, but Chin Sun loved her too dearly to fault her for it.

"I'm glad you told me." She lifted her mouth into a grin despite the flames shooting through her arm.

Sang Mi smiled back. "Of course. I wanted to make sure you were all right, too. You are all right, aren't you?"

Chin Sun nodded. "Yeh, but I am very tired. It was a long day. Might we discuss this more in the morning?"

"Oh, yeh. I'm sorry." Sang Mi bowed, cracked open the paper doors, and scampered out.

Chin Sun stared at the door long after her cousin was gone, stomach still tight. Another night, another crisis averted.

But what would happen when she wasn't fast enough to get away?

Chapter 2

The Bodyguard

Sunlight and the sweet scent of spider lilies announced the morning as Chin Sun opened her eyes. The shuffling feet of servants on the other side of her latticed doors were comforting, easing the tension that remained in her shoulders even though five days had passed since she'd fled the magistrate's office.

"Everything is fine," she repeated for the hundredth time. No one knew anything; if they did, they would have already come for her. Everything was normal.

Chin Sun hadn't fully convinced herself, but she began the lengthy process of dressing for the day, taking care with her pink jeogori jacket as it slid over her arms. Her wound wasn't healing as quickly as she'd like, but so far, the orchid root had kept it from getting infected. Someone with more medical expertise would be helpful, but she couldn't risk calling for an uinyeo right now. With the neighbors whispering about Gwishin potentially having an accomplice, she wasn't going to do anything to cause suspicion. And a nurse's aid was hardly necessary when she'd be fully recovered in a few days anyway.

Chin Sun deftly arranged her long black hair, parting it down the middle before sweeping it back into a simple braid and securing it with a red ribbon. Once her pink hairpin was in place atop her head, she needed but one final adornment to be ready for the day: a smile.

She practiced a few times, forcing her muscles into something friendly yet refined. But the maroon of her chima skirt was a little too similar to the blood stains she still needed to wash out of her hanbok, and her stomach turned.

She clenched her fists, willing the nausea back. One would have thought she'd be immune to such things after all the blood she'd spilled since becoming Gwishin a year and a half ago.

"Chin Sun-ah, are you ready?" Sang Mi opened the hanji doors and peeked inside, bubbly as ever.

Chin Sun's smile reached her eyes for the first time that morning. "Yeh, I am. But, Sang Mi-yah, you really should be dressed before you leave your chambers. What if someone sees you?"

Sang Mi looked down at her sokgot undergarments and grimaced. "Ah, you're quite right, Cousin. Excuse me." She zipped out, moving much more swiftly than a lady should.

Chin Sun chuckled. Sang Mi would have to mature soon. Once Chin Sun was married, her samchon would waste no time in arranging a suitable match for his daughter.

Married . . . Anxiety swirled in Chin Sun's stomach. Negotiations were already underway for Chin Sun's union with one of the local nobles. She was eighteen, and Kang Dol Sam was only a few years older, but he was already a widower, his first wife having succumbed to illness shortly after they'd married. As Confucianism dictated, he'd lived in mourning for the past three years, but now that the mandatory grieving period was over, he was ready to take a new wife. The fact that he was the only son and heir of Lord Kang Ki Yong, the most powerful yangban in all of Sokju, made him the ideal match.

Other than the fact that his father was one of the most corrupt individuals in the city, of course. If only she and Kang Min Joon had enough evidence to prove it, she wouldn't have to go through with this.

Uncle had been overjoyed when Lord Kang had first sent a matchmaker to their home to discuss the possibility of uniting their families. Though wealthy, the Lees were still technically jungin, not yangban, making Chin Sun a less desirable future daughter-in-law than some of the other maidens in the city.

Still, she was esteemed throughout the Gangwon Province, not only for her grace and beauty but also for her avid mind. Her samchon had noticed her intellect at a young age and, rather than squelching it as others would have, had chosen to teach her much as one would a son. Besides her impressive education, she was also skilled in music, embroidery, and painting.

Upon receiving the news, Uncle had happily told the matchmaker that Chin Sun would be delighted to marry Young Master Kang, marking the beginning of euihon, the marriage negotiations.

Since then, the matchmaker had traveled back and forth between both families, asking questions about the prospective bride's and groom's family histories, personalities, and talents. While the Lee family sent the matchmaker very little to inquire about, out of courtesy so as not to seem like they were prying, the Kang family's questions were almost . . . invasive.

"It is to be expected," Chin Sun had explained to her

younger cousin, Sang Ook, when he wondered why Lord Kang cared if Chin Sun had suffered any grave illnesses as a child. "He wants to ensure his future grandchildren will be healthy and that I will be able to take care of his son as a good wife should."

On this particular morning, Young Master Kang himself would be coming for a visit. So far, Chin Sun had only gotten rare glimpses of him from a distance. Curiosity tugged at her almost as much as it did Sang Mi, who blushed anytime the young lord's name was mentioned. Her cousin's voice twittered in her head: *Do you think he's handsome, Unni?"*

But that wasn't what Chin Sun wanted to know most. What she was interested in learning was whether he would be easy to lie to, seeing as she'd have to do that for the rest of her life.

She sashayed to the sangbang, the main room where the family ate together, chin held high despite her slight tardiness. Breakfast porridge and side dishes sat upon a low-legged table, along with a fresh pot of tea. Uncle was already waiting, biting his lip in the way he always did when perturbed. His son, Sang Ook, sat on his left and smiled when he saw Chin Sun. The young boy was only seven and often didn't notice the subtleties of his father's expressions.

"How are you this morning, Niece?" Uncle greeted.

Chin Sun bowed deeply in a show of respect. "Quite well, thank you, Samchon." She lowered herself into her usual seat, hoping Sang Mi would arrive soon. If not, Uncle would surely scold her for being late. Again.

"Did you forget whom we're expecting?" Samchon's tone deepened.

"Of course not, Uncle. I instructed the servants to prepare our best food."

Ever since Chin Sun's sungmo had passed away four years ago, Chin Sun had taken over managing the household in her aunt's stead. Such a responsibility might have been too great for some fourteen-year-olds, but Chin Sun had been eager to do her part to help the family.

Especially considering her role in Sungmo's demise.

He gestured to the empty place next to Sang Ook. "It appears Sang Mi's punctuality is even more lacking."

"She was feeling unwell, Uncle. Please don't hold it against her." Chin Sun's voice was smooth, calm. The result of years spent lying for her irresponsible cousin.

When the girls had been younger, Uncle had been much more easily fooled by Chin Sun's excuses. Now, he saw them for the falsehoods they were.

"Sang Mi cannot hide behind you forever, Chin Sun."

She dipped her head. "You're right, Samchon. I apologize for misleading you."

When he dropped the subject, Chin Sun took a sip of tea, glad he had been so easily placated. He must have been feeling generous because of Young Master Kang's visit.

It wasn't completely appropriate for him to be coming to his betrothed's home. He should have been waiting to meet Chin Sun at their wedding. His desire to come early suggested great eagerness—or that something was very wrong.

Sang Mi's arrival at the table was far less frazzled than when she'd departed Chin Sun's quarters. She carried herself with dignity, but she tucked her chin too tightly as she bowed, betraying her nervousness.

Uncle was an understanding man, but even the most understanding of men required order in their household.

"Such tardiness is not befitting of a woman of your station. Do not disappoint me again, Sang Mi-yah."

"I understand, Father." Sang Mi didn't look up, but the shame billowing off her was palpable.

Maybe it would be enough to help her change this time. Uncle was right. A sapling couldn't grow if it forever lived in the shade.

"Then do your father a favor and let me see your lovely face." Uncle's tone was softer now, and when Sang Mi raised her head, his eyes twinkled with affection. For all his efforts to be stern, Samchon had a soft spot for Sang Mi. He couldn't help it any more than Chin Sun could.

Sang Mi's mouth spread into a relieved smile, and she sat down next to her brother just as a servant shuffled into the room, head low. He stopped at Uncle's side and bowed. "Young Master Kang is here."

"Excellent. Send him in."

Kang Dol Sam stepped through the doorway, his floral green robes spotless as always. An elegant strand of beads hung from his wide-brimmed hat, symbols of his wealth and social status. He walked over to Uncle stiffly but with purpose, and before Samchon could stand, Young Master Kang bowed, much deeper than rank required. "Lord Lee."

Uncle leaped to his feet and bowed in return. "Please do not be so formal, nauri. After all, we're soon to be family."

Kang Dol Sam lifted his head, eyes guarded. His gaze snapped to Chin Sun, then back to Uncle. "As the guardian of my future bride, you are worthy of the highest respect."

Sang Mi giggled, earning a hard look from Chin Sun. Sang Ook glanced between the two of them, face riddled with confusion.

Uncle pointedly ignored the girls' exchange and nodded

to Young Master Kang. "Please have a seat." He gestured to the one remaining spot, the place of honor at his right hand.

Once a servant had given the family's guest refreshments, Sang Mi asked, "Did you hear about what happened the other night?"

"Daughter," Uncle warned, "you know we don't discuss him in this home."

Young Master Kang tugged at his ear, then brought his hand into his lap. "I did hear about Gwishin, if that's whom you're referring to." He took a sip of barley tea.

Chin Sun was fairly good at reading people, but the man's vague response and the way his gaze darted about the room were concerning. Something was clearly on his mind.

Was he uncertain about this union? Kang Dol Sam's father had been the one to reach out to make the arrangements, as was customary. Perhaps Young Master Kang wasn't as keen on the match.

Did he already have someone in his heart? Or did he despise Chin Sun for being an orphan?

Her lack of parents was a slight some families would be opposed to, and, as a child, she had once asked her uncle if anyone would want her as a wife when she was a flower without roots.

"A peony among weeds," Samchon had said, "is no less a flower just because it does not grow in a garden."

"Does that make your home the weeds?" she'd asked with a smirk.

Uncle's boisterous laugh had filled the room, casting the anxiety from her young heart. She'd not known then of her gumiho heritage; otherwise she would not have been so easily comforted. Even so, Chin Sun clung to the warmth she'd felt then, wielding it as a shield against the doubts pricking at her mind.

Perhaps the food didn't suit him. Young Master Kang *was* picking at his greens as if he were displeased. Chin Sun grabbed her chopsticks and took a bite of hers. Her lips lifted instinctively. Na Ri had truly outdone herself this time. Hmm . . .

Chin Sun tried to meet Young Master Kang's gaze, but he seemed determined to look everywhere else. Finally, she said in a demure voice, "I hope the meal is to your liking."

Kang Dol Sam slowly locked eyes with her, his throat bobbing. "Indeed. It is all quite delectable." His mouth tilted into a smile that seemed sincere until his lips twitched and he turned to Uncle. "Actually, I need to make an announcement."

Ah. So, there *was* something wrong. Chin Sun's heart quickened, but she kept her expression neutral.

"Oh?" Uncle set down his cup.

"I probably should have discussed it with you beforehand, but when news reached me of a vigilante sighting just outside your home, I panicked at the thought of my fiancée not being protected."

Samchon's eyebrows pinched together. "I assure you, my niece is not in any dang—"

"That is why I sent word to a friend of mine from the capital who has agreed to be her bodyguard. He used to be part of his Majesty's royal guard, and he's the best swordsman I've ever encountered. Meet Mr. Park Hyun Soo."

A young man clad in black robes stepped silently into the room, bowing once to Uncle, then to Chin Sun. The first thing she noticed was that his hair was neither braided down his back like that of single men and boys nor tied up in a topknot as was customary for married men. Instead, it was gathered at the back of his head, with some shorter strands framing his stubbled face. Short enough that it must have been cut at some point, though such a thing was so shameful it was never done willingly.

The second was that his eyes were almost as piercing as the arrow from the other night.

Chin Sun's hand trembled before she clasped it in the other.

Mr. Park's gaze followed the movement. "It is my honor to serve you, Lady Lee." His voice was steady, confident. "You have my word that no harm will befall you while I'm here. If Gwishin so much as shows himself, I *will* strike him down."

Rather than instilling the comfort he undoubtedly aimed to provide, anxiety pooled in Chin Sun's stomach as Mr. Park moved to stand behind Young Master Kang. She raised her chin, poised as ever. "Thank you for your offer, but"—her gaze shifted from Mr. Park to her fiancé—"I neither need nor desire this man's protection."

Kang Dol Sam frowned. "I will compensate Mr. Park for his service. You need not—"

"It is not a matter of lack of funds," she interrupted sharply. "Suggesting such a thing is an insult to the Lee family." Uncle's countenance darkened, but Chin Sun pressed on. "As is the assumption that my samchon cannot provide the necessary protection on his own."

Sang Mi gasped, hand hovering over her open mouth, and Uncle's face reddened.

To speak to one's future husband so brazenly went against etiquette, but Chin Sun wouldn't allow anyone, *anyone*, to disrespect her family. They may not be her blood relatives, but they had raised her as one of their own. She would defend them to her dying breath.

Even though they would surely turn on her if they knew what she truly was.

Mr. Park spoke up, eyes locked on the floor. "Young Master Kang meant nothing of the kind. He simply wished to do his duty, as your betrothed, in keeping you safe. However, if you would prefer to spurn his kindness, it is your right to do so."

Silence descended over the room like falling snow, everyone watching Chin Sun to see how she would respond to the man's bold statement.

Chin Sun dug her suddenly too-sharp fingernails into her palms, maintaining her poise despite the seething anger in her belly. How dare he insert himself into the conversation.

Her eyes flicked to Young Master Kang, wondering if he would reprimand his friend. But, rather than expressing disapproval with Mr. Park, he was staring at her with unmistakable hurt.

Guilt pinched her heart. She wouldn't have spoken so harshly had the stakes not been so high. To allow a stranger such close access would make it more difficult to maintain her facade as a gentle noblewoman. Her words had been meant to surprise her fiancé enough that he would retract his offer, not make him think she disliked him.

But now that this Mr. Park had turned her insult around on her, she couldn't refuse without looking heartless —and possibly making her fiancé rethink their betrothal.

Chin Sun pressed her lips into a thin smile. "If it is meant as a gift of affection, I am happy to receive it."

Kang Dol Sam's expression brightened. "It is," he exclaimed quickly. "That's exactly what I meant by it."

Uncle cleared his throat. "In that case, thank you for

your generosity, my lord. It will do my heart good to know my dear niece is so well looked after."

"Excellent. I'm so glad you see it that way. Park Hyun Soo will remain here while the marriage talks are still underway."

Sang Ook, who'd kept surprisingly quiet throughout the conversation, cried, "You are so lucky you get to have a bodyguard, Chin Sun Noona."

Chin Sun started to cough, then took a quick sip of tea to steady herself. "Indeed."

"It is very thoughtful of you, Young Master Kang." Sang Mi pressed her hands to her cheeks, smiling at the young nobleman like a girl in love. "I wish I had a fiancé who was so devoted to me."

"Daughter . . ."

Chin Sun barely heard her uncle's rebuke, for Mr. Park had lifted his gaze and met hers across the room. Her eyes narrowed, silently conveying her displeasure at his meddling. She would not let this go. Nor would she make his job easy.

Something flashed in his dark eyes for a split second before he ducked his head, going so still he seemed almost one with the furniture.

But Chin Sun recognized the emotions he'd so expertly concealed—confusion and just a hint of curiosity. Neither boded well.

Chapter 3

The Enemy

Once Young Master Kang had taken his leave and arrangements had been made for where Mr. Park would stay, Samchon pulled Chin Sun into the jeongjugan next to the kitchen.

"What were you thinking?"

"I was thinking of the family," she said meekly, hoping he'd hear her earnestness.

Uncle shook his head. "A pretty lie, Chin Sun-ah. If you'd been thinking of the family, you'd have remembered how important this marriage is. Don't you want Sang Mi to find a good husband? And Sang Ook, too—your connection to the Kangs could help him attain a higher position. Much better than a simple interpreter."

She dropped her head, cheeks blazing with shame. In a low voice, she said, "I thought you liked your job, Samchon."

"Yeh, but I was very limited in my choices. I want more than that for Sang Ook. For all of you. I thought you understood that when you agreed to this match."

Chin Sun swallowed, unable to look him in the eye. "Yeh."

"Then you also understand what it could do to our family if the Kangs change their minds about you. . . ."

He didn't need to spell out the consequences of a broken engagement. Dishonor. Losing face with the community. And it wouldn't just be Chin Sun who was affected. All of the Lee family would suffer.

Uncle seemed to take her silence as an answer. He left in a whoosh of yellow robes, but his disappointment lingered in the air like the stench of smoke.

Now she wasn't just heartless but unfilial as well. Chin Sun gnashed her teeth to keep from crying.

"Unni, are you all right?" Sang Mi's voice floated through the wall.

Chin Sun rejoined her cousins in the sangbang. She smiled reassuringly at Sang Mi. "Yeh. All is well. Are you ready to go to the market?"

Sang Mi grimaced. "Oh . . . about that . . ." She rubbed at her sleeve. "I actually wanted to do some painting this morning. Would you mind going without me?"

Chin Sun held back a sigh. How would Sang Mi learn to take care of the household if she didn't watch how Chin Sun did things?

She was about to say as much when she noticed the moisture in her cousin's eyes. Had something upset her while Chin Sun was talking with Samchon?

There was a crumpled piece of paper in the girl's hand that hadn't been there before. Chin Sun glanced at Sang Ook, hoping he might know what was wrong, but the boy was paying more attention to Chin Sun's new bodyguard than to Sang Mi.

"That would be fine," she told Sang Mi, giving her cousin a small smile.

The other girl bowed, then left the room at almost a run, disappearing down the corridor that led to her bedroom. How peculiar . . .

Chin Sun swung around to Sang Ook, who was in the midst of reaching for the long sword at Mr. Park's hip. "Sang Ook-ah!"

The boy froze, then pulled back his wayward hand. "Sorry, Noona."

"It's not me you should apologize to." She jerked her chin toward Mr. Park.

"The young master did nothing wrong, agasshi," Mr. Park said, lifting his head for the first time since she'd come back into the room. "I was well aware of his intentions."

"Yet you did nothing to stop him?"

"Is it wrong to be curious?" Mr. Park pulled the hwando from its sheath and laid it flat against his palms. He turned to Sang Ook. "Should you wish to see it, you need only ask."

The boy's eyes widened, but he glanced at Chin Sun to make sure it was all right.

She didn't want to agree, but the hopefulness in her cousin's eyes was her undoing. "Aigoo, I suppose."

Sang Ook marveled at the gleaming metal, but when he went to grab the blade, Mr. Park shifted his body away, the movement so swift it was almost fox-like. Sang Ook looked up at him curiously.

"I said you could look, but to place this in the hands of one so young would be irresponsible." His tone was kind but firm, and Chin Sun got the distinct impression that if she hadn't interrupted earlier, Mr. Park would have moved before the boy's fingers had reached the sword. "But don't worry, Young Master Lee. Your day will surely come."

Sang Ook's shoulders fell, but he didn't protest. Instead, he stared up at Mr. Park with unadulterated admiration, as only the young were bold enough to do.

The bodyguard grinned. "In the meantime, your cousin here will look after you, I'm sure."

Chin Sun's lips twisted into a ghost of a smile before a thought shattered her composure. An opponent with such quick reflexes might prove difficult to defeat.

Gone was the flicker of respect she'd felt toward the mysterious man her fiancé had entrusted with her safety. At best, he was an obstacle to her plans. At worst, an enemy she might have to kill one day.

Mr. Park's gaze slid toward her, but Chin Sun refused to meet his eye, focusing instead on Sang Ook. "Dongsaeng, you really should be getting to school."

The boy gasped, then turned sheepish. "Ah, yeh. I'll be going, then." He bowed before scurrying off.

Leaving Chin Sun alone with the man who'd sworn to kill her.

The boy's padded footsteps became muffled as soon as the screen door shut behind him, but Hyun Soo's ears stayed alert. Attacks often came when one was least expecting them, and he was nothing if not prepared.

His mistress didn't acknowledge him, instead staring in the direction her female cousin had gone as though considering whether or not to follow her. Finally, Lady Lee turned away and floated into the courtyard with all the grace of a crane. Hyun Soo followed softly behind her, keeping three steps between them as she entered a separate building he assumed was the kitchen.

"Good morning, agasshi," the servants greeted, bowing politely. There were four in total, three women and a man. Two of the women were much younger than the third, who stood near the hearth with a nervous expression and so many frown lines it looked as if she'd never smiled a day in her life. The man held a long broom that could be a formidable weapon if wielded properly.

Could he be Gwishin? He looked well-fed and was fairly young, perhaps in his early thirties. Gwishin was known for his ability to easily scale buildings and dodge arrows.

But Kang Dol Sam had told him Gwishin got shot in the arm the other night. . . .

"Everyone, I want you to meet Mr. Park Hyun Soo," Lady Lee announced. She turned to him with tight lips. "He'll be staying in the spare room at the servants' quarters for the foreseeable future. Young Master Kang hired him to be my bodyguard."

The servants bowed in greeting but didn't speak, instead eying him with a mixture of suspicion and curiosity.

"It's good to meet you." Hyun Soo bowed in turn.

Lady Lee gestured first to the man, then to the young women. "This is Pyung Ho, and these ladies are Ah In and Ye Seul." She turned to the older woman. "And this is Na Ri, the most wonderful cook in all of Sokju."

Na Ri flushed but didn't contradict the claim. "I trust breakfast was satisfactory?" she asked Lady Lee. Her hands shook with what was probably arthritis.

"Indeed. It was quite excellent," Lady Lee replied, voice ringing with sincerity. "Thank you all for your efforts. I know it must have taken a long time to put together."

The older woman beamed with pride, transforming her wrinkled features from off-putting to welcoming. "Yeh, but it was worth it to make your first meal with your betrothed special. He did like it, didn't he?"

Lady Lee nodded. "He was very complimentary, as is only fitting for someone lucky enough to enjoy your cooking."

Hyun Soo watched the exchange with puzzlement, wondering at the relationship between the two. It seemed far too intimate for people of such different social standing. Did this servant have some kind of hold over Lady Lee to the point that she felt the need to fawn over her like this?

Movement caught Hyun Soo's eye. The male servant was sneaking out of the back door. Without hesitation, Hyun Soo marched over and grabbed the man's arms, digging his fingers in.

The servant lurched back with a yelp.

"What are you doing?!" Lady Lee jumped between them, planting herself in front of the servant like a shield. Her eyes blazed, much as they had when he'd accused her of looking down on Kang Dol Sam's affection. It was a look that said, *Remember your place, or I shall make you remember it.*

But no matter how she glared, Hyun Soo had a job to do, one he wouldn't be swayed from. "What Young Master Kang hired me to do."

Lady Lee's brow furrowed. "Young Master Kang told you to . . ." Her mouth formed a small O, then she turned to the servants. "Leave us."

Once the two of them were alone, she swung back, pinning Hyun Soo with her stormy gaze again. "Regardless of what Young Master Kang said, while you are here, you follow what I tell you. Agreed?"

"Yeh." He dipped his head, hoping she wouldn't see through the bald-faced lie. He'd already upset her once today. It would make this assignment much more difficult if she continued to oppose him.

He peeked back up. Some of the fire had faded from Lady Lee's eyes, but suspicion remained. "Tell me, why did Young Master Kang ask you to frighten my servants?"

"Not frighten," he corrected, "investigate. I've been charged with protecting you at all costs. When Gwishin was sighted at the magistrate's office, one of the guards shot him in the arm. Your servant was acting suspicious. I needed to eliminate him as a suspect."

"Pyung Ho is *not* a suspect. How dare you," she rebutted, sparks flying once again.

Hyun Soo shook his head in silent frustration. "Everyone is a suspect until proven otherwise."

"Then why didn't you do the same to Samchon?"

Hyun Soo's eyes nearly popped out of his head. "You want me to investigate your own uncle?" He almost asked if she had no filial piety, but he restrained himself at the last second.

Lady Lee huffed as though his question were ridiculous. "Of course I don't, but you said you considered everyone a suspect. If I'm going to trust you to protect me, I need to know your word means something."

Hyun Soo winced. "I apologize for my word choice, but I assumed you knew I wasn't including your family."

"My servants *are* family. You do not touch them." She spoke slowly, calmly, but beneath her response lurked an unmistakable threat.

What in the world? He wasn't the enemy here. Why did she seem so determined to turn him into one?

"Now, I'm about to leave for the market," Lady Lee

continued, "but if you can keep your opinions—and hands—to yourself, you may accompany me."

Before he could answer, she strode off like a tidal wave returning to sea, unconcerned with the destruction it left behind.

So radically different from the way Dol Sam had described her that Hyun Soo could scarcely believe his friend had been speaking of the same woman.

When Dol Sam had written to request a favor, Hyun Soo had spared no time in traveling to the city of Sokju, not knowing what to expect. After Dol Sam's first wife had passed, he hadn't seemed interested in remarrying. It was only after a round of drinks that Dol Sam had opened up about his earnest affection for his future bride.

"Lady Lee is a moonbeam, bringing light and happiness to the darkest of nights, with eyes like twin dewdrops on a blade of grass. Her voice is more stirring than the gentle notes of the gayageum when—" Dol Sam broke off at Hyun Soo's raised eyebrow, then crossed his arms. "What?"

"You always were the poetic one," Hyun Soo replied with a grin. "If she's that mesmerizing, aren't you worried I'll fall in love with her, too?"

Dol Sam playfully shoved his arm. "If you do, I would not blame you. Just keep your feelings to yourself."

Hyun Soo scowled at his mistress's retreating form. How disappointed his friend would be if he found out whom he was truly betrothed to.

Chapter 4

The Liar

The streets of Sokju teemed with people as merchants proudly displayed their wares to passersby. One could buy almost anything at the market stalls, from hats to sweet potatoes to wine. Some of the wealthier establishments had separate buildings to purchase goods and services at, such as the bookstore and clothing shops. Most of the pedestrians were commoners in white cotton robes, but a few nobles eyed the expensive fabrics and jewelry. Their bright silk hanbok made them stand out like butterflies in a cloud-filled sky.

Chin Sun perusued the various hairpins and fans with a practiced ease, but she was painfully aware of the presence shadowing her steps. Ah In normally accompanied her to the market, but she'd dismissed her young servant since Mr. Park could help carry anything she purchased.

She already regretted that decision.

Chin Sun cast a sharp glance behind her. Mr. Park's attention was on a pair of commoners chatting together, and there was a good amount of space between them. Hmm, perhaps she should find out just how skilled he was.

A trio of gisaengs, female entertainers owned by the state, stood just in front of her, giggling as they ogled Mr. Park. Their brightly colored hats and clothing reminded Chin Sun of beautiful wildflowers, but she knew they were just as much slaves as those forced to live with yangban nobles. They could be bought or sold on a whim, nothing more than property in the eyes of the highborn. The Lees' own servants were treated well, but they, too, were bound to the household, unable to leave without the Lees' permission. Such was the Joseon way, though it was a flawed system Chin Sun despised.

She stepped forward, placing the gisaengs between herself and Mr. Park, then veered to the right. She dashed into the yard of a nearby inn that seemed to always be bursting with customers, no matter what time of day it was. Guests huddled together in small groups, some on the ground but others on raised platforms, enjoying trays of steaming food and soju. Female servants darted here and there like anxious rabbits, trying to keep even the most irritable guests satisfied. Noise flooded Chin Sun's hypersensitive ears: commoners complaining about taxes, drunkards laughing at the innkeeper's threats to throw them out, meat sizzling in the kitchen.

She smiled. She couldn't have picked a better place to lose someone.

Chin Sun weaved around the distracted patrons and disappeared out through the back, which deposited her on an empty side street. Most nobles avoided this part of town since it was a poorer area, but Chin Sun liked the straight route it provided to Mr. Han's bookstore.

A quick check over her shoulder told her she'd lost Mr. Park. She smirked. Some bodyguard he'd turned out to be.

She slowed her pace, spirits lifting. If it was this easy to get rid of Mr. Park, she should have no trouble delivering a message to Kim Min Joon. She and the young police inspector had been working together for months now, meeting up frequently to practice swordfighting and help each other with any problems they couldn't deal with individually. Min Joon's connections were useful for opening doors Gwishin couldn't, and while a police inspector was duty-bound to uphold the law, a vigilante was unencumbered.

Chin Sun's eyes crinkled at the corners. She was grateful to have someone she could depend on, someone who knew her true identity. That hadn't always been the case.

Though the two had been childhood friends, she and Min Joon had been separated for years when he'd gone to study in Ming, as many bright, young yangban did when they reached adulthood. Chin Sun hadn't even known he was back until he'd happened upon her a year ago while she was fighting a policeman on a market street and, mistaking her for an average criminal, had chased her all across the city. They'd scaled buildings, darted down alleys, and even clashed swords a few times before Chin Sun had successfully escaped his grasp. Or so she'd thought.

She hadn't expected him to track her into the woods and shoot her down.

The memory was amusing now. Min Joon had surprised her in many ways that night. Though she'd tried to frighten him off by revealing her gumiho nature, he'd kept his wits about him, pinning her with his sword before forcing her to remove her mask. The utter shock on his face would have been laughable, were the situation not so dire.

But instead of turning Chin Sun in, he'd demanded she explain herself. Not many would have believed her when she'd told him the officer she'd been fighting had stolen from a poor commoner family and she'd been trying to recover what they were owed.

But Kim Min Joon had. He'd even investigated the matter himself and seen to it that the family's goods were returned. After that, he'd tried to convince her to stop moonlighting as a vigilante, but she'd told him he could either help her or get out of her way. That had been the start of Min Joon and Chin Sun's alliance, though the relationship was more like that of siblings than colleagues. Min Joon couldn't help but act like an overprotective older brother, and Chin Sun couldn't help but put herself in situations where she worried him to death.

The two had worked out a secret means to pass messages—by leaving a drawing of a fox tucked under a vase at the bookstore. Depending on what the sketch looked like, it could mean the sender wished to meet in person, had information that would be left in a secure location, or had been found out by the authorities. The fox Chin Sun carried indicated she had important information that she would leave in the abandoned hut at the edge of the woods.

Though she would have preferred speaking with Min Joon in person, she didn't dare ask him to meet, not with this new bodyguard on her back. She may have lost him for now, but she didn't want to push her luck. Once Min Joon knew everything she'd overheard at the magistrate's office, he could leave another note for her, detailing what he thought they should do next.

She pulled a pouch of rice from one of her wide sleeves, hoping the bookstore wouldn't be as crowded as the inn. Perhaps she'd also get Sang Mi that new romance novel she'd been asking for. That should cheer her up.

She also needed to buy some paper, and Uncle had

asked her to pick out a new pipe for him as well. Though the country had used a coin currency in the past when it had been called Goryeo, after King Taejo had overthrown the old dynasty and founded the Joseon nation, people had returned to their traditional bartering systems. Grain and cloth were most commonly used, and the white millet rice Chin Sun carried should be more than enough for what she needed.

Her destination was almost in view when a tall figure blocked her path.

"Did you hear what happened to Gwishin the other night at the magistrate's office?" a low voice asked.

Hyun Soo froze, then swiveled to the right.

Two merchants stood behind their stalls on the opposite side of the street, oblivious to Hyun Soo's scrutiny. One stall displayed several pairs of straw sandals, while the other sold baskets of various sizes. The men themselves were older, both with gray hair and beards, and one leaned upon a cane.

"Yeh," the man with the cane replied, "no one has seen him since. You don't think . . . ?"

The other man laughed and clapped his friend on the back. "The wound was only in his arm, Woo Tak-ah. Gwishin isn't about to let something like that stop him. He'll be back."

Woo Tak grinned. "I hope you're right. If not—"

A police officer passed in front of their stalls, spear clasped in his right hand. He glared at the merchants before tapping his spear against one of the public walls. A handbill featuring a sketch of a man in black was plastered there. A cowl covered the bottom half of the figure's face, and his hair was pulled up in a topknot. Beside the sketch was a notice, written in Hanja, classical Chinese.

The GANGWON PROVINCE POLICE BUREAU INSTRUCTS ANYONE WHO HAS INFORMATION REGARDING the IDENTITY or LOCATION of the REBEL KNOWN as GWISHIN to COME FORWARD. INFORMATION THAT RESULTS in the CAPTURE of THIS DANGEROUS CRIMINAL WILL BE GREATLY REWARDED.

"Gwishin is a criminal, not a hero, and if I hear you openly supporting him again, I will have you both tried as conspirators. Is that clear?" the officer sneered.

The merchants kowtowed, bodies trembling. "We apologize, sir. We meant nothing by it."

"That better be true, but in case you're prone to forgetfulness . . ." The policeman marched over and cracked both men across the back with his spear. The merchants groaned but stayed still, heads pressed into the dirt.

The policeman spat on the ground, then knocked down a few of the baskets as he turned away. "Parasites."

Once the officer was gone, Hyun Soo hurried over and grabbed the shorter man's cane.

"Are you all right?" he asked as the merchants pushed themselves to their feet.

The shorter man—Woo Tak, Hyun Soo thought his name was—stared at the proffered cane in confusion. "T-thank you, sir." He bowed, then hesitantly took his cane, as if he feared Hyun Soo was about to strike him.

Hyun Soo wasn't surprised at the man's apprehension. Most looked down upon merchants since they earned their wealth through trade rather than hard work. But Confucianism called the highborn to display kindness toward those below them, and unlike some yangban, Hyun Soo took his moral responsibilities seriously.

"Ahjussi, why did that officer think you supported Gwishin?" he asked. "Do you happen to know—"

"We don't know anything!" Woo Tak covered his face with his free hand while the other merchant scuttled to the farthest corner of his stall.

Hyun Soo's brow furrowed. "Be more careful in how you talk when the police are around," he warned, then turned back to his charge.

His stomach dropped. She hadn't been moving quickly; she should have been just ahead on the road. "Agasshi?" He surveyed the crowd for her pink jeogori and reddish-purple skirt in the sea of white hanbok, but there was no sign of her. Fear shot through him as he hurried into the throng, pushing past peasants with one hand wrapped around his sword hilt.

Lady Lee knew better than to wander off alone with Gwishin still at large. Something must have happened to her.

A vision of her body lying broken and bloody on the street appeared in his thoughts. Dol Sam was counting on him to protect his beloved. He couldn't fail his friend.

Hyun Soo picked up the pace, earning a few quizzical looks from the locals, but he couldn't be bothered with propriety right now. Not when every second could be the difference between life and death.

"Leave me be, if you know what's good for you," snapped a familiar voice.

Hyun Soo's heartbeat spiked as he lurched in the direction of Lady Lee's words. He found himself on a side street dotted with thatched huts. Three men armed with knives surrounded Lady Lee, whom they'd cornered against a house wall. Bandits, by the looks of their dirty white robes.

Hyun Soo kicked the fellow nearest him in the back. The thug went sprawling forward onto his face before the other two could react. Hyun Soo rushed to Lady Lee, unsheathing his hwando while she gaped.

"Are you injured?" He scanned her form, but nothing seemed out of place, aside from the blades clenched in her dainty hands.

"No, I—Watch out!"

Hyun Soo dodged a wildly thrown punch, then grabbed the cutthroat's arm and swung him away from Lady Lee. The bandit slammed his head into one of the hut's clay walls and fell to his knees with a loud cry.

Hyun Soo aimed the tip of his sword at the final man still standing. The bandit paled, but he didn't lower the knife in his trembling fingers. He glanced at his companions, who were slowly rising to their feet.

The three squared off for another round, fists and knives raised, but the fear dancing in their gazes made it clear this was a fight they'd lost their appetites for.

"Those blades are no match for my hwando," Hyun Soo pointed out. "If you don't wish to die today—because that's what will happen if you touch her—I suggest you get out of here."

The gang looked at each other, then scattered like beetles. If anyone was a parasite in Joseon, it was people like them—stealing from the vulnerable rather than earning an honest living.

Hyun Soo turned to Lady Lee. "Are you all right?"

"Yeh, I'm fine," she replied, so calmly one might have thought they were discussing the weather.

"Why did those men attack you?"

She rubbed at the jade ring on her forefinger. "They wanted me to hand over my valuables"—her face darkened—"but I refused."

It was then that Hyun Soo noticed the daggers she'd held before were gone. "What happened to your knives?"

"Knives?" Lady Lee blinked her large, doe-like eyes. "I don't know what you mean. I never had a knife."

Hyun Soo frowned. The past few minutes were a bit of a blur, but he was almost certain she'd been wielding multiple daggers in each hand. Perhaps he'd been wrong.

He stared at Lady Lee for a few more seconds, then looked away as a wave of guilt came over him. Knives or not, he definitely hadn't imagined her dauntless expression when he'd first arrived. No woman should be put in such a perilous position, and certainly not often enough that it hardly phased her.

The fact that *he'd* been the one who'd allowed her to walk into danger today simply made the knot in his stomach worse.

Hyun Soo dipped his head. "I apologize, agasshi, for failing in my duty. If I'd kept a better eye on you, this never would have happened."

Lady Lee's slender brows pulled inward. "It wasn't your fault. I should have stayed closer to your side." She spread her fingers over her mouth as though embarrassed. "I'm so glad you found me when you did. If you hadn't, I don't know what I would have done."

When moisture began to gather in the woman's eyes, Hyun Soo drew back, disoriented by her sudden shift in attitude. She'd been fine a moment ago. Why was she—

Lady Lee stepped toward him, a nervous hand pressed over her chest. "What's the matter, Mr. Park? Did you get injured? Should I ask someone to find a physician?" The syrupy-sweet quality in her voice was indeed as enchanting as the gayageum, but unlike the precious instrument, her words elicited a thrum of dread in his heart.

For even the prettiest of strings could strangle someone.

He'd only met her this morning, but at that moment, there was one thing Hyun Soo was absolutely certain of: this woman was a liar.

And he hated liars.

Chapter 5

The Partner

The pair headed home once they'd collected all the items Chin Sun needed, with nary another word between them. Mr. Park didn't seem to be a talkative sort, which she was glad of. His heroic rescue had made quite an impression on her, and she needed time to sift through her thoughts.

He'd overtaken the bandits so quickly that it was difficult to gauge just how skilled of a fighter he was. Still, he'd proven himself both levelheaded and a man of sharp reflexes. If he was also an expert swordsman, he might be more than Chin Sun could handle.

For while her gumiho nature afforded her greater speed and strength than the average human, she was far from invincible. Oftentimes when she accessed her powers, she felt like she was hitting an invisible wall, one she had no idea how to overcome. She'd only barely surpassed Kim Min Joon during their last sword fight. And though her old friend was a skilled opponent, he couldn't be the best there was.

What concerned her more than Hyun Soo's swordsmanship, though, was that he'd noticed her claws.

How could she have been so reckless!

He'd mistaken them for knives, of course, but that was only because she'd come to her senses before he'd scared off the idiots who'd been foolish enough to try to rob her. Maybe she *should* start carrying a dagger during the day. That was much easier to explain than claws suddenly growing out of her fingertips.

This was the first time someone had threatened her while she was dressed as a noblewoman. Most thieves were either simple pickpockets or smart enough to wait until nightfall before they made their move. Those men, though, had practically reeked of desperation.

Chin Sun sighed. While she didn't condone their actions, such behavior was just another symptom of the city's growing problems. Commoners were forced to pay higher and higher taxes that ultimately went to yangban pockets, and rather than helping those less fortunate than themselves as they were instructed to in school, most nobles were only interested in increasing their wealth and position.

If she weren't an orphan, would she have turned out the same way? It was only thanks to her aunt and uncle's benevolence that Chin Sun enjoyed such a privileged life. She saw herself in every beggar she passed, every gisaeng faking a smile on her powdered face, every slave crying out to his master for mercy.

Once they arrived at the Lee residence, Mr. Park took his leave so he could guard the perimeter while Chin Sun went about her household chores. She tried to talk to Sang Mi, but the girl refused to leave her room, so Chin Sun simply placed the new book she'd purchased on the floor outside.

When the family came together for the evening meal, Sang Mi finally emerged from her bedroom, eyes puffy and red. The two locked gazes as Sang Mi sat down at the low table next to her brother, and though neither spoke a word, a silent conversation passed between them:

Please don't tell Father, Sang Mi pleaded.

All right, Chin Sun replied, *but I expect a full explanation later.*

They broke eye contact when the servants brought out trays of hot food and alcohol. The heady aroma of hotpot, pickled cucumbers, seasoned bean sprouts, and rice filled the air, making Chin Sun realize she'd been so worked up by the morning's events that she'd forgotten to eat lunch.

"How was school today, Sang Ook?" Uncle asked.

The boy began sharing what he'd studied, and Samchon happily talked with him for the next several minutes. The girls chimed in a few times when they had something to add, but both were quieter than usual, and Sang Mi ate hardly anything.

"Did you find everything you needed at the market?" Uncle finally asked, gaze going from Sang Mi to Chin Sun.

Sang Mi paled, her grip on her chopsticks a bit more rigid, but Chin Sun spoke up. "Yeh, we did, Samchon."

"I trust your new bodyguard was helpful?" Uncle's tone was casual, but Chin Sun could tell by the way he leaned slightly closer that he was very interested in her response.

Chin Sun debated how much she should share about the incident with the thieves. She didn't want Uncle worried about her safety—then he would agree with Young Master Kang that a bodyguard was necessary. But she could accuse Mr. Park of negligence, as the man himself had confessed to, and perhaps that would result in his dismissal.

She opened her mouth to do just that, but to her shock,

she hesitated, a vision filling her mind of him leaping to her rescue with no regard for his own safety.

She was the one who'd put herself in danger by willfully running away from him. Was it wrong to call his capability into question when it was her fault she'd gotten into trouble?

No, it didn't matter if it was right or wrong. It was too risky to keep him around. If he found out she was Gwishin, everything would be ruined. His reputation was a small price to keep her life intact.

"Actually, he—"

"His presence was most comforting," Sang Mi interjected.

Chin Sun's hand slipped, but she barely noticed the broth that sloshed out of her bowl. She glanced at Sang Mi, but the girl was focused on Uncle.

"After all these Gwi—" She cut off at her father's sharp look, then stumbled onward. "Uhh . . . sightings, I was glad to have him there to keep us safe."

Heat rose in Chin Sun's belly. If Sang Mi had just kept her mouth shut, she could have gotten rid of Mr. Park and not had to worry about him anymore. Why had she gone and—

"Is that true, Chin Sun?" Samchon turned, a single eyebrow raised.

"Y-yeh, of course." She smoothed away the anger from her expression, though it still blew over her heart. Sang Mi had unwittingly backed Chin Sun into a corner; now there was no way she could share what had happened with the bandits without exposing her cousin's lie.

"Hmm . . ." Uncle took a bite of cucumber, chewing it slowly as he continued to watch her.

Chin Sun smiled innocently until he looked away and

directed another school-related question to Sang Ook. She tried not to sigh in relief.

Did I say something wrong? Sang Mi mouthed across the table.

Chin Sun broke eye contact, too frustrated to give her a response. Covering up for her cousin was taking more of a toll than she wished.

When the meal came to a close, Chin Sun announced, "I believe I shall retire for the evening."

"Did you not want to read with me?" Sang Mi asked. The two of them had a habit of enjoying stories together in the evenings whenever Chin Sun brought home a new book. It was also a good time to discuss the things they didn't want Samchon or Sang Ook to know about, which mostly involved Sang Mi's frequent romantic interests.

Chin Sun shook her head. "I have a slight headache coming on. Forgive me."

Her voice was perfectly sweet, concealing the bitterness swimming through her thoughts. Sang Mi may be ready to talk now after ignoring her all afternoon, but the girl's impulsiveness had ruined Chin Sun's mood. Perhaps it would do her good to be the one snubbed this time.

Aren't you being rather petty, Chin Sun? her conscience argued.

She brushed aside the invoked twinge of guilt. She had the right to be petty after all the trouble Sang Mi had caused.

Uncle frowned. Chin Sun wasn't prone to poor health, so even something as mild as a headache must have sounded odd to him. "Should I ask Ah In to bring you some tea?"

She shook her head a little too strongly. "No, I should be fine once I get some rest. Thank you, Samchon." She bowed and took her leave, ignoring Sang Mi's puzzled brow.

The sky was coated with pearly white stars when Chin Sun crept into the courtyard, then leaped over the wall and onto the main road. She'd observed Mr. Park patrolling the property for almost an hour before she'd made her move. He always paused in his sweep when he reached the back of the manor, giving her ample time to slip out unseen.

No men besides police officers were about now, for it was after curfew and only women were allowed on the city's streets. On three occasions, patrolmen marched by, so she hid behind the nearest building until their clomping footsteps faded into the night. She knew the officers' routes so well now, she could practically skirt by them in her sleep.

She told herself to stay alert. Her carelessness at the magistrate's office had given her the wound in her shoulder. She didn't want any further mistakes.

The injured area was still very tender, but the brief skirmish this afternoon didn't seem to have done her any harm. She didn't like admitting it, but it had been a good thing Mr. Park was there. While she could have taken them all on and won, she may not have been able to walk away unscathed. Especially not while pretending to be a delicate noblewoman.

By all rights, she should still be resting, but the conversation she'd overheard at the magistrate's office contained valuable information Min Joon would want to know about.

"In ten days' time, meet at the agreed-upon location to trade," Hong whispered, his Japanese so stilted Chin Sun almost couldn't decipher it.

"What guarantee do we have that you'll be there?" the pirate asked.

Hong didn't speak for a moment. "How could you doubt me when my entire reputation is on the line?" His voice was low, angry. "You just make sure all the sulfur is ready for transport."

If the pirates were smuggling sulfur into the country, it could only be for a single purpose: gunpowder. What Hong needed it for, Chin Sun had no idea, but if she got the information to Min Joon quickly enough, perhaps he could intercept the goods and stop whatever the magistrate was planning. Or maybe he'd want to watch the exchange to find out where the sulfur was being delivered. Either way, all she needed to do for now was drop her note off at the abandoned hut at the edge of the woods, then she could sneak back into her bedroom and get some much-needed rest.

Chin Sun hadn't been to the hut since Min Joon had tipped her off about the magistrate's clandestine meeting. The inspector lacked Gwishin's stealth and had asked her to listen in on Hong's conversation. He'd also advised her to be discreet, which certainly *hadn't* happened, so he would probably give her a good tongue-lashing the next time they met.

The moon was bright as Chin Sun arrived and stepped into the straw-roofed hut, illuminating the dark space and casting ominous shadows along the inner walls. Neatly stacked papers rested atop an old table, along with a small lantern ready for use. Two chairs leaned against the wall nearby.

Chin Sun approached the table, note in hand.

Her gaze darted to the back corner where a tall silhouette lurked, barely visible even with her fox senses. She whipped forward, unsheathing her sword and addressing the intruder. "Show yourself."

"Is that any way to treat your partner?"

Chin Sun huffed as she put away her sword, annoyance overtaking her alarm. "You could have announced yourself from the start, Min Joon-ah."

The young police inspector stepped forward, a grin on his lips. "Where's the fun in that?" He lit the lantern and took a seat.

"I'd say not getting impaled is fun enough," she replied gruffly. "I thought you weren't returning until tomorrow."

"I came back early when I heard you'd been wounded." All traces of humor vanished from his face. "Are you all right?"

Chin Sun reached for the map on the table, avoiding his eye so she didn't have to see the worry on his face. "News travels fast. I didn't think you'd have heard about it all the way in Geungmeung already. Speaking of which, I need to tell you what I learned while I was there."

Min Joon moved the map out of reach. "Don't avoid the question. Did you really get shot?"

"I'm not that easy of a target," she hissed, the lie stinging her lips. "Now, can we get on to more important things?"

Her friend's expression remained hard, stubbornly resisting her attempts to ignore his concern. "It's all right to be weak sometimes, you know. You may not be human, but you still bleed like the rest of us."

When she didn't answer, Min Joon sighed and relinquished his hold on the map. "What did you find out?"

Chapter 6

The Goblin

After Chin Sun and Min Joon had gone over the details, they concluded that surveillance was the best course of action. Min Joon had a contact south of Sokju he wanted to visit to find out whether there had been any other pirate sightings in the next province. If this operation stretched beyond their city's borders, it might be too big for them to handle on their own. Chin Sun would watch Hong for any other suspicious behavior, and then the pair would reconvene here the night before the magistrate's planned deal.

Once they'd finalized everything, Chin Sun was quick to depart. Normally, she would have stayed longer to cross blades a few times, but she wasn't up for the exertion right now, and she didn't want Min Joon discovering the severity of her injury. He would have told her not to come when they went to spy on Hong's operation.

Not that she would have listened if he'd urged her to stay away. Her healing abilities were more than sufficient to have her in good condition by the night of the deal. It was just easier to keep Min Joon in the dark; then she didn't have to worry about questions—or worse, concern.

Chin Sun darted across the tiles of a rooftop, the crisp air invigorating her lungs. It would be Chuseok soon, a time which always evoked a pang of sorrow within her. The annual celebration of the harvest was a three-day holiday full of laughter and joy for most, but for Chin Sun, it was also a time of grief. As much as she loved her family and was grateful they'd taken her in, she couldn't help but long for the mother and father she couldn't remember.

A silly desire when they'd died long ago.

The story her uncle and aunt told of her origins was that Uncle's younger brother had gotten a lowly peasant girl pregnant and agreed to marry her, but then he'd been killed by ruffians, leaving his bride-to-be penniless and alone. Uncle and Aunt had taken the girl in, but she'd passed shortly after giving birth, so Uncle and Aunt had raised baby Chin Sun themselves.

It had always been a sensitive subject that tended to make Aunt burst into tears. When Chin Sun's gumiho abilities had emerged, though, she'd discovered their reluctance to talk about the past had really been because it was a lie. What had actually happened was far worse.

Chin Sun swallowed, hating the emotions such memories dredged up. She jumped to the ground as her family's residence came into view. Her neighbors' homes sat on either side of her, hidden behind their stone walls and eaves. As if they wanted to keep out anyone who didn't fit the perfect mold they'd created.

She cut off the thought. She needed to focus on the present. That was what she could control.

A soft swish was her only warning before a blade arced toward her.

Chin Sun leaped into a front flip, then pulled her sword from its scabbard and swung around. The sharp ring of metal filled the night as the two swords collided. Her eyes widened when she recognized her assailant, foot slipping before she righted herself.

Mr. Park. She shouldn't have been surprised to see him, but somehow, in all the planning with Min Joon, her nuisance of a bodyguard had slipped her mind.

Mr. Park pressed harder, straining to get the upper hand, but Chin Sun shoved him back. "Get out of my way," she growled, then turned to leave. Despite the complications his presence brought to her life, he seemed to be a decent person. It would be a shame to have to kill him.

But Mr. Park jumped into her path once more, weapon raised. "I'm afraid I can't do that. You see, I swore if we ever crossed paths, I would kill you."

"I'm flattered." Chin Sun noted the self-assurance in the man's eyes, the wide stance of his legs. Curiosity sparked within her. "But what makes you so certain I'll let you?"

She advanced, not moving at full speed, but he easily deflected the blade. She struck again, faster this time, but the result was identical.

Mr. Park raised his eyebrows as if to say, *Is that the best you can do?*

Chin Sun smirked, injury forgotten. This was going to be fun. She thrust her sword forward, so quickly she was almost a blur, and Mr. Park parried just in time. He struck toward her core, but she evaded him gracefully, sliding to the right before moving into a defensive pose.

Mr. Park attacked a second time to the same effect. Chin Sun tried to knock his legs out from under him, but he lurched out of the way. Back and forth the two moved, almost in a dance as their swords clashed again and again, neither able to overtake the other. Chin Sun pressed into her gifts as hard as she could, but again, she came up against that mental wall, leaving her wondering what might lie on the other side.

"Impressive," Mr. Park admitted. Chin Sun had purposely led him away from the center of the city, and they now stood at its very edge. Rice paddy fields stretched out at her back, and great mountains rose in the distance. "I see why no one has captured you."

"They don't call me the Ghost for nothing." She blocked a weak attack to her right, then twirled out of reach. "But I'm more curious about you. Did Hong send you? He must be desperate if he's hiring common thugs now."

A muscle twitched in her opponent's jaw, sending a ripple of pleasure through her. She'd gotten under his skin. Perfect.

What she couldn't do through skill with a blade she'd accomplish with her barbed tongue. There was more than one way to overpower an enemy. And distracted ones were prone to all kinds of mistakes.

Chin Sun swung at his chest. He blocked with his sword before metal met skin, his mouth curving with amusement.

Not as distracted as she'd thought.

"Since you're so interested, there *is* something you should know about me," he said.

"What's that?" Chin Sun stepped back, allowing him the next move. She purposely left her chest unguarded to see if he would go for the obvious play. Then she could knock the sword out of his hand and flee to the woods at the mountains' base. As entertaining as this back-and-forth was, she was growing tired. She needed to end this before things got messy.

He sliced toward her center, then at the last second, pivoted to the right. Chin Sun swerved to counter the attack, realizing his intent just before he made contact. She was too late. He cut into her left arm, right where she'd been injured.

Chin Sun gasped as pain ricocheted through her body, her blade clattering to the ground. She grabbed her arm; the sleeve was already damp with blood.

A second strike sliced just below her ribs, and she dropped to one knee with an all-too-feminine cry. Her head swam, black spots peppering her vision.

Mr. Park hesitated for a split second before moving closer, victory flashing in his eyes. "I never start a fight without first knowing my enemy's weakness."

Irritation surged through her, hot and overpowering. And strong enough to break through the fog descending on her mind. She gave his legs a great push, knocking him off his feet, then drew herself up and raced toward the mountains, her sword abandoned in the dirt.

Mr. Park's feet pounded behind her. The forest lay ahead, growing thicker the farther she fled from the city. She weaved in and out of the trees, trying to lose the stubborn bodyguard, but he clung to her trail like a dog after a fox. Her energy was fading, draining out of her with the blood dripping onto the cold ground.

Chin Sun scrambled over a thick log, searching for a place to hide. Her dizzy mind spun in circles. Had she already gone this way? She'd grown up playing in these woods with Min Joon, but now everything looked the same. Sweat gathered on her skin, her breath coming in short pants.

The hair on the back of her neck prickled. Mr. Park was getting closer.

This form made her too big of a target. It might be time to resort to extreme measures.

Chin Sun blinked a few times, trying to shake off the idea, though she couldn't remember why it was unwise anymore. She was so tired.

Heavy footsteps made her rapid heart fly faster, and before she could stop herself, her human form slipped away.

Hyun Soo dashed after the vigilante, amazed at the fellow's breakneck pace after sustaining such heavy injuries. He seemed almost more like a ghost than a man, and when he slipped into the woods, it was all Hyun Soo could do to keep from losing him completely.

But he'd promised Dol Sam he'd protect Lady Lee, and that was what he was going to do. Once Gwishin was eliminated, he could ask Dol Sam to help him acquire a government position. From there, he'd work his way up until he'd rebuilt the reputation he'd lost. Then Father would realize he'd made a mistake, and the two of them could—

He needed to slow down. There were too many variables still up in the air. Too many things that could go wrong.

Even so, stopping Gwishin was a step in the right direction, and the hope of restoration bolstered his endurance despite the fatigue creeping into his muscles.

A strange scraping sound to the right drew his attention, and he veered toward it. A wild boar lifted its head from the base of a nearby tree, staring straight at him. Hyun Soo carefully backed away from the animal, not wanting to startle it. After a moment, it seemed to lose interest in him and returned to scratching at the tree bark.

Hyun Soo sighed in relief, then hurried off in the direction Gwishin had fled. Where had that fiend gone?

The screeching of bats and chirping of insects inundated his ears, but he could no longer detect Gwishin's light steps. The terrain was rockier now, with several drop-offs and dangerously steep inclines. Hyun Soo picked up his pace, praying he hadn't let the elusive criminal slip away.

He wandered onto a precipice and peered down. About ten paces below was a brook that flowed into a pool of water. Several rocks jutted out of and around the pool, and a lone musk deer leaned over it to get a drink.

Hyun Soo started to lean back to search elsewhere, then froze. A second animal was crouched against the rocks, so well hidden he'd almost missed it. Wait, was that—it couldn't be—

Hyun Soo gawked, unable to believe what was right there in front of him: a small white fox with, not one, but nine tails. A gumiho. The monster Grandmother had claimed would snatch him away in the dead of night if he didn't respect his elders.

But gumiho weren't real. They were figments of the imagination, created for the sole purpose of frightening children into good behavior. Like goblins or haetae.

He rubbed his eyes, but the scene before him remained. The creature was exactly as his grandmother had described, except . . .

"If you see a gumiho, you must run to the safety of home as quickly as you can, little one. If you don't, it will trick you into swallowing its fox bead. And if it can't do that, it will eat your liver."

"Why does it do that, Halmeoni?"

"Because a gumiho has one desire above all else: to become human. If it takes enough human lifeforce, it will obtain its wish. It gains the most lifeforce by sharing its bead, but when that's not an option, a few human livers will do nicely instead."

"But you said gumiho could transform into people. Why would they need my lifeforce if they can already become human?"

"Monsters come in many forms, but no matter what shape they take, their evil nature remains the same. Theirs is a life without joy, without honor, without love. That's why they envy us. And that is why we must appreciate how precious our humanity is. Do you understand, my treasure?"

"Yeh, Grandmother."

Except in the story of the great dragon, the gumiho from his grandmother's tales had always been evil, and regardless of their shapeshifting and trickery, they were unable to fully conceal their true natures. Something would always give them away, whether it was a sharp word, a sadistic aura, or a blood-stained hand.

But while the animal cowering at the water's edge was undoubtedly gumiho, seeing it didn't evoke fear within him. Instead, he was overcome by a sense of awe, as if his whole life had been building to this very moment. He remained absolutely still so as not to make a sound, watching this beautiful creature that had walked straight out of a fairytale.

But why did it seem so scared? He followed the gumiho's line of sight, and his blood ran cold.

Something *else* was here.

Blue flames flickered atop a stone on the opposite side of the pool, and within the blaze stood a being Hyun Soo struggled to describe. Such terror seized him that he found himself clamping his eyes shut without even realizing it, a scream lodged in his throat.

What was wrong with him? It hadn't even done anything and he was already terrified? He needed to assess the threat like he would have when he was still a royal guard, not get worked up like this.

He forced himself to open his eyes, though that same, almost-debilitating panic latched on to his heart as soon as he took a second look.

The willowy figure at the edge of the water resembled a human in many ways. It had the same build, height, and even wore white hanbok. Long black hair hung in messy strings around its angular face, and a thick beard covered its chin, reminding Hyun Soo very much of the homeless ahjussis one might see on the streets. But its body radiated with an eerie shimmer unlike anything he'd ever seen before, and the hungry expression on its face was too feral to belong to a human.

Worst of all was the malicious energy wafting off it. Whatever that thing was, Hyun Soo knew without a doubt that it was evil.

And it had its sights set on the fox.

The gumiho took a hesitant step to the side, but its front leg gave out, sending the animal to its knees. That was when Hyun Soo spotted the blood gathered at its feet, no doubt the reason it hadn't already bolted as the musk deer had a few minutes ago.

It was injured, maybe even dying.

The monster surged forward, the movement so fluid it was like water sliding over rock. The blue fire that had heralded its arrival evaporated, but the unearthly glow on the creature's skin remained, a chilling reminder that this was no human. Its long fingers reached toward the gumiho, which snarled and bared its teeth.

Just before the monster made contact with the fox's fur, it paused. "Thank you for your sacrifice," it rasped, its gentle voice like sweet poison.

The figure tapped one sharp nail on the gumiho's chest, sending something shooting out of the fox's mouth and into the air. The gumiho howled before collapsing, but the thing it had expelled, a glowing blue orb, hovered just above its head.

Its fox bead.

The source of the gumiho's magical essence. Hyun Soo's grandmother hadn't explained all the details when he was a child, but he'd heard enough since then. Young men must be cautious around beautiful women, for they could be gumiho in disguise, and if one were to receive a kiss, his death was almost guaranteed.

For a gumiho's kiss was much more than a kiss.

It was the method by which they transferred their fox bead into a human's body, where it would then absorb its host's lifeforce. Once swallowed, the gumiho must remove the bead in a relatively short span of time; otherwise, the human would perish. And gumiho were not known for being kind.

But to just stand here and let this one die . . .

Hyun Soo lurched out of hiding and launched himself at the monster, sword aimed for its stomach. Maybe it was a horrible idea that would end in his death, but he couldn't allow something so dangerous to remain in these woods, not when they were so close to the city—and Lady Lee's residence.

The monster shrieked when his blade struck true, piercing the creature's flesh and releasing a stream of silver blood. The monster fell back, eyes wide with shock, and a cold wind brushed over Hyun Soo's open mouth.

"You will regret that." The monster reached for him, then stopped with a wince. One thin hand went to its gushing wound, conflict written all over its fearsome face. It let out a dry laugh. "Do you truly think you can keep that from me? I'll be back for what's mine very soon, thief." The fiend smiled, two sharp canines digging into its upper lip, then stepped back and vanished in a curtain of blue flame.

Hyun Soo stood motionless, trying to wrap his head around what had just happened. His eyes flicked to his sword, now stained with blood. That definitely wasn't his imagination.

What had happened to the fox bead? He'd lost sight of it during his rush to protect the gumiho, but the monster certainly hadn't taken it. Perhaps—

Hyun Soo spun around, but his eyebrows bunched together at the empty stone behind him.

The gumiho was gone.

Chapter 7

The Nurse

Chin Sun dragged herself back to the Lee residence and over the courtyard wall, relieved when Mr. Park didn't come bounding out of the shadows. She'd managed to sneak away while he was busy with the goblin, but she'd nearly passed out on the trek back to town.

Her arm seemed to have stopped bleeding on its own, but she could still feel liquid trickling from the wound in her side. Never had she been more grateful for her healing abilities than she was tonight, for this was the closest she'd ever come to death. She didn't even have the energy to clean herself up and simply collapsed on her sleeping mat, still clad in her black hanbok.

Sleep embraced her like a long-lost friend, welcoming her into its blissful darkness, yet even as Chin Sun faded, a pang of awareness went through her. She'd lost something far more precious than blood tonight.

The monster's cold sneer burned the back of Chin Sun's eyelids, forcing her awake before her body was ready to comply. She shivered, almost as frightened now as she'd been in its presence. She tried to pull herself up into a sitting position, but a wave of pain sent her falling back to the floor.

She'd never encountered a goblin before, but the blue fire around it had been a dead giveaway. They were shapeshifters like her, but they weren't restricted in the forms they could take. Legend claimed their true shape was horned and one-legged, but Chin Sun wondered how anyone could know that for sure.

What could it have wanted with her bead? She'd not heard of a goblin showing interest in one, and though her memories of last night were hazy, she was certain that had been the monster's target.

Chin Sun pressed her hand to her stomach, the place where her bead resided, then let out a yelp.

Where there should have been an outflow of warmth and tranquility there was only emptiness. Panic blanketed her soul like fog spreading over the mountains. The goblin must have gotten it.

She had to stay calm. If she figured out where the goblin had taken it, she could make a plan to steal it back. She'd always been able to sense the bead before. Maybe she still could.

Though she wasn't exactly sure what she was doing, she pictured the bead in her mind and then extended the image outward, beyond herself. At first, she felt nothing, not even a flicker of her fox power, but then—like a firefly in the dark —she sensed the bead.

But as soon as she found it, she also felt the energy it was absorbing. And she instinctively knew it was human.

What? That meant it wasn't the goblin who had taken it. Who could have?

She pressed her fingers to her temple. Someone *else* had been there, someone who'd interrupted the goblin's plan, but she couldn't recall who.

Without her bead, Chin Sun couldn't use her gumiho powers. Her strength, speed, heightened senses, and fox form were inaccessible.

But that meant she also couldn't—

Chin Sun pulled her hanbok away from her torso, sucking her teeth to hold back a cry. She stared at the gaping wound in her side with horror. She'd sustained stab wounds before, but her healing abilities had always lessened their impact. Not so this time. It was a miracle she hadn't bled out, but her undergarments were soaked. There was no way she could hide this.

Unless . . . She hadn't wanted to do this before, but it seemed she had no choice now.

"Ah In," she called, flinching at how much it hurt to speak.

Footsteps padded down the hallway. "Yeh, my lady?" came a voice from the other side of the screened door.

"Send for a nurse."

"For your head, my lady?" The servant started to pull open the screened door.

"Please waste no time in calling for one," Chin Sun replied a little too shrilly. Pain rolled through her body, but she had to keep it tamped down. Her survival depended on it. "I fear I shall faint if I don't receive aid soon."

Her words had the desired effect, for Ah In stepped away from the door to do as she'd been bidden. "I'll go to the nearest clinic and—"

"Actually, see if there's one available at the police bureau. It's much closer."

Dead silence followed for several seconds until Ah In hesitantly inquired, "A damo, my lady? Are you certain?"

Damos were the lowest-ranking female nurses, sent to work for the police bureaus as punishment for receiving low grades in their schooling. They handled the tasks men couldn't perform, such as examining female corpses. Confucianism decreed men were not to touch women who weren't close relatives, even in death.

"I may be ill, but my judgment is still sound," Chin Sun said, adding some bite to her tone. "Fetch one at once."

When Ah In scurried off, Chin Sun anxiously counted the minutes until her return. It was still early morning, which was a miracle in itself, but the day wouldn't tarry for her sake. If the damo didn't show up soon, someone else would come to check on her, whether it was another servant or a family member. She wished she could remove her soiled clothes, but moving too much could reopen her wounds, and she doubted she could handle losing any more blood.

"I've brought Hae Rim and a bowl of water in case you need it, my lady," came Ah In's voice.

Chin Sun made sure her clothes were completely covered by the sleeping mat before she uttered a soft, "Send her in."

A young woman stepped into the room, head lowered, so Chin Sun couldn't get a clear view of her face. She wore a white apron, and her hair was tied back with a long red ribbon. A small bag hung from her shoulder, and an oddly shaped ring rested on her forefinger.

Once the door was shut and it was just the two of them, Chin Sun pulled back the blanket. "Thank you for coming."

"How may I assist you, agasshi?" The nurse finally raised her head, revealing a pretty face with round cheeks, but her genial countenance fell away at the sight of the blood, replaced by eyes as large as deep-fried honey cookies. A green pallor came over her skin like she was about to vomit.

Chin Sun's lips thinned with irritation. This Hae Rim was supposed to be a nurse, and a damo at that. Surely she was familiar with sword wounds.

"I should think you'd know the answer to that."

Chin Sun's words jarred Hae Rim from her paralysis, the stunned look on her face disappearing behind a serious expression. "Let's see what we're working with, agasshi."

For the next several minutes, the damo inspected, cleaned, stitched up, and bound Chin Sun's wounds. She also managed to get Chin Sun out of her ruined hanbok and into some clean clothes. There were no broken ribs or signs of infection, but it was crucial that Chin Sun stay in the bed for several days; otherwise, she would slow down her recovery or perhaps even bleed to death. Rest would be the best medicine, though Hae Rim did sprinkle some powdered herbs onto the injured areas to help with the healing process.

Chin Sun said little during her visit, not wanting the nurse to start asking questions about the cause of her injuries. But when Hae Rim stated that she was finished and needed to speak with the rest of the family, Chin Sun grabbed her wrist.

Something almost like disdain flickered in the damo's eyes before she ducked her head in submission. "Is there something else?"

"What you've seen here does not travel beyond this room. Is that clear?"

"But, agasshi, your family needs to—"

Chin Sun shook her head. "No one can know. I don't care how much it costs to keep you quiet. You will not speak of this, or there will be consequences you won't like." She increased the pressure on the woman's wrist.

The damo winced a bit but nodded. "I understand. If you'd rather it be a secret than let your family ease your suffering, I will keep my mouth shut."

Chin Sun didn't appreciate the jab, but she released her.

Hae Rim rubbed her wrist, then gathered her things. "But do you truly think this will stay quiet? I'm sure your servant has already told the rest of the household about my visit."

Chin Sun's lip curled back. She was liking this girl less and less. "I'll handle that. Ask Ah In to pay you on your way out."

"I'll return tomorrow to change the dressings. Try not to move too much, or you may reopen your wounds."

Hae Rim didn't wait for a response before she bowed and departed, but as she stepped out of the screened doors, Sang Mi burst inside.

"Unni, what happened?" She dropped to the floor beside the mat, eyes red and face flushed. "Are you all right?"

Chin Sun patted her cousin's hand. "I'll be fine. The nurse gave me some medicine that should help, and she's going to return tomorrow to check on me. In the meantime, she said I shouldn't overwork myself."

"You *are* very pale." Sang Mi's gaze was skeptical. "Was it truly just a headache?"

"It's also the time of my monthly cycle, so it made every-thing worse." Chin Sun had thought up the lie while the nurse was here. Although all the sullied clothes had been taken care of, there was still the possibility that Chin Sun might bleed through her dressings. Her monthly cycle was an easy excuse.

"Ah." Sang Mi nodded in understanding.

"But since I need to be careful, that means you'll have to take on more of the responsibilities for the household. Can you do that?"

The younger girl cringed before she lifted her mouth into a smile. "Of course, Unni. What would you like me to do?"

Chin Sun drummed her fingers against her blanket. Sang Mi hated anything even close to physical labor. Her idea of exertion was a stroll through town or a dance. Chin Sun was tempted to tell her something strenuous, like scrubbing the floors, but Sang Mi was just too pitiful.

Plus she didn't want to hear Sang Mi complain about how the work ruined the orange bongsunghwa dye on her fingernails.

"The first thing you can do is go get your new book so we can read it together."

"Really?" Sang Mi's eyes lit up, then she stiffened. "But I thought you were angry with me."

Chin Sun frowned. "Should I be? You never did tell me what happened yesterday."

"Oh, that . . ." Sang Mi blushed and looked away. "You know Yong Ha down at the market?"

"The hat maker's son? What about him?"

The younger girl started playing with her skirt. "Well . . . about a month ago, he asked if Father had received any requests for my hand."

"What?" Chin Sun kept her voice from rising to a shout at the last instant, then grimaced apologetically. Yong Ha was a nice young man and, as far as she could tell, very respected among the merchants and commoners. Still, Uncle would never approve of such a match. "And how did you respond?"

Sang Mi looked up, searching Chin Sun's gaze as though hunting for any trace of criticism. Finding none, she mumbled, "I told him I hadn't yet, but now that negotiations for your marriage were underway, I expected Father would start looking for a husband for me soon." She dropped her head again. "And that I hoped he would reach out."

"Sang Mi-yah!" This time, Chin Sun couldn't restrain herself. "However did you grow up to be so brazen?"

When her cousin crumpled like hanji paper, Chin Sun placed her fingers on Sang Mi's cheek, drawing the girl's eyes to hers. A soft smile spread over Chin Sun's face. "If only we all were courageous enough to share our hearts like you do."

Sang Mi's eyes crinkled. "You really think so? That it was courage and not just me being stupid?"

Chin Sun nodded, then playfully tapped her nose. "Perhaps a bit of both."

Sang Mi giggled, the sound as warm and refreshing as spring sunshine.

But all was not well—it couldn't be when something had made this sweet, pure, sometimes foolish, girl cry. Chin Sun hated to ruin the moment, especially after the awful night she'd had, but she had to know. "That doesn't explain why you were upset yesterday."

Sang Mi's shoulders fell. "Ah, yeh. Yong Ha sent me a letter." She twisted her hands together, voice breaking. "He and his father were robbed. They've . . . lost everything."

"Robbed? Do they know who did it?"

"Yeh, but the police are refusing to investigate him

because he's the chief's nephew. It all sounds so hopeless, and now Yong Ha doesn't feel like he can approach Father. He said—" Sang Mi sniffled, then rose to her feet. "I better go get that book." She bowed and darted out.

Chin Sun's muscles were tense, rage boiling in her stomach. This was exactly why Gwishin was needed. Sokju's government was so crippled by nepotism and bribery that true justice felt like an impossible dream. But even as a vigilante, she was only a dewdrop in a scorching desert. If the common people were going to thrive, it was going to take a rainstorm.

She took a deep breath, reminding herself she couldn't even help one thirsty soul while stuck in this state. She had to get her bead back first.

Who had that second figure been? Chin Sun's head was pounding, but she forced herself to think back. A silhouette slowly came into focus. Black hanbok much like her own. Tall. A sword in his right hand. Wisps of hair framing a handsome, stubbled face—

Chin Sun gasped as everything clicked into place. The sword fight, the chase through the woods, shifting into fox form.

And her rescuer.

Dread flooded her insides as her bodyguard's face flashed through her mind. Of all people, why did it have to be Mr. Park? He was the worst person it could possibly be.

While not all of the humans' beliefs about gumiho were correct, they had gotten some things right. And though Chin Sun hadn't grown up among gumiho, she knew in her soul what she had to do.

The only way to retrieve a swallowed fox bead was with a kiss.

Chapter 8

The Investigator

Hyun Soo tried not to let his dissatisfaction show when he returned to the Lee residence empty-handed. One of Lord Lee's servants opened the door to allow him entrance, a question flickering in his eyes, but the young man dared not ask it. Hyun Soo didn't bother explaining his late arrival. Instead, he made his way to his small sleeping area and took a much-needed break, knowing he'd only have a few hours before his duties would begin again.

Such was the life of a soldier, and Hyun Soo had grown accustomed to surviving on the bare minimum. His comrades had often joked around that he was more than human, for no human could function on as little sleep as he got.

He wondered what they'd say if they'd been there tonight. Tae Min would probably have made a joke about how Hyun Soo had done fairly well, but if it had been him, he wouldn't have let Gwishin escape. Then Byung Hun would have shoved Tae Min and told him to stop lying.

His old friends' laughing faces were bittersweet, for it

was impossible to think of them without also remembering how they'd abandoned him when he'd needed them most.

Hyun Soo pressed his fist against his forehead, wishing sleep would snatch him away from his thoughts. He didn't need to be thinking about his comrades now; he had other disappointments to rectify.

When he woke, one of the servants told him Lady Lee had taken ill with a fierce headache and would be staying in her quarters for a few days, so he would only be needed at night for keeping the residence secure.

A headache? More like the fight in the alley yesterday had her too frightened to go outdoors.

Guilt skittered across his chest. She wouldn't be frightened if he'd done his job properly.

No matter. This was actually helpful since it gave him some time to gather information.

Hyun Soo spent the extra time investigating, first with a visit to the police bureau, then to the yangban and jungin in the center of Sokju. It took quite a bit of effort, and sometimes outright bribery, but he managed to get statements from just about every officer and highborn who claimed to have seen the infamous vigilante. The only ones he didn't talk with were the Kangs, Lees, and a certain inspector Kim who was away on business.

He also manned his nightly post over the Lee residence until his reprieve, and though he didn't have any other encounters with the vigilante, he couldn't escape a nearly constant feeling of being watched. It would come upon him as soon as the sun set each night, starting with an eerie chill down his spine that would spread through his limbs and settle around his heart. Every time he tried to dismiss it as paranoia, he'd remember the monster from the forest and check the perimeter again. He never found anything, but that didn't mean the creature wasn't out there. Watching. Waiting.

Between questioning people by day and standing guard by night, Hyun Soo barely stopped to eat or rest, and by the time he'd finished speaking to the last witness, he was exhausted. It was lunchtime, so he headed to the closest inn, ordered a hearty bowl of janggukbap, soju, and side dishes, and sat down to sort through everything he'd collected about Gwishin.

He'd asked the police to share what they'd learned about the vigilante, specifically when and where he'd been spotted. They hadn't wanted to tell him anything at first, but mentioning the Kang family name had been like a key that unlocked a treasure trove of information.

From what Hyun Soo could tell, Gwishin had only become a serious problem in the last couple of years, though vague reports of masked men in black spanned back in the city's records for decades. People hadn't officially named the vigilante "the Ghost" until about a year ago when he'd raided a yangban's storage building and bags of grain had subsequently appeared in front of several commoners' huts. Eyewitnesses placed him all over the city. From the quaintest clay hut to the most luxurious yangban estate, almost every area of Sokju had a story of the infamous Gwishin. He'd been accused of assault, armed robbery, destruction of property, and the murders of over thirty individuals, a few of whom were civilians.

Physical descriptions of the man were sparse, aside from his black hanbok and covered face. Some said he was taller than any man they'd ever seen while others claimed he was on the short side. Hyun Soo recalled a short adversary with slight features, which had made the vigilante all the more elusive during their skirmish.

He wasn't even a man, according to a few, but a real ghost who'd returned from the grave to settle an old score with the government. Some of the reports even used phrases like "too fast to be human" and "he cast a spell on me so I couldn't move until he was gone." Hyun Soo's encounter last night *had* been strange. He'd assumed he'd be dealing with someone fairly skilled in martial arts, not someone who seemed to disappear like the mist.

But Hyun Soo hadn't believed in ghost stories since he was a child, and he wasn't about to start now. Ghosts didn't bleed.

The yangban and jungin he'd spoken with had been happy to hear someone besides the police was finally getting involved in this whole mess. They'd lost a great deal because of Gwishin and hoped he would soon be brought to justice. Among the highborn, there was a common thread of hatred toward the infamous criminal.

But then there were the others, mostly testimonies from commoners and lowborn, that painted a starkly different portrait. "He's not a criminal. He's the savior of Sokju," one merchant had claimed after the vigilante had saved his daughter from drowning.

"We've needed him around for a long time," a disgruntled citizen had told the police after a nobleman's home was looted. "This yangban stole from me on three occasions, and the government did nothing about it. Gwishin is standing up for the common people."

Hyun Soo gulped down his soju, then called for a refill.

Such contradictory evidence was giving him a headache of his own. Just who was Gwishin?

The innkeeper brought him some more alcohol, and Hyun Soo thanked her despite the critical look she gave him before bustling off. He raised his drinking bowl back to his lips.

"I should have known I'd find you here," said a familiar voice.

Hyun Soo looked up as his friend waltzed over from the entrance and plopped into the seat across from him. Dol Sam smirked in that annoying "I know you better than you know yourself" way, and Hyun Soo set his bowl down with a scowl.

"Dol Sam-ah, I know you told me I should come see you when I got the chance. I've just been busy."

"Clearly," was the yangban's dry response, but the crinkle at the corners of his eyes revealed he was only jesting.

Hyun Soo ran a hand down his face. "Stopping Gwishin has proven more . . . difficult than I anticipated."

Dol Sam nodded sympathetically before calling the innkeeper over to ask for some stew and a second bottle of soju. Once she'd brought him his meal, he took a swig of alcohol before asking, "Have you found any leads at all? Any clue as to where he might be hiding?"

Hyun Soo glared at the innkeeper, who was overtly eavesdropping a few tables over. She huffed and stomped off to another table, but still, Hyun Soo kept his voice hushed. "Actually, I met him a few nights ago."

Dol Sam slammed his bowl down, catching everyone's attention and sloshing so much liquid onto the floor that the innkeeper hissed in disapproval. "Where? Where did you see him?" Gone was Dol Sam's teasing tone, replaced by a fierce urgency that bordered on hysteria.

"Calm down." Hyun Soo grabbed his arm, surprised at the man's visceral reaction. Hadn't he not even blinked when he'd been under an assassin's knife three years ago? "Do you want to get us kicked out?"

"Sorry." Dol Sam waved to the innkeeper and apologized again, dipping his head a few times until the woman seemed reasonably placated. He turned back to Hyun Soo. "Please tell me what happened."

"I ran into him just outside the Lee residence a few nights ago. I fought him, injuring him just below the ribs, but the coward escaped into the woods."

"You hurt him, but he still got away? Gwishin must be slipperier than I thought."

Guilt weighed heavily on Hyun Soo's heart. His friend had entrusted him with his betrothed's safety, yet with Gwishin still out there, he wasn't able to guarantee it. "I'm sorry, Dol Sam-ah. I wish I had better news to tell you."

The two fell into silence, the only sound between them the slurping of janggukbap. Finally, Hyun Soo ventured, "About Lady Lee, are you sure she's the right woman for you? From what I've seen, she's—" He broke off at the dark look on his friend's face, then tried again. "I just don't think the two of you are a good fit."

"And you figured this out after only knowing her for a few days?"

Hyun Soo didn't miss the sharp undercurrent in Dol Sam's voice warning him not to discuss the matter further, but Hyun Soo wasn't going to let it go that easily. No matter how much Dol Sam liked Lady Lee, he didn't want his friend making a mistake. The noblewoman was argumentative, moody, and deceptive. She may be beautiful and good at managing her household, but Dol Sam needed someone who would support him, not question his decisions at every turn. "I can't say anything for certain, but she seems very different from the woman you made her out to be."

Dol Sam crossed his arms. "After everything we've been through together, I thought you of all people would understand and be on my side. But you're just like everyone else, looking down on her because she's jungin."

The jab stung, but Hyun Soo forced his pride down. "I *am* on your side. It's not because she's jungin."

"Then you don't like that she's an orphan? She had no choice in that. The Lees raised her as their own, and Lord Lee is perfectly respectable."

Hyun Soo held up his hand. "Please, you've got it all wrong. I'm not against Lady Lee because of anything like that."

"But you are against her." It wasn't a question, and though Dol Sam hadn't raised his voice, there was no mistaking the anger simmering within the young yangban. If Hyun Soo didn't calm him down soon, this conversation might turn into a full-fledged argument.

"I'm just worried about you."

Dol Sam sighed, some of the fire leaving his eyes, and took a bite of stew. "Well, you don't need to. I know what I'm doing. I've known the Lees for years, and Lady Lee is everything a man could wish for."

You may have known her family for years, but how much have you actually spoken to her? Hyun Soo wanted to ask, but he held back, knowing that question wouldn't help anything. Perhaps a different approach would be better.

"What do your parents think of her?"

Dol Sam didn't respond at first—a bad sign—and then he said, "Mother is very happy for me."

"And your father?"

"He's . . . he's not opposed to the Lees, but they're not his first choice," Dol Sam admitted. "That's why it's so important you stop Gwishin, and soon. Father doesn't want me anywhere near the Lees until the vigilante is no longer a threat. He's even suggested moving somewhere safer."

"Moving? But what about your wedding?"

The stricken expression on his friend's face was answer enough.

Compassion welled up in Hyun Soo's chest. He may not like Lady Lee, but he didn't want to see his friend hurting. "Doesn't he know how much you care for Lady Lee?"

"That hardly matters to him. Connections are what's important. The Lees are wealthy and respectable, but there are plenty of other families who fit that description. Plenty of *yangban* families who would love the chance to form ties with my father." Dol Sam fixed his attention on his food, lip quivering like he was holding back how much it bothered him.

But it was a pathetic attempt to hide his true feelings, especially after he'd just defended his betrothed so vehemently. It would devastate Dol Sam if he couldn't be with Lady Lee; Hyun Soo was certain of it.

And if he was the friend he claimed to be, there was only one thing left to do. How he felt about Lady Lee personally was immaterial. If Dol Sam was sure she was the one for him, far be it from Hyun Soo to oppose him.

"Don't worry, Dol Sam-ah," Hyun Soo assured him, "I won't let anything or anyone get in the way of you and Lady Lee. Be it this vigilante or even your father. You can count on me."

Dol Sam's lips lifted into a weak smile. "I hope so. And if there's anything I can do to help—"

"Actually, maybe you can. Let me tell you what I've found so far. . . ."

Chapter 9

The Gamble

"Hold still," Hae Rim snapped, pulling the bandage tighter around Chin Sun's middle.

Chin Sun gritted her teeth as she stared at the midmorning sunlight streaming through her window onto the floor. This nurse grew more insufferable by the day. Any leverage Chin Sun had thought she'd had over her as a jungin had disappeared by the nurse's second visit. In fact, it seemed the tables had completely turned, and now Hae Rim was the one with all the power.

But Chin Sun forced herself to bear it, no matter how acerbic Hae Rim was, for she couldn't risk the truth of her injuries coming to light.

"There, that should do it." Hae Rim sat back with a satisfied grin. "You're healing remarkably fast. I'd say you should be able to move around now, if you feel up for it." When Chin Sun's expression brightened, the nurse wagged her finger. "But nothing strenuous. I don't want you ruining all the progress you've made."

Chin Sun glared. "Are you certain of that? A longer recovery would mean more income for you."

Hae Rim didn't respond to the quip and simply packed up her things. "Send for me if you have any more . . . issues."

"Does that mean you're not coming back?"

"You sound so excited one might almost think you disliked my company." The nurse's head didn't lift, and her tone stayed as flat as ever, and yet . . .

Amusement twitched at Chin Sun's lips, but she concealed it behind a well-placed frown. "I'm sure I don't know what you mean. Thank you for your service."

When Hae Rim bowed and turned away, Chin Sun could have sworn there was a grin at the edge of the grumpy woman's mouth.

Once she was gone, Chin Sun practically leaped off her bed mat and retrieved a sheet of paper from her desk. She peered down at it for a moment, then tucked it safely away in her sleeve. All that time on bed rest had allowed her to plan out her next steps accordingly. Now, it was time to execute them.

"Ah In," she called cheerily.

The young servant bustled into the room with a deep bow. She lifted her head and smiled. "You're looking well, my lady. What did the nurse say?"

"She said I'm no longer confined to my chambers." Chin Sun giggled with glee. "Oh, when does Mr. Park take time to rest? I'd love to go out into the city, but I don't want to interrupt him if he's asleep." She spoke nonchalantly, as if she was only mildly curious, but inside, she couldn't be more invested in the answer.

"He stops working at about midnight and goes back on duty at eight o' clock, so there's no need to worry about waking him."

"Wonderful. Then would you call him? I'd like to buy some fabric for new curtains."

Ah In's eyebrows knit together. "I'm afraid Mr. Park isn't here at the moment."

Chin Sun blinked. "What? Not here? Where else would he be?"

"Ever since you took ill, he's been scouring the city for information about"—Ah In dropped her volume to a whisper—"Gwishin."

Chin Sun took a deep breath. This man just didn't know when to stop. Wasn't it enough that he'd almost killed her and stolen her bead? She'd been stuck in this room ever since, and instead of waiting patiently at home like a body-guard should, he was out there, trying to find her so he could make sure she was dead.

"Oh." She spoke through her teeth. "How *thoughtful* of him."

Ah In shivered. "My lady? Are you sure you're all right? You seem . . . tense."

Chin Sun threw back her head and laughed, a sharp, frustrated sound. "I don't know why you'd think so. I'm feeling better than I have in days." She wandered over to the window and peered at the lily pond in the courtyard. Sang Mi was taking a stroll out there, as her cousin often did in the mornings. "I suppose I'll go see Sang Mi instead. Perhaps she has some extra fabric I can use."

"Would you like me to send someone to go find Mr. Park?"

"No, it's fine. I'm sure he's busy. Actually . . ." She whirled around and met Ah In's eye. "Don't bother telling him I'm feeling better until tomorrow. He can have one last day before he resumes his normal guard duties."

"That's . . . very generous of you, my lady." Ah In excused herself with a nervous bow.

Chin Sun pressed a smile to her lips and sauntered out to the courtyard. "Dongsaeng, may I join you?"

Sang Mi's eyes lit up as she turned. "Unni!" She ran over and squeezed Chin Sun in an embrace that was slightly painful before pulling back. "I take it this means you're free to go wherever you'd like again?"

Chin Sun nodded. "I don't suppose you'd like to join me on a walk through the market?"

"Oh, yeh!"

The cousins locked arms and wandered out, one jabbering away about how she wanted to look at the fans while the other toyed with the fox sketch hidden in her sleeve.

She hoped Min Joon wouldn't be too angry with her for missing the stakeout on the magistrate. If they met up tonight—after midnight when Mr. Park was sleeping—she could apologize properly.

And tell him they had far bigger problems than Magistrate Hong.

Slipping out of the city came almost as easily as breathing now, and before long, Chin Sun was stalking up to the hut she and Min Joon had deemed their "hideout" back when they were children, innocent to the evils of the world. Little had they known how accurate the title would become.

The house was in shambles, clay walls covered in fingers of ivy she'd traced with her eyes dozens of times. Chin Sun swept past the brushwood gate rendered useless long ago and stepped inside.

"I wasn't sure you'd show," came a harsh voice. Min Joon leaned against the far wall, arms crossed.

Chin Sun grimaced. "Min Joon-ah, I'm sorry I couldn't make it before. What happened with the sulfur?"

"I was so worried about you that I lost Hong in the woods before the exchange happened. So, you better have a good reason for why you didn't meet me."

"I would have, only—something came up." Her gaze darted away. Why was it so hard to admit she'd gotten into more than she could handle?

He pushed himself off the wall and closed the distance between them, bending down until they were at eye level. "Something came up? That's your reason?"

She wrung her hands. "No, it's . . ." She sighed. As much as it pained her to tell him, protecting the people of Sokju was more important than her pride. "After I left you here last time, someone attacked me on the road. He was—it didn't end well, and I had to make a run for it. I—"

Min Joon waved his hand. "Wait, wait, wait. What do you mean, 'it didn't end well'? Did you get hurt?"

Chin Sun's cheeks bloomed under his scrutiny, but she nodded. "Yeh, but that's not the worst of it."

She told him how she'd run off to the forest, how she'd thought she'd lost her pursuer after shifting into fox form— and what had found her in the darkness.

"A goblin?" Min Joon's brow furrowed. "I thought you'd never come across any other creatures of magic."

"I hadn't until then. But that's what it was, I'm sure of it."

"But you said you were injured. How did you fend off a goblin on top of that?"

She shook her head. "That's the thing. I didn't. When

the goblin appeared, I was so weak I couldn't stop him. He nearly killed me. Nearly stole my bead."

Her chest went tight at the memory. She'd never been so terrified in all her life.

"But he didn't?" Min Joon pressed.

"The man who attacked me found us and fought it off."

"So you didn't lose your bead." The relief in her friend's voice was palpable.

Chin Sun rolled her lips, wishing she didn't need to share this next part. "Well, that's not exactly true. . . . When the man who attacked me showed up, he—he swallowed it."

Min Joon's eyes nearly popped out of his head. "What? Someone swallowed your bead? But don't fox beads store human energy?"

She nodded. "If I don't get it back from him soon, he's going to die."

Her friend turned away and plopped into one of the chairs. His mouth was a tight line. "If he tried to kill you, perhaps it's better if he's gone."

Chin Sun blinked. Min Joon wasn't usually so callous. Out of the two of them, she'd always thought him the better person, the more reluctant to leave casualties.

She took the seat next to him, wishing the situation were that simple. "I can't do that."

"Why not?"

"You know why."

Chin Sun may be an outlaw, but she still had honor. Those who'd met their end at her hand had either been vile transgressors of the law or had given her no choice. And as easy as it would be to do nothing, if she allowed Mr. Park to perish because of the bead, she would be no better than the people she was fighting against.

Luckily for him, absorbing human energy took time, and Chin Sun could sense that her bead was nowhere near full. She wasn't entirely certain how long it would take, but she guessed she had about a month before Mr. Park's lifeforce ran out.

One month to fix this.

But she needed that bead now; otherwise, how could she protect the citizens of Sokju?

"Besides, he's not just anyone," she added. "He's Kang Dol Sam's friend—and my new bodyguard."

"Bodyguard?" His tone was incredulous. "Since when do you need a bodyguard?"

She raised her eyebrows with a deadpan look.

"Ah. The delicate Lady Lee needed protection, so her rich fiancé made sure she was well taken care of."

"Don't talk about Kang Dol Sam like that," she snapped.

"Sorry, it's just difficult to think highly of someone whose family has gotten away with so many crimes against mine."

It was hard to argue with him there. As two of the oldest yangban families in Gangwon Province, the Kims and the Kangs had a long-standing enmity, always trying to dominate the other. The Kangs were the more powerful right now, but that could change at any time.

She had never met Kang Dol Sam's father, Lord Kang Ki Yong, personally, but the man was highly respected throughout the region for both his wisdom and dedication to Joseon's well-being.

Too bad his patriotism didn't extend to the people who got in his way.

Chin Sun hadn't been able to pin anything on Lord Kang yet, but she'd uncovered plenty of unsavory information about his associates. Bribery, kidnapping, assault—it seemed Lord Kang's men would stoop to anything to expand their lord's power.

She and Min Joon had gotten quite a few arrested in the last six months, looking forward to the day they could finally take the greedy lord down, too.

Her betrothal to his son was a complication she hadn't expected.

"Forget about your hatred for the Kangs for one moment, and listen to what I'm saying. *Mr. Park has my fox bead.*"

He shrugged. "And? I still like my idea of letting him die. If he's a friend of the Kangs—"

Chin Sun groaned. "That's not an option, all right? And I need the bead back as soon as possible anyway."

"Why's that?"

"Because as soon as he swallowed it, I lost my powers."

Min Joon's mouth fell open. "All of them? What about your speed, your strength?"

"All of them." She held her palms up. "Right now, for all intents and purposes, I'm only human."

Something flashed in her friend's eyes, but before she could discern it, his hand had shot out and slammed into her shoulder.

"Aigoo!" She leaned away with a glower. "What did you do that for?"

"Just checking."

"Do *you* want to die?"

Min Joon chuckled, then turned contemplative. He drummed his fingers on the table, no doubt considering the dangers involved in attempting to recover the bead. Chin Sun waited, nervously, desperately, for him to come up with an idea that didn't involve destroying the reputation she'd spent her whole life building.

In a world that valued virtue above all else, anything that even hinted at sexual misconduct would taint not only her but also her entire family. Marriage talks with the Kangs would be a thing of the past—and Uncle would likely struggle to find anyone in Sokju willing to marry her or Sang Mi.

Finally, Min Joon paused. He turned to her with a weak smile. "I might know something you could do. But you won't like it."

Chin Sun crept past the servants' rooms as furtively as a weasel, single-minded in her goal. She couldn't afford any slip-ups. She just hoped Mr. Park was a hard sleeper.

The only extra room in the house was at the end of the hall, so she hadn't needed to ask where he'd been placed. It had functioned as a storage room until now, mostly for the books and documents Uncle didn't use on a regular basis.

She felt a little bad to be doing this without his consent, but it wasn't like there were any good options. When Min Joon had suggested this idea, it had at least sounded viable. She could hardly expect Mr. Park to just *let* her kiss him, or keep it a secret from her fiancé.

CREAK.

Chin Sun's foot froze on the loose floorboard. She was just outside Mr. Park's room now, close enough to be heard if the troublesome bodyguard wasn't actually asleep. She held her breath, heart thumping in her ears.

When no sounds emerged from the man's room, she crept closer and pulled open the door.

Mr. Park's sleeping form lay a few inches within,

stretched out in a room barely wide enough to accommodate him.

Chin Sun threw her hand over her mouth to stifle a gasp. She hadn't expected the room to be *this* small. Mr. Park's chest rose and fell steadily, his face more carefree than she'd ever seen. A thick green blanket covered all but his head and neck, and his hair fanned out over his small pillow.

Her heart leaped at the sight of a trio of swords to the man's right. Two belonged to him, but the other was her hwando, the sword she'd lost the night of their fight. She reached over Mr. Park and took it, clutching it to her chest. Gratitude surged through her. Even though it hadn't been intentional, retrieving her precious blade felt like receiving a gift.

Her gaze fell to Mr. Park's lips. She'd never kissed a man before, but from what she'd heard, it could either feel delightful or horrendous. Sang Mi had confessed to having done it about a year ago, and she'd compared one's first kiss to the first blooms of spring—hesitant, tender, and a little magical.

But Sang Mi was a hopeless romantic, so Chin Sun didn't completely trust her judgment.

It was only a kiss. She needed to stop overthinking it. And not even a real kiss either—she was just getting her fox bead back, so there was no need for all the anxiety.

Unless she woke him up, of course.

Chin Sun swallowed, sweat forming on her temples. The bead was right there; she could feel its gentle hum at the edge of her consciousness. She got down on her knees.

Mr. Park was awfully handsome. She hadn't taken the time to notice before, but now that he was just a hairsbreadth away, it was rather distracting. The almost perfect symmetry of his face was marred only by a thin scar on his right eyebrow. All that was left of an old battle wound perhaps. His mouth was relaxed in sleep, his smooth lips slightly parted.

If she had to lose her first kiss to someone besides her future husband, she could have done much worse.

But what if *he* was married? She couldn't kiss a married man! Panic flared within her, but then she reminded herself that a married man would have his hair tied up, not loose. No wife would stand for such dishonor. Mr. Park was, without a doubt, unbound, meaning she could kiss him with a clear conscience.

She had to hurry up.

She leaned forward, but then a groan from a nearby room cut through the silence. Her eyes widened, limbs turning to ice when Mr. Park began to stir.

His eyelids fluttered, breaking the spell over her, and she stumbled out of the room. Chin Sun's footsteps were clumsy, and altogether too loud, but she had to get out of there. The rustle of waking servants sent her heart pattering, so she threw herself down the hallway and out into the courtyard.

She ducked behind the storage shed and crouched down in the darkness. Listening. Waiting. Wind whistled through the trees, followed by the screech of an owl. Crickets hummed from the bushes, oblivious to the tension running through Chin Sun's veins.

But neither footfalls nor voices reached her ears.

After a few minutes, she peeked around the shed. The courtyard was empty, and the only lights were the paper lanterns that always hung from the main pavilion's eaves. She'd gotten away.

Chin Sun sighed, but her relief quickly shifted to

dismay. She'd been so close to getting the bead! It had been *right* there.

She shook her head. More like so close to getting caught. That couldn't happen again. She had to come up with a new plan.

Chapter 10

The Dream

Hyun Soo woke with a start, images of terrifying monsters lingering at the back of his mind. He'd been having nightmares ever since he'd attacked that creature in the woods; he could still hear its haunting voice, feel its murderous aura brushing against his skin.

He opened his door and grabbed the small basin and washcloth the servants left outside his room every morning. He splashed some water on his face, effectively banishing the visions, then took a deep breath. Maybe he'd find something useful today.

He and Dol Sam had discussed everything he'd learned about Gwishin the day before, concluding that if the yangban and jungin had nothing more to give, it was time to start questioning the lower classes directly. That meant not only talking to sangmin, the commoners, but even going so far as to meet with cheonmin, the lowest class in the Joseon caste system. Jail keepers, butchers, entertainers, and the rest of the unclean were people Hyun Soo typically avoided. But if that was what it took to find Gwishin, so be it. Their testimonies were the most sparse in the police reports, but also the most positive. Perhaps the police hadn't questioned them as thoroughly for fear of stirring up the highborns with talk of Gwishin being a hero to the masses.

Hyun Soo turned to gather his weapons, then paused. Hadn't the vigilante's hwando been beside his own last night? He checked the small room, trying to recall where else he might have lain it, but neither the sword nor a memory of moving it surfaced.

A sour taste filled Hyun Soo's mouth. If he hadn't misplaced the sword, that meant someone had taken it while he was sleeping. But who would be bold enough to—

His nostrils flared. A burglar would have taken Hyun Soo's sword as well, yet only the vigilante's blade was missing. And who had even known it was in his possession?

Only Gwishin himself.

Hyun Soo finished getting ready, letting the revelation sink deep into his bones. But as sure as he was that the vigilante must have taken the sword, there was one detail he couldn't make sense of.

Why hadn't Gwishin killed him when he'd had the chance?

A thorough search of the room and corridor revealed no evidence of the vigilante's visit, and when he questioned the servants—subtly, so as not to raise alarm—they told him they hadn't heard or seen anything out of the ordinary the night before. Which left him with nothing to go on, except the knowledge that the vigilante had eluded him. Again.

The other servants ate together in the kitchen, but Hyun Soo's working hours were so different from theirs he had his meals on his own, which typically consisted of leftovers from the previous meal. The cook made some of the most delicious stew he'd ever eaten, and that was saying something when the food was usually cold by the time he got some.

Once he'd finished his breakfast, he marched past the pond in the courtyard and headed toward the main gate to continue his hunt. There had to be something out there, some clue to track him down and stop this criminal for good.

"Mr. Park," a servant called. It was the young man Lady Lee had defended so vehemently—Pyung Ho, if Hyun Soo wasn't mistaken. The servant scurried over and bowed. "Lady Lee has requested your presence in her chambers."

"Is she all right?" Hyun Soo gripped the hilt of his sword. He hadn't seen his charge since she'd fallen ill; perhaps something had happened to her in his absence.

Pyung Ho's complexion whitened, eyes homing in on Hyun Soo's blade. "Sh-she's fine. She's feeling better, actually, so she's ready for you to resume guarding her."

Hyun Soo's hand relaxed. "Ah. Thank you for letting me know."

"The Lees already ate their breakfast, so she's waiting in her chambers." Pyung Ho bowed sharply before darting toward the kitchen like a mouse fleeing a cat.

Maybe he'd been a bit too harsh with him the other day.

. . .

When Hyun Soo reached the lady's quarters, he announced his arrival and waited for a soft "you may enter," then stepped inside.

Lady Lee sat with a needle and thread in front of a folding screen depicting a flock of cranes. Her green jeogori bore a black floral pattern, while her skirt was a deep burgundy. A black flower pin rested just above her forehead against her hair. Her face was paler than usual, as though she truly had been fighting an illness, but her expression was pleasant as she stitched a butterfly into a small pillow.

And then she looked up.

The moment their gazes met, a vision flashed through Hyun Soo's mind. Lady Lee hovering over him in the shadows, lips poised for a kiss.

Heat filled Hyun Soo's cheeks, as much from shock as embarrassment. Though his charge was strikingly beautiful, he'd never been one to indulge in fantasies. Especially about his friend's fiancée.

Or so he'd thought.

His memory of the dream ended there, but that split second of recollection was enough to completely unnerve him.

"Mr. Park, are you well?"

"Of c-course, agasshi." He tried to even out his voice. "Why wouldn't I be?"

She nodded toward his hands. "You're shaking."

Hyun Soo peered down. Indeed, both his hands were trembling as though wracked with cold. He clasped them behind his back. "It's nothing. How are you feeling? I was glad to receive your summons."

"I'm feeling rather . . . bored, actually. It's a good thing you're here."

Hyun Soo frowned, unsure how to respond. What was she . . . ? Her tone almost sounded suggestive, but that didn't make any sense. She disliked him as much as he disliked her. Perhaps he was still under the influence of that strange dream.

"Mr. Park?"

"Hmm?"

"I said I need you to escort me to the school where my uncle works."

"Oh." Hyun Soo winced. "I apologize, my lady. I assure you, I'm not usually absent-minded."

"I should hope not," she replied, a mild, almost playful rebuke in her voice. She set aside the pillow and thread and rose to her feet. "Ah In!"

One of the young servant girls entered and gave Lady Lee two small bags.

"Thank you," she said.

The two shared a smile before Ah In bowed and hurried out. Lady Lee turned to him. "Would you carry these for me?"

Hyun Soo silently accepted the bags, then followed behind her as she exited the pavilion and crossed the courtyard. A canopy of clouds hung low in the sky as they passed through the main gate and onto the city streets. They took a different route than last time, avoiding the busy market. Lady Lee's gait was brisk, focused, but unlike the last time he'd escorted her, there was an added mindfulness to her steps, and she kept glancing back as if to make sure he was still with her.

She must still have been shaken up from those thieves in the market. Hyun Soo quickened his pace until they were side by side. He may not be fond of her, but he didn't want her fearing for her safety.

"You're probably wondering why I wanted to visit my uncle's workplace," she said, turning to him expectantly.

"Uhh . . ." No, he hadn't been. Truth be told, Hyun Soo had been scanning the periphery for threats. The nature of her visit was of no concern to him.

She grinned as she pointed to the bags in his hands. "Uncle has been working so hard lately he's missed lunch the last few days. I wanted to make sure he gets enough to eat."

Hyun Soo nodded but said nothing. At least she was

filial. He didn't need to worry about Dol Sam starving once they were married.

"I'm sure you're very dedicated to your family as well?" She ended the sentence as a question, her expression tentative yet inviting.

What *was* this? Lady Lee's personality seemed to shift like sand on the seashore. One moment, she was downright antagonistic, and the next, she was asking about his family. It left him so flustered, he didn't know what to make of her. Had he misjudged her before? Was he misjudging her now?

Or could it be that she'd changed her opinion of him since he'd saved her?

That idea did make a certain sort of sense. Perhaps she'd been angry with him before because she'd believed she didn't need a bodyguard, but after the incident in the market, she'd realized she was wrong.

Hyun Soo's chest tightened. Maybe they'd misjudged each other?

She was still waiting for a response, her honey-brown eyes full of curiosity rather than spite. He cleared his throat and looked away, trying to remember what she'd asked. He'd figure out the answers to his own questions later.

"I . . . don't have much in the way of family." He tried to smile, but it came out as a grimace. This wasn't a topic he wanted to discuss. Not with her, not with anyone.

Lady Lee seemed to pick up on his discomfort and looked away. They walked in silence for a few minutes before she asked, "How did you and Young Master Kang meet?"

A bit of the tension eased from Hyun Soo's shoulders. Kang Dol Sam was someone he had no trouble talking about. "We met at the palace a few years ago when Kang Dol Sam and his father were there for an assembly. An assassin infiltrated the palace, but he was spotted before he'd shot his first arrow. My comrades and I pursued, but he happened upon Kang Dol Sam and pressed a dagger to his throat, threatening to kill him if we came any closer. I tried to get him to calm down so Kang Dol Sam didn't get hurt, but the man panicked and tried to stab him. My comrades and I got the assassin to the ground before he did any real damage."

"So, you saved Young Master Kang's life."

Hyun Soo rubbed the back of his neck, uncomfortable when she put it that way. "I was just doing my job, and I wasn't acting alone. Even so, Kang Dol Sam felt indebted to me, and the two of us quickly became friends after that. You couldn't have wished for a better man to marry."

Dol Sam had more than made up for what Hyun Soo had done by standing beside him when no one else would. By all rights, Dol Sam should have abandoned him when he'd been suspected of espionage. Instead, he'd refused to believe Hyun Soo capable of such a grievous crime, even after he'd been tried and convicted.

"It sounds like he would say the same thing about you. You're a hero," Lady Lee pointed out.

Hyun Soo shook his head. "I'm far from a hero." He couldn't keep the bitterness out of his voice.

A hero wouldn't be estranged from his father. He would have proven his innocence instead of giving up.

Dol Sam's words came back to him: "*There was nothing else you could have done. If your father can't see the good person you are, that's his own problem. Your conduct was completely honorable. I've only known you for a short time, and there's not a doubt in my mind that you were framed.*"

He appreciated his friend's support, but Hyun Soo's

discharge hadn't affected the Kangs' family name. It had affected the Parks'.

"Don't devalue yourself, Mr. Park." Lady Lee was firm, gaze unwavering. "When I was in danger, you jumped in to save me, too, and that was completely on your own. So even if you try to convince me otherwise, I'll still say you're a hero."

"You really believe that?"

"I do. And even though we didn't start out on the best of terms, I also know you would have done it even if it wasn't your job."

"There's no way you could know that."

Something flickered in the woman's eyes, like she was recalling a memory. "Yeh, there is."

Before Hyun Soo could respond, Lady Lee halted in front of a blacksmith shop. Scythes, knives, hoes, and sickles hung on the wall next to a small stone forge with still-glowing embers. A large water wheel was situated outside, tirelessly revolving to power the blacksmith's craft. "Stop here for a moment."

Hyun Soo wrinkled his nose, keeping some distance between himself and the entrance. Of all places, why here? If the family needed tools, surely Pyung Ho could have made the trek. Blacksmiths were cheonmin, not people a noblewoman should be associating with.

"Ahjussi," Lady Lee called, seemingly unaffected by her slovenly surroundings.

A stinky ahjussi emerged from the back of the shop, clothing in tatters and hammer in hand. His hulking form was reminiscent of a moon bear, with small, sad eyes and a wide, upturned nose. He frowned at Lady Lee before dipping his head in a deep bow. "Agasshi, it's an honor to have you in my shop, but I'm afraid I'm not ready with your order just yet."

The noblewoman bowed in return. "That's not why I'm here. How is young Hee Joo?"

The burly man's expression softened. "She's doing as well as can be expected. I'm hoping to be able to get some medicine for her soon, but until then, she has to stay close to home to preserve her strength. Thank you for asking after her."

She motioned for Hyun Soo to come over. "This is Mr. Park Hyun Soo, my new bodyguard. He has something for you that may help."

He sidled up on Lady Lee's right, eyebrows squished together. What was she talking about? He didn't have any—

Lady Lee snatched a bag from his hand and passed it to the blacksmith. The man accepted it with a blank look, then his bearded face split into an overwhelmed grin.

"Thank you, agasshi," he sputtered, tears forming in his eyes. "This will mean so much to my family." He bowed to her, then Hyun Soo. "Thank you. Thank you both."

Lady Lee's lips turned up. "Please give my best to your wife and daughter."

After the blacksmith had promised to do so, the pair turned to leave, only to be blocked by a troupe of performers and onlookers gathering in the street. Spectators laughed and clapped as men with multicolored robes and long white streamers sang and danced in time with drums and gongs.

Hyun Soo stretched out his arm to keep people from getting too close to his mistress, but the crowd was too big. A man in a straw hat shoved between them, and before Hyun Soo knew it, Lady Lee was lost amidst the unfamiliar faces.

"My lady? Lady Lee!" he cried, head swiveling in all directions.

A hand latched onto his, and when he looked down, there was his mistress, grinning up at him. "It's all right, Mr. Park. I'm here." She pointed down a bend. "That direction will take us to my uncle's school."

Hyun Soo tried not to notice how warm her hand felt in his as she led him away from the throng. Tried not to think about how happy she'd looked when she'd given that blacksmith rice for his sick daughter. Tried not to remember that cursed dream of her leaning in to kiss him.

But when she finally let go, he gave up trying, unable to shake the disappointment flooding his veins.

He closed his empty hand into a fist and nodded toward a group of buildings just ahead. "Is that it?"

"Yeh," Chin Sun answered. They approached the large compound, which was situated on the southern end of Sokju. The school was a branch of the Bureau of Interpreters, responsible for both training up official interpreters and producing textbooks about the languages of Joseon's neighbors. Most schools specialized in the language of the country nearest them, but Sokju's school employed experts in Mandarin, Japanese, and Jurchen. Uncle was one of Sokju's most esteemed interpreters, for he was fluent in all three languages and had single-handedly translated more foreign books than any other interpreter in Joseon.

Chin Sun smiled at Mr. Park as she made her way to the entrance gate. Her decision to try befriending the enigmatic bodyguard so she could learn his weaknesses was going well so far. The way he'd clammed up when she'd mentioned family hinted at a traumatic past, whereas the warmth in his eyes while speaking of Young Master Kang had revealed his deep respect for her betrothed.

Unfortunately, neither tidbit seemed helpful for retrieving her fox bead. She had to keep digging. Eventually, he'd share something she could exploit.

Besides, it was in her best interest to be on good terms with Mr. Park since he and Young Master Kang were friends, and she'd probably have to see him from time to time. She wasn't being friendly because she was interested in him.

Not even a little.

Inside the compound, scholars, teachers, and servants sauntered about the grounds. A group of students circled around a teacher in the midst of a lecture about Japanese funeral rites while male servants used brooms to sweep up fallen leaves around the pavilions. The school included an examination hall, cafeteria, library, assembly hall, and various classrooms. Small storage sheds sat at the back of the compound. Beautiful red maple trees towered in clusters around the pavilions, providing lovely shaded areas for outdoor study.

Women weren't normally allowed on campus, but Uncle's prestige at the school allowed Chin Sun to come and go as she pleased. Not that she abused this privilege, for she knew how important Samchon's reputation was. She'd only been to the school a half dozen times or so over the years, but taking Uncle some lunch was a great excuse to chat with Mr. Park about topics she might not otherwise have been able to.

Chin Sun meandered across the compound, keeping her pace slow. Samchon was probably in his classroom right now, preparing for his next lesson. "So, Mr. Park, how long are you—"

A high-pitched scream rent the peaceful atmosphere, drawing several scholars and teachers outside, Uncle included. Mr. Park leaped in front of Chin Sun, while she instinctively got into a defensive stance before she remembered she was supposed to be a defenseless noblewoman right now.

"Who was that?" someone asked, nearly identical expressions of fear on everyone's faces.

A young scholar stumbled out of the library, red streaming down his robe and face ghastly pale. He held one hand tight to his stomach, fingers drenched with blood. He stopped in front of the nearest group of scholars.

Those in the courtyard gathered around him, talking all at once. "What happened, Tae Hee-ah?" "Are you all right?" "We should call for a physician."

The young man, Tae Hee, took a gasping breath. "Gwishin!" He gestured back to the pavilion, then collapsed on the ground, blood pooling around his body.

What? Chin Sun's mouth went dry. An impostor? Her gaze went to the library, hand itching to grab the eunjangdo dagger concealed in her hanbok.

Mr. Park strode forward and gently rolled the scholar over, exposing what was clearly a stab wound to his stomach. He knelt down and pressed two fingers to his neck. After a moment, he rose and said in a somber voice, "Someone go to the police bureau and tell them there's been a murder."

The entire compound went as silent as a tomb; even the birds, which had been twittering happily up until now, seemed to sense the gravity of the announcement and ceased their songs.

When no one moved to do as he'd directed, Mr. Park clasped the nearest student's arm. "Did you not hear me? A student has been stabbed to death. Go!" He shoved the young man toward the gate, then pulled out his hwando. "Everyone else, get to safety. Gwishin might still be on the premises."

Panic ensued as everyone scrambled for the exit, knocking each other over in their haste. Mr. Park ducked into the library alone, a single salmon swimming against a current of chaos. Uncle spotted Chin Sun in the crowd and urged her to follow, hiking up his robe so he could move faster.

She nodded, but as soon as he turned, she hurried toward the library. Powers or no powers—she wasn't going to run away when people were in danger. She pulled out the knife she'd brought in case of emergency, ready to cut down this impostor or die trying.

Chapter 11

The Reaper

Hyun Soo barreled forward, adrenaline shooting through his veins. This was it. The chance he'd been waiting for. Gwishin wouldn't escape him a second time, especially not now that a student lay dead who would still be alive if he'd only caught the vigilante sooner. He'd wavered the past few days, wondering whether Gwishin thought himself some sort of hero to the common people, but now Hyun Soo was certain—for a cold-blooded killer like Gwishin, justice couldn't come swiftly enough.

He pulled open the library's latticed door and stepped into a forest of books. Stacks upon stacks filled the shelves, hitting him with a pungent dose of their earthy scent. His eyes homed in on a red trail along the floor, so he followed it to a back corner. Where it stopped, papers lay scattered about the floor, along with a candlestick and writing brush. Signs of a struggle.

But no sign of the perpetrator.

Hyun Soo's eyebrows drew together. The library had a single door, and no one had left after the victim. Had Gwishin gotten out before the scholar did?

Something about that conclusion didn't make sense, but nothing about this incident was adding up. Gwishin had never been spotted in broad daylight before, nor had he ever attacked someone on school grounds.

A flash of white drew Hyun Soo's attention back toward the front of the library. Flowing robes and a gleaming sword—

Hyun Soo hurtled forward, blade clashing with the intruder's before he'd even fully registered whom he was fighting. A bearded ahjussi with a large nose and crazed eyes smiled at him, his manic expression catching Hyun Soo off guard. His opponent took advantage of Hyun Soo's distraction and knocked his sword out of his hand.

"How wonderfully lucky." The man laughed, making his long, unbound hair shake. "I was hoping I wouldn't have to search for you long."

Hyun Soo dove for his sword, then jumped back up, holding it between himself and the ahjussi. "You were searching for me? Why? Who are you?"

The ahjussi's mouth spread impossibly wide, teeth sharpening to fine points. "Oh, you didn't know? Funny, I thought I heard someone announce me." His body rose from the floor as though weightless, his white robe swirling around him.

Hyun Soo's blood ran cold. Someone *had* announced him. When the victim had called his attacker "Gwishin," he hadn't been talking about the vigilante. He'd meant an actual ghost.

The spirit gave him a patronizing nod. "Yeh, you're seeing it now, aren't you?" He gestured to his clothes. "I really thought the white hanbok would be enough, but you humans are denser than I expected."

Hyun Soo knew he should feel insulted right now, but

he was still reeling with shock. A ghost? Had Grandmother been right about everything? He couldn't remember how she'd said one could dispel malignant spirits.

"What do you want?"

The ghost shut his eyes with a frustrated groan. "Must I explain that as well? You, of all humans, should understand why I was drawn here. And why others of my kind will be here soon."

"Others?" Hyun Soo didn't like the sound of that.

The ghost waved his hand dismissively. "Not to worry. It won't come to that if you simply give me what I'm after."

"But you haven't told me what that is," Hyun Soo pointed out. Like he'd told the vigilante, he never started a fight until he knew his enemy's weakness. What was a ghost's? He racked his brain, conjuring up stories of deceased spirits seeking to set right the unresolved issues of their lives. "Do you want me to help you get revenge on someone?"

The ghost covered his face, thoroughly exasperated. "Trying to reason with you is a waste of time." When he removed his hand, his eyes were narrow with malice. "The only thing left to do is take it."

He flew forward, reaching for Hyun Soo's torso.

"Stop right there," came a commanding voice.

The ghost froze, then turned to the newcomer behind him.

Sunlight blazed in from the open doorway, making it impossible to discern the features of the figure standing there, sword raised. Hyun Soo blinked a few times, trying to restore his impaired vision. The voice had been female; familiar, even. Surely it couldn't belong to—

"Don't touch what belongs to me," the woman declared, "or I will end you."

The ghost shrieked as he launched an attack, meeting his new adversary's blade. Blue fire crackled where their swords met, and the woman fell back with a gasp.

Hyun Soo's spotty eyesight began to clear, revealing what he hadn't wanted to believe: his rescuer was none other than Lady Lee.

"Get back," he warned, jumping into the fray as the ghost swung its sword at the woman's head. Hyun Soo blocked the blow, but upon contact, a searing heat ran up his arm and he nearly lost his weapon a second time.

Lady Lee scooted backward just as Hyun Soo dropped to the ground and rolled to the side. The ghost's sword tip hit the dirt, and the fiend pulled back with a frustrated hiss.

"Stay still," the spirit shouted.

When Hyun Soo sprang to his feet, Lady Lee was beside him, brandishing a dagger. "Are you all right, Mr. Park?"

"What are you still doing here? I told you to get to safety."

The ghost advanced, aiming for Hyun Soo. The two exchanged blows, shuffling across the school courtyard, and all the while, Lady Lee looked on.

Why wasn't she leaving?

Hyun Soo blocked a strike near his chest, then spun around and pierced his opponent's exposed back, the blade digging into the flesh between his shoulder blades.

"Agh!" The ghost fell to his knees.

Hyun Soo drew back, the sword coming away covered with silver blood.

The ghost lifted off the ground, his body whirling until they faced each other again. "You'll pay for that." The sword in his hand vanished, only for blue flames to appear in its place. He lifted his palm, then sent a burst of fire at Hyun Soo's face.

Hyun Soo leaned back as it flew past him, but a second fireball struck him in the leg. He collapsed to the ground, groaning as pain shot through his body.

The spirit hovered over him, victory gleaming in his dark eyes. "Now, for my prize."

Lady Lee leaped into view, plunging her dagger into the ghost's side.

The spirit wheezed, then threw her off with a burst of fire. She landed hard on her back with a loud grunt. "You just don't know when to give up, do you?" The ghost raised both hands, summoning a whirlwind of blue fire.

Hyun Soo staggered to his feet, then threw himself over Lady Lee just before the world exploded.

Warmth encompassed Chin Sun's body, along with an unknown scent that reminded her of four-footed walks in the forest. Memories passed through her mind like prancing deer, flowing from one to the next. She hadn't realized how much she missed those times, when she could shed her human skin and all its expectations, free to wander and hunt among the trees.

Those times would come again, if she could just figure out how to get her fox bead back from Mr. Park.

Mr. Park! Chin Sun opened her eyes, only to discover a body lying on top of her. Heat flooded her cheeks as she realized the source of the warmth surrounding her was none other than her bodyguard, who'd gone completely limp.

Pain ricocheted through her torso. Had she reopened her wound?

She craned her neck back, gaze landing on the figure floating just above them, hand outstretched. Chin Sun rolled Mr. Park off her and grabbed his sword, which was lying a few inches away in the dirt. She lifted it just as the goblin's hand came forward, his fingers colliding with the cool metal.

Liquid silver dripped from the fresh cuts in his forefinger and thumb, landing on Chin Sun's cheek. The goblin howled in pain, cradling his injured hand to his chest. He peered at her in disbelief. "How did you . . .? That blast should have taken you out."

Chin Sun rose on shaky legs. Fighting took a lot more energy without her gumiho powers, but she was holding her own better than she'd expected. Maybe she could keep going long enough for the police to arrive.

"I'm not as helpless as you think, goblin."

The monster's eyes widened, then he let out a dry laugh. "I suppose it was silly of me to think a gumiho wouldn't see through my disguise."

It had been a clever trick, posing as a ghost. Chin Sun had nearly been fooled, were it not for the signature blue flames emanating from his body. No wonder that student had come out of the library crying "Gwishin."

"I don't appreciate you confusing the humans. Now, tell me what your purpose is for coming here. Is it just to spread havoc?" She raised her sword to remind him it was in his best interest to answer her. Unlike her last goblin encounter, she wasn't so incapacitated that she couldn't fight back. And this goblin didn't seem nearly as dangerous as the one from before.

"You think you can scare me because you drew blood?"

He shook his head, the humor in his expression shifting to outrage. He clapped his hands together, and when they parted, a stream of blue fire stretched between his palms. "See if you can handle this without your little human shield to save you."

"That's enough," bellowed an agitated voice.

Gumiho and goblin turned in sync to a handsome young man at the edge of the courtyard. He stood as still as death, clad in black hanbok and a wide-brimmed hat. When combined with his pale complexion, steely eyes, and lack of fear in the face of the supernatural, this newcomer's identity was almost certain.

"A grim reaper?" Chin Sun stammered.

Stories claimed these frightening figures, whose name literally meant "afterworld messenger," were tasked with guiding the departed to Jeoseung, the land of spirits. Seeing a grim reaper was an omen of imminent death, and if you were foolish enough to look one in the eye, that death would most certainly be your own.

The goblin gasped and then raced off toward the school gate.

The grim reaper sighed and shook his head. He disappeared in a puff of black smoke, then re-formed directly in front of the goblin. "Did you really think you could get away? Since when has your kind escaped mine?"

The goblin dissolved into pathetic sobs, pleading that he hadn't done anything wrong, that all of this was simply a misunderstanding.

Chin Sun watched the interaction as if it were some children's tale being performed and she was only a simple bystander, safe and far removed from the dangerous characters standing before her. Being a gumiho may have made her wonder if there were other magical creatures in the world, but in her heart of hearts, she hadn't truly believed it. Even the goblin attack in the woods had been something she'd almost written off as a dream, an anomaly she would never encounter again.

But seeing this new goblin groveling at a grim reaper's feet made her realize just how naive she'd been. A whole other world existed, one where beings like herself lived and fought and loved and died. A place with rules and history and, by the looks of it, a social hierarchy.

Questions burst in Chin Sun's mind. Where did gumiho fit into the social order? What was life like for them? How many different creatures were out there?

The grim reaper wrinkled his nose at the goblin, then turned his hand palm up. A red rope materialized, and he wrapped it around the sobbing goblin's wrists. "Save your excuses for the trial."

He tapped the goblin's shoulder, sending his captive off in a plume of smoke.

Chin Sun waited for him to vanish, too, but instead he walked over to her and bowed.

"I apologize for the inconvenience, agasshi."

"I-it's no problem." She bowed in response, doing her best not to look him in the eye. Maybe the superstitions about direct eye contact with a grim reaper were wrong, or maybe they didn't apply to gumiho, but she wasn't going to risk it. Especially not after seeing how easily he'd dispatched the goblin.

When he didn't leave, she hesitantly asked, "Was there something else you needed?"

Had she broken some law she didn't know about? Was he going to take her next?

"Per regulations, I have to ask: how much more lifeforce do you intend to collect before you retrieve your bead?"

Chin Sun's mouth fell open. "You mean"—she glanced at her bodyguard and back at the reaper, completely forgetting not to make eye contact—"you can sense my fox bead?"

"Do you think I'm a novice?" The reaper scoffed. "I've been in this position for four years now. I know a beaded human when I see one."

"A beaded human . . ." she echoed. Not because she was confused—the term was completely self-explanatory—but because it drove home the feelings of ignorance brought on by the grim reaper's arrival. It seemed he knew more about her kind than she did.

"Nauri, may I ask you something?" When he didn't say anything, she continued, "That goblin—he was after my bead. What would he have done if he'd gotten hold of it?"

"He was?" His brow furrowed. "Hmm, perhaps he intended to sell it to another gumiho in need of one. They go for quite a high price on the black market. But stealing a gumiho's bead is a serious offense. I'll make sure that gets added to his list of crimes when he stands trial. If he pleads innocent, I may need to call on you to testify."

Chin Sun paled. "Me, testify?"

"I doubt you'll need to. If he's smart, he'll admit to everything in the hopes of reducing his sentence."

She nodded woodenly. "That's a relief. But if I do get called in, where—"

The reaper held up his hand. "I answered your question, but you've yet to answer mine. How much longer are you going to wait before you collect your bead?"

Mr. Park was beginning to stir. Chin Sun needed to finish this conversation quickly. "Oh, not much longer. I promise."

The reaper hummed. "I hope so, for your sake. The goblins have been unruly of late, making more and more problems in the human realm. Best keep your bead close. And remember, the punishment for needless killing of humans is execution or imprisonment. So it would be wise to retrieve the bead in the next eighteen days. Otherwise"—his voice rippled with cruelty—"you'll be the one getting dragged off to Jeoseung."

Eighteen days? That was all the time she had left?

The reaper must have noticed the surprise in her eyes, for his brow wrinkled in suspicion. Chin Sun dropped her gaze to his black boots. "You don't need to worry. I'll be sure to retrieve it in time."

"We shall see. I'll be back to check very soon," the reaper whispered, then vanished like the apparition he was.

Chapter 12

The Interrogation

"Lady Lee!" Hyun Soo shouted as he came to, fingers grasping at the air in a vain effort to lift a hwando that was no longer in his hand. He groaned at the throbbing pain in his back; it felt like the ghost's fire was still blazing under his skin. He swiveled his head, taking in the empty courtyard.

Panic rose in his chest. What had happened to the ghost? And where was—

His breath caught at the sight of a burgundy skirt. Lady Lee stood under a maple tree a few yards away. Her face was whiter than bone, and the dagger she'd wielded earlier was clenched in her fist, shining with silver blood.

Hyun Soo pulled himself up and bounded over to her, eyes peeled for any trace of their ghostly foe. "Lady Lee, are you all right?" He grabbed her wrist when she didn't respond. "Lady Lee?"

She blinked as though coming out of a daze, then peered up at him with a soft smile. "Mr. Park, I'm glad to see you're awake."

Her gentle response threw him off. Again, she hadn't

reacted the way he'd expected her to after a fight. Why wasn't she crying or screaming like any other woman would be?

He released her wrist, a line forming between his brows. "What happened? Where's the ghost?"

Lady Lee shuddered as though recalling something painful, then shook her head. "He's gone."

"Gone? How? Did you—" He broke off. The idea that she could have fended off the ghost seemed laughable, and yet he couldn't help but remember how fearlessly she'd come to his rescue. And her voice when she'd confronted the spirit—it hadn't been the voice of a helpless noblewoman, but rather, the command of a warrior.

"Don't touch what belongs to me, or I will tear you apart."

A flush broke out over Hyun Soo's neck despite himself. What could she have meant by that? She couldn't have been referring to him. . . .

But if not him, what else could she have been talking about?

The answer hit him like a splash of cold water. It was because he was her bodyguard. That had to be it.

"There was . . . someone else," Lady Lee replied. "He came and—and took him away."

"Someone else? Who?"

"It was a—"

Clomping footsteps drew their attention to the main gate. A dozen black-robed police officers swarmed into the school courtyard like wasps, spreading out in all directions with spears ready. One policeman branched off to inspect the corpse, then gestured to the others. From the back of the group came a tall officer in a blue inspector uniform, a sword fastened to his side. He spoke with the policeman kneeling by the dead scholar, expression grave, then seemed to notice Hyun Soo and Lady Lee for the first time.

The officer strode up to them, the amber beads on his police hat swinging back and forth. He bowed before addressing Hyun Soo. "Thank you for your patience. I'll just need to ask the two of you a few—" His eyes slid over to Lady Lee and widened in surprise. "Chin Sun, what are you doing here?"

Hyun Soo stepped in front of his mistress, blocking the officer's view. "Who are you?" He did nothing to disguise the indignation burning within him. How dare this man address her so informally! Not even Dol Sam spoke to Lady Lee like that.

The officer frowned and took a moment to size Hyun Soo up, wrinkling his nose. "I'm Inspector Kim. And you are?" His voice was sharp with annoyance.

Hyun Soo glared in return. "Park Hyun Soo, *Lady Lee's* new bodyguard."

"Bodyguard?" Inspector Kim's jaw tightened. "Chin— Lady Lee, is that true?"

Lady Lee stepped out from behind Hyun Soo, much to his disappointment, and bowed to the officer. "Yeh. You're looking well. And you're an inspector now—very impressive."

Hyun Soo's head whipped between the two in confusion. He didn't like the friendly, almost affectionate, grin on Lady Lee's face. She was Dol Sam's fiancée. She shouldn't be giving others false hope, especially not this policeman who looked much too young to be an inspector. "You . . . how do you two know each other?"

"Inspector Kim's family used to live next to mine. We often played together as children, but we haven't seen each other in a very long time." Lady Lee gave the inspector a pointed glance, something unspoken passing between them.

"I got you out of quite a few scrapes, didn't I?" Inspector Kim leered.

Hyun Soo waited for Lady Lee to shut him down, to remind him of proper decorum between grown men and women. Especially when one of them was betrothed.

Instead, a teasing glint came into Lady Lee's eye. "Is that how you remember our childhood? Funny, I thought I got you out of trouble far more often."

Inspector Kim had the gall to look sheepish. "Perhaps my memory is faulty. I—"

"Aren't you here on official police business?" Hyun Soo interrupted. "Or do I need to complain to your supervisor?"

"Mr. Park," Lady Lee snapped, "there's no need for such rudeness."

Inspector Kim held up his hand. "No, he's right. We can reminisce about the old days another time. The scholar who came to us explained what happened"—he jerked his chin toward the corpse—"but he also said someone went hunting for the killer. I assume he meant you?" He raised his eyebrows at Hyun Soo as if he didn't think the bodyguard was brave enough to do such a thing.

Hyun Soo responded with a haughty smile. "I'm always ready to defend those who need it. As an officer, I'm sure you understand."

Inspector Kim rolled his eyes. "Well? Did you find the killer then?"

Hyun Soo grimaced, the bravado whooshing out of him as he recalled their fearsome adversary. "Yeh, but . . ."

How would this inspector take it if he told him there was a real ghost here? Hyun Soo hadn't been in Sokju long, but from what he'd seen, superstition didn't hold much weight with most of the citizens.

After a few beats, the inspector added, "The scholar said the victim shouted 'Gwishin' before he passed. Is that true?"

Lady Lee jumped in before Hyun Soo could answer. "He did, but it's not what you're thinking, Inspector. He wasn't talking about the vigilante."

"He wasn't? But then, why would he say that?"

"I . . ." Her gaze flicked to Hyun Soo, but he had no idea what to say either, so he gave her a subtle head shake. There was something a little off in her behavior, something he couldn't quite put his finger on.

She said to the inspector, "He must have made a mistake. I know for a fact that the vigilante didn't do this."

Hyun Soo cocked his head to the side, curiosity snagging his thoughts. Lady Lee's voice had wavered when she'd begun speaking, but during that last sentence, it had hardened with resolve. Why? Why was it so important that the inspector knew Gwishin wasn't responsible for this? She couldn't be a supporter, could she?

"Did you see the perpetrator?" Inspector Kim pressed.

"Yeh, we did," Hyun Soo supplied. "He got past me and ran off."

The inspector glanced between the two suspiciously, then his expression turned smug. "Not a very proud moment for you as a bodyguard, hmm?"

A barb danced on Hyun Soo's tongue. "Actually—"

"He did his job very proficiently," Lady Lee cut in. "If he hadn't protected me, I wouldn't be standing here, Inspector. I'd be lying on the ground with that scholar."

Hyun Soo gaped at her. She was defending his honor now? Even though they'd both nearly died? There was no need for her to do that. He hadn't protected her as he should have. Why was she helping him?

She met his eye and gave him an encouraging nod, which sent warmth skittering through his heart. She didn't see him as the enemy anymore, did she? She was helping him because she wanted to.

Just like when she'd put herself in harm's way to save him.

He'd been wondering if he'd misjudged her before—now he had his answer. Lady Lee might be headstrong and more prone to join a fight than flee one, but she wasn't a bad person. She was . . . well, Hyun Soo didn't quite know what she was, but he felt better now about Dol Sam marrying her. It seemed his friend had made a wise choice, after all.

Inspector Kim asked a few more probing questions, to which Lady Lee and Hyun Soo answered honestly whenever possible, though there were a few times when the best they could offer were half-truths.

"Chin Sun-ah?" came a strained voice.

The trio turned as Lord Lee scurried over to them and caught his niece up in an embrace. "Oh, my dear one. I thought I'd lost you. How is it you're still here? Why didn't you stick closer behind me? You're not hurt, are you?" He examined her face and hands for marks and, finding only some dirt and scratches, hugged her again.

Lady Lee readily accepted his affection, squeezing him back. "I'm all right, Uncle. I'm sorry I lost you in the crowd. You don't need to worry. Mr. Park took care of me."

Lord Lee drew back and addressed Hyun Soo, gratitude sparkling in his eyes. He bowed. "Thank you, Mr. Park, for watching over my niece. I wasn't sure about you initially, but now I'm relieved Young Master Kang hired you."

"So, you were here when the murder took place, Lord Lee?" Inspector Kim asked.

Lord Lee lit up in recognition as he turned to the officer. "Kim Min Joon, I almost didn't recognize you! The last I heard, you were leaving to study in Ming. When did you get back?"

Inspector Kim grinned. "I've been home for a year now, but I became an inspector about six months ago."

"How exciting. You'll need to tell me all about what you thought of Ming—" He broke off with a wince. "After you're finished with the investigation, of course. I'm happy to do what I can to help you. What was it you were asking?"

Teachers and scholars started drifting back into the courtyard, so the inspector pulled Lord Lee aside to speak privately.

Hyun Soo wandered over to Lady Lee, eager to get his own private word in. "My lady, you didn't finish what you were trying to tell me before. Who took the ghost away?"

The young woman peeked over at her uncle and the inspector, then leaned in to whisper near his ear. "He didn't identify himself, but he looked like . . . a grim reaper."

Ice seeped into Hyun Soo's bones as she described a dark figure that had appeared at the edge of the schoolyard and overpowered the ghost as if it were child's play. He'd summoned a red rope out of nowhere, tapped the monster's shoulder, and then both had vanished.

Gumiho, ghosts, and now grim reapers? Was he in some kind of nightmare? All his training, all his battles, none of it had prepared him for enemies like these. Monsters straight from folklore that were nigh unbeatable.

His chest tightened. The vigilante was nothing compared to this. This was an entirely new level of danger.

Threats that weren't bound by the laws of nature. Threats that could disappear and reappear at will.

He gripped the back of his neck, knowing his unease must be bleeding onto his face. He had to get it together.

His gaze turned to his charge, wondering how she was so calm, so collected, even in the face of such frightening circumstances. Her hands were steady at her sides, her mouth a neutral line.

She had to be faking it. Didn't she know how close they'd come to perishing? Only a fool would be unaffected by something like that. It must be that she just didn't want him to know how upset she was.

Hyun Soo took a deep breath and spread his lips into a grin. If she didn't want to admit how she truly felt about the incident, he supposed he could indulge her. Pretending everything was fine was better than bursting into tears. If Lady Lee did that, he didn't know what he would do.

"Ah, now everything makes sense," he said. "Who better to get rid of an unruly ghost than a grim reaper?"

Lady Lee's mouth moved downward instead of into a smile, a clear sign his attempt at humor had failed. She continued to speak in a hushed tone. "That's something else I wanted to tell you. The creature we fought—he wasn't actually a ghost. He was a goblin."

Hyun Soo blinked. "A goblin? Are you sure?"

She nodded. "The blue fire is what tipped me off. That and . . ." She fidgeted with the red ribbon in her hair. "He admitted it himself when I called him out for it."

She said it so matter-of-factly, almost trivially, that something inside Hyun Soo snapped. "Have you no fear, woman?"

Lady Lee tensed, indignation flashing across her face, but he wasn't finished. Now that the dam holding back his pent-up feelings on the matter had burst, everything flooded out before he could stop it.

"How am I supposed to protect you if you have no sense of self-preservation? Is jumping into fights you can't win a habit of yours?"

She crossed her arms. "I never asked you to protect me. That was all Young Master Kang's idea. I was doing just fine before you showed up."

Hyun Soo threw his hands in the air, his temperature rising. "You tried to take on a goblin. You were about to take on those thugs in the alley last week"—he pointed a furious finger at her when she started to protest—"don't try to deny it! Just who do you think you are to be going around doing these dangerous things? It's almost like you think you're . . . you're . . ."

Lady Lee leaned back, the outrage clearing from her eyes. Maybe his words were getting through to her, and she realized now how foolish she'd been. He waited for her to mumble an apology or at least an admission of wrongdoing.

But instead of guilt or regret, a different emotion bloomed on her face. And it was the last one he would have expected.

Fear.

Chapter 13

The Offer

Chin Sun tried to speak, but her throat was so tight nothing would come out. She stared up into her bodyguard's eyes, and within those dark orbs, she could almost see the life she'd built falling apart. Had he put the pieces together? Did he know she was Gwishin? Or worse, the gumiho from the woods?

She stumbled back a few steps, eyes darting about for an escape. Uncle was completely focused on Inspector Kim right now; he wouldn't notice if she disappeared. The other officers were busy moving the body and questioning witnesses. If she made a break for the gate, she could make it.

She started to lift her foot, then hesitated. What difference would it make if she ran? Mr. Park wouldn't keep her secret.

"Lady Lee," the bodyguard said, drawing her eye. He ducked his head, chagrin marring his handsome features. "I apologize for my outburst. I didn't mean to startle you."

Chin Sun nearly toppled to the ground. What? He . . . he thought she was scared because he'd shouted?

Her shoulders sagged with relief, a laugh bubbling up in her chest. She coughed to hide her amusement. "Thank you for apologizing, Mr. Park. I—"

"But that doesn't mean I'm wrong." His gaze locked with hers. "Even if it's inappropriate for me to reprimand you, it doesn't change the fact that you're reckless. And since my ultimate priority is to protect you, that includes protecting you from yourself. Going into a fight unprepared is the quickest way to lose your life."

Chin Sun took a breath to say that it was her choice which fights she engaged in, but before she could, he continued, "And since I get the feeling you don't intend to stay out of trouble anytime soon"—his lips quirked up into an almost teasing smirk—"that leaves me with only one option."

She closed her eyes, waiting to hear the words, "I'll have to tell your uncle to lock you up" or "I'll have to let your fiancé know you're unfit to be his wife." That was how the general public would deal with a rebellious maiden like herself. She tried her best to be virtuous in the ways a noblewoman should be, but she couldn't fully tamp down her willful spirit. Instead, she'd hidden it behind demure smiles by day so she could embrace it as Gwishin by night.

Until this infuriating bodyguard had pierced her facade.

And now she was about to lose the little freedom she'd carved out for herself. Reckless was a good word to describe her. Far too reckless.

"I'll just have to train you myself," he finished.

"What?" Chin Sun opened her eyes. "You want to . . . train me?"

It was a joke, right? He couldn't actually—

But there was no humor, no trickery in his steady gaze. Her jaw dropped, all thoughts of maintaining composure forgotten. This bodyguard—this former soldier—wanted to teach her, *her*, how to fight. "You're serious."

Mr. Park nodded. "Once Gwishin is no longer at large, I won't be needed anymore. It would put my heart at ease if I knew you could defend yourself when I'm not around."

Chin Sun stiffened, something stirring within her at his words. Or maybe it was the way he'd said them, as if his desire to protect her had nothing to do with duty.

"Lee Chin Sun-sshi!" a voice cried.

The two of them whirled toward it and found a familiar figure sprinting across the courtyard, unconcerned with the impropriety of his actions. His black robe bore a pattern of purple peonies that matched the soft purple sleeves under his jeogori. He careened to a stop a few paces in front of them, eyes fixed on Chin Sun.

"Young Master Kang, I didn't expect to see—"

He gripped her hands, panting like he'd just run halfway across the city. "Lee Chin Sun-sshi, I heard what happened. What are you doing here? Is your uncle all right?"

Chin Sun gestured to Uncle and Kim Min Joon. "He's fine. Thank you for your concern."

Young Master Kang let out a sigh. "What a relief. I'm so glad Gwishin didn't hurt him."

"Gwishin?" She drew her hands away, feeling light-headed all of a sudden. "What are you talking about? Gwishin didn't do this."

"It's all over Sokju. The vigilante killed a scholar in cold blood. There are multiple witnesses who attest to it."

"Witnesses? That can't be. . . . We saw the killer ourselves." She turned to her bodyguard. "Tell him, Mr. Park."

Mr. Park bowed in greeting. "What she says is true. The

cre—person we encountered was most definitely not Gwishin."

Young Master Kang rubbed at his forehead. "Are you sure? Everyone else is saying so. It sounds like the magistrate intends to tighten security around the city. More officers on patrol, and not even women will be allowed out after curfew."

"He can't do that," Chin Sun blurted. "The other yangban would never allow it."

"I don't know. . . ." Young Master Kang said vaguely. "The people are more upset than I've ever seen them, nobles and peasants alike."

What? The sangmin, too? Had one false accusation been enough for even the common people to lose faith in her?

"But they'll listen to you, right? If you tell them they're overreacting?" She tried to keep her anger pinned down, but her tone came out a little too biting.

How could they do this to her? She'd fought for them, bled for them, and instead of believing in her when she needed them most, they'd rally against her?

"Are they overreacting though? Someone is dead, and this time, there's no way it can be justified."

"But it wasn't Gwishin who did it," she insisted. "You don't want them to arrest the wrong person, do you?"

Young Master Kang leaned back, visibly startled by her intensity. "Even if Gwishin didn't do this, he's still a criminal, Lady Lee. I don't understand why you're defending him."

Chin Sun slammed her mouth shut, the blood draining from her face. She'd made a mistake. She patted her hair as if trying to make sure it was neat, then put on her most innocent expression. "Me, defend that lowlife? I'm not sure how you reached that conclusion. I just don't want to see my beloved Sokju in a state of panic. It could be dangerous."

Mr. Park snorted, which earned a subtle glare from Chin Sun and a confused look from Young Master Kang before her betrothed smiled at her like she was both charming and hopelessly naive.

"Your kind heart is admirable, Lady Lee, but I'm afraid this is out of my hands. Anyway, I'm glad to see you and your uncle are well." He turned to Mr. Park and encouraged his friend to come by for a visit when he got the chance, then excused himself.

Leaving Lee Chin Sun to try her best not to show how distraught his news had made her. Were the people really going to abandon her so easily?

She glanced at the faces of the scholars and teachers around her. She took in their fear, their hopelessness, their grief. She'd wanted to save them.

But now she knew they'd have responded the same way Aunt had when she'd found out what Chin Sun truly was. The moment was just as clear and heart-wrenching as it had been four years ago.

Chin Sun was only fourteen, in the thick of learning all that was expected of a noblewoman. She and her sungmo were walking at the edge of town, by the rice paddy fields, and Chin Sun was angry with herself for making so many mistakes with her sewing. She'd messed up five times and even pricked Aunt's hand. She felt like such a failure, but Sungmo kindly told her it took time to gain skills, and the important thing was to keep trying.

Chin Sun glanced over at her aunt with a grateful smile, but then something flashed in the corner of her eye.

A dagger catching the sunlight.

"Aunt, watch out!" she cried.

But the call came too late. By the time her aunt had turned, the man wielding the blade had already stabbed her stomach.

Aunt fell to the ground, blood pouring from the open wound. The cutthroat grabbed at her clothes, searching for valuables even as she struggled to stay conscious.

Rage flooded Chin Sun's heart, lining her vision red and sending energy through her limbs. She charged at the thug and slammed his body into the dirt with a strength she hadn't known she possessed.

He let out a cry of alarm and tried to get back up, but she ripped his knife from his hands, then drove it straight into his chest.

He fell backward, red seeping into his jeogori and a look of shock all over his face.

Chin Sun dropped the dagger and turned to her aunt. She was still on the ground, but she'd pulled herself into a sitting position. Her pallor was ghostly pale, her gaze unfocused. The scent of blood was over-whelming.

"Sungmo!"

The older woman's eyes locked with Chin Sun's, then widened in fear. "M-monster." She scooted back, then yelped in pain. "Don't come any closer."

"Aunt, it's me, Chin Sun. What are you—I need to get you help. Can you stand?" She moved to touch her sungmo's shoulder, but Aunt flinched away.

That was when Chin Sun noticed the claws on her hands. Long and thin—like an animal's. Nausea rose in her gut. "W-what is this? Aunt? What's happened to me?"

A dreadful sort of resignation settled over Aunt's features. "I should have known. The night we found you—I should have known then. If only I hadn't been so happy to *find a baby, I would have realized you were just like the dying monster I saved you from."*

"Monster? Sungmo, you're frightening me." She reached out again, but Aunt slapped her hand away.

"Don't touch me! Do you still not understand? I'm not your aunt. You're not even human. And now I'm going to die and your horrible face will be the last thing I see."

Hot tears dripped down Chin Sun's cheeks. She couldn't process everything, but she knew she didn't want Aunt to die. "I'm going to get you help." She stumbled to her feet. "Just stay there, and I'll be right back."

Water blurring her vision, Chin Sun sprinted back into town, not stopping until she reached her house. She banged on the gate, crying for someone to let her in. When Uncle appeared on the other side, she fell into his arms, sobbing. Between breaths, she told him where Aunt was—how they'd been attacked.

The two of them hurried back to Aunt, but by the time they reached her, she was already gone. Chin Sun had been too slow to save her.

Footsteps interrupted the downward spiral of her thoughts. It was Uncle and Kim Min Joon coming back over. Chin Sun took in a sharp breath, forcing back the tears that threatened to fall anytime she thought about what happened to Aunt. She'd never told anyone all the details from that day, and she never would.

"Was that Young Master Kang?" Uncle asked.

Chin Sun shared what Kang Dol Sam had told her, making sure to mention the people's change in sentiment toward Gwishin so Kim Min Joon would hear. When she mentioned the magistrate's call for a manhunt, the inspector's expression darkened before he excused himself on "official business."

Relief blossomed in Chin Sun's chest as she watched him march out of the gate in the direction of the magistrate's office. If anyone could stop Magistrate Hong from this madness, it was Min Joon.

"Chin Sun-ah?" Uncle stood in front of her with a concerned look. "You've had a long day. In fact, we both have." Uncle took her hand and gave it a gentle squeeze before nodding to Mr. Park behind her. "Let's all go home."

As they made their way out, Chin Sun peered into the eyes of those she passed, wondering if they all were as hostile toward Gwishin as Young Master Kang claimed.

It's not true, she wanted to tell them. Gwishin didn't hurt the innocent. The real danger was gone.

But such words had to remain buried inside her, never to see the light of day. The people weren't ready for the truth. She could hardly believe it herself. No one would have taken her seriously if she'd admitted a goblin was responsible for the scholar's murder. Maybe in a smaller village where the old lore was more than fairytales but not here in Sokju. The people were too wise, too advanced, to believe such nonsense.

She needed to focus on the bigger problem. This was the second time a goblin had shown up and tried to steal her fox bead. A scholar had died, and without her powers to protect her, she'd nearly died, too.

She glanced at Mr. Park with a renewed sense of determination. The longer he had her fox bead, the greater the risk for the people of Sokju. And even if they'd abandoned her, she refused to abandon them.

An idea began to form in her mind. He'd offered to train her, which meant they'd have to go somewhere private to avoid being seen. A small smile spread over her face.

How wonderful.

Chapter 14

The Promise

Hyun Soo marched to Lady Lee's quarters with a strange tingling in his stomach. It had been a few days since the goblin incident, and Lord Lee had finally calmed down enough to return to work. Meaning Hyun Soo and Lady Lee could start her training under the ruse of him taking her to the market.

When Lady Lee had brought it up to the family at breakfast that morning, he'd stood silently outside in the courtyard, worried Lord Lee wouldn't allow her to go out after the attack at the school. But the middle-aged interpreter had simply warned her to stick close to her bodyguard at all times, then commented that perhaps he should acquire a guard for himself as well. Young Sang Ook then offered to protect him, which had caused not only a ruckus of laughter but also a tight squeeze in Hyun Soo's ribs at the reminder of the family he was missing.

Though his mother had passed too soon after having him to bear any other children, Hyun Soo had often imagined what it would be like to have siblings. Would he dote on them like Lady Lee doted on her younger cousins? She

132

seemed to have become a motherly figure to them, and while she maintained high expectations, she was also sweet with them in a way that seemed completely unlike the hard woman he'd first met. It was fascinating seeing so many different sides to her, and he couldn't help but wonder if there were any more.

He'd never trained a woman before. The skills he'd learned in the army would have to be altered to accommodate for her size and strength, but he was sure he could help her at least a little bit. She'd already shown she had the courage and motivation, which were the most essential elements when it came to swordfighting.

So, why was he nervous? He tugged at the collar of his hanbok as he remembered the moment he'd thrown himself over Lady Lee to protect her in the schoolyard. He'd tucked her head into the crook of his neck, trying to shield as much of her as he could from the goblin's attack. A peach scent had tickled his nose just before he'd passed out.

Try as he might, he hadn't been able to forget that smell ever since.

The hanji paper doors slid open before he could announce himself, and Lady Lee stepped out, a vision in a blue jeogori and bright red skirt. Her expression was tense, impatient, as her head dipped in a quick bow. "Mr. Park, are you ready to go?"

He studied her intently. "Why are you in such a rush? Your uncle won't be back until this evening."

The woman twisted her jade ring, gaze darting back and forth before she gave him a weak smile. "I just don't want anyone to find out what we're doing."

"If today is a bad day, we can start la—"

"No," she cut in. "I need to do this now." She fluttered past him down the hall, steps jerky and nervous.

Hyun Soo trailed behind her, saying nothing as he tried to make sense of her word choice. She "needed" to do this today. Need, not want. Why? He understood being anxious at the possibility of being caught. What they were about to do was far from proper and could easily be misconstrued. In order to train her, they would have to touch each other, something Confucius said should never happen between men and women who weren't closely related. And even more than that, Lady Lee was engaged. If someone were to see them, it could cause quite a scandal.

Dol Sam had been adamant that Hyun Soo keep her safe. He was simply doing what his friend had asked him to when he'd hired him.

Some of the tightness in his chest lifted. He'd always been a man of honor, and even if others wouldn't support this decision, he was sure his dear friend would understand.

Then why hadn't he told him what he was planning?

The question stopped Hyun Soo in his tracks. He'd had every opportunity to share it with Kang Dol Sam yesterday when they'd spoken at the school. And yet he hadn't said a word.

Why?

"Mr. Park? Are you coming?" Lady Lee called. The distance between them was much farther than it had been a moment ago.

Too far.

Hyun Soo frowned, unsure why he felt that way. The risk of danger within the walls of her own home was relatively low, especially with him here, too. Maybe the attack yesterday had set him on edge, made him overly suspicious.

Lady Lee turned and stepped out into the courtyard, disappearing from view. An invisible tether suddenly yanked on Hyun Soo's heart, compelling him to follow. And whether he wanted to or not, he was powerless to resist its pull.

Chin Sun led Mr. Park out of Sokju, away from nosy neighbors and wagging tongues, past clay huts and rice paddy fields, until they reached the forest's edge. Pine and fir trees stared down at them like jangseung poles, warning of evil spirits lurking within their dark expanse. Indeed, an ominous aura hung over this section of woods like a dark cloud, and many claimed it was haunted.

Which had worked out very nicely for her and Min Joon when they'd decided to use it as their secret meeting spot as children. In all the years they'd played here, they'd never once been disturbed.

She kept walking, head held high despite the conflict raging within her. She'd been arguing with herself about this idea ever since she'd come up with it, putting their training off in the hopes that she'd think of some other way to get the bead back.

But when she'd met with Min Joon last night at the abandoned hut—after midnight to ensure Mr. Park didn't follow her—the only other idea he'd come up with had involved alcohol, and she wasn't about to resort to that.

The bodyguard paused behind her, so she swung around, hiding her feelings with a well-placed smirk. "Not frightened, are you?"

He scowled, the movement forming a deep groove in his forehead.

She couldn't help but chuckle, for his expression was so

similar to Min Joon's when she teased him. "Not to worry. I'll protect you from anything we may find."

She stepped into the trees' shade, then hesitated, her careless words coming back to bite her. The last time she'd been here, she'd lost her bead at the hands of a goblin. Maybe venturing into the woods again wasn't the best idea.

Mr. Park strolled past and called over his shoulder, "Not frightened, are you?"

Chin Sun glared daggers at the back of his head before hurrying to catch up. "Just trying to remember which way to go. There's an old path here somewhere. . . ." She scanned the area, eyes homing in on a spot where the undergrowth wasn't as thick. "Ah, there it is."

She motioned for him to follow, and soon they found themselves in a clearing, completely hidden from the forest's entrance. The space seemed smaller than she remembered, but perhaps that was simply because she was an adult now instead of a child. Still, it should suit her purposes.

"Here we are. What do you think?"

The bodyguard cast his gaze about the perimeter, but the only other creatures around were a few magpies and pheasants watching from the tree line. Hardly worth noticing in human form, and since Chin Sun's fox form was inaccessible, it was better not to dwell on meals she couldn't have.

Mr. Park grabbed the sword he'd strapped to his back and gave it to her. A hwando that had seen many battles, judging by the cracks along the blade. It was more curved and not as comfortable in her grip as her own, but it would do. Still . . .

"This sword looks like it's taken quite a beating in your care. You should get it replaced."

The bodyguard didn't answer and instead took a few steps back before unsheathing his second sword, which hung from his waist. He held it parallel to the ground, gaze never leaving hers. The curiosity she'd glimpsed a flicker of when they'd first met had returned, but this time, it burned brightly in his eyes.

"First, I want to know how much training you've already had," he said. "You're obviously comfortable with a blade."

Chin Sun faltered, nearly dropping the sword before she steadied herself. Maybe she *should* drop it. Or would that seem even more suspicious?

"Wh-what makes you say that?" She fumbled again, trying to look like she had no idea what she was doing.

Mr. Park raised his eyebrows.

She sighed, giving up the act. "Yeh, I admit it. When I was young, Kim Min Joon taught me how to fight. This"— she gestured around the clearing—"was our place."

"Kim Min . . . you mean that inspector?" There was a hardness in his voice that hadn't been there before, as if he disapproved. He *had* been rather rude to Min Joon earlier, though she couldn't think of why he would dislike her childhood friend.

"Yeh, the inspector," she replied. "I know it's not something he should have done, but I begged him to. I . . . I just wanted to be able to defend myself."

Mr. Park didn't respond and instead lifted his sword. He nodded for her to do the same, so she made a weak attempt to block him when he swung his hwando toward her.

He knocked the sword out of her hand. She glowered at him like she was offended, but he just gave her an innocent look and gestured for her to retrieve it.

She picked up the sword and attacked again, this time with a little more speed than before. Mr. Park parried, then stepped back and lowered his sword. He let out a small sigh that almost sounded disappointed.

What was that about?

She almost called him out for it, but before she could, he asked, "Defend yourself from whom?"

"What?"

"You said you begged Inspector Kim to teach you how to fight so you could defend yourself."

"Oh." Chin Sun swallowed. "From . . . the other children." She kept her tone completely flat, as if she were recounting someone else's history rather than her own. It was better that way. If she kept her distance from it, it couldn't hurt her anymore.

"Of course your parents didn't want you. Why would they?" "You're nothing special. Your aunt and uncle must be so disappointed." "I bet your parents wanted a boy, so they got rid of you."

The taunts had started as early as she could remember. The hitting and shoving soon after that. Always when Aunt wasn't looking, and once Sang Mi was walking, that happened more and more. Not that Chin Sun blamed Aunt. She couldn't have kept an eye on Chin Sun every second they were out in public; she'd had to take care of the whole household, not just her orphaned niece.

Mr. Park's expression softened. "Because you didn't have parents?"

Chin Sun looked away. "Does it matter? Min Joon helped me for as long as he could. Once my uncle found out what we were doing, he told Min Joon's parents and they moved to the other side of the city to keep us apart."

Her cheeks tinged. She hadn't intended for it to sound

so dramatic. Like childhood sweethearts separated, only for fate to bring them together again years later.

"I didn't mean it like that. Our relationship never went beyond friendship, I assure you. Min Joon is only—"

She winced. Calling him by his given name instead of Inspector Kim certainly wasn't helping her case. She didn't even use Young Master Kang's given name, and he was her fiancé.

She peeked at Mr. Park, fear skipping through her chest. He and Young Master Kang were friends. If he claimed something inappropriate was going on between her and Min Joon, Young Master Kang might call off the marriage.

The bodyguard was watching her carefully, but beyond that, his face was impassive. Finally, he said, "So, I have him to thank for your poor technique?"

P-poor technique?

Her eyes narrowed just before she lunged, blade crashing into his with a zing. "You call this poor technique?"

Mr. Park pushed her away with a laugh. "There we go. Now you're not holding back."

Chin Sun's lip curled. She didn't like being baited. Even more than that, she didn't like falling for it.

Time to return the favor.

"Are you sure that's what you want?"

Mr. Park's wicked grin was all the answer she needed.

She flew forward in a blaze of movement, striking again and again. She may not be as fast without her bead, but that didn't mean she'd forgotten the intricacies of swordplay. For the next half hour or so, they sparred, testing each other for weaknesses, goading each other to try harder. Chin Sun was the more cunning of the two, her attacks less predictable. But Mr. Park was the greater swordsman by far, besting her three times to her one. He not only had experience on his side but also strength and speed.

Once they'd gotten into a good rhythm, Chin Sun changed tactics, doing all she could to keep Mr. Park on the defensive so he wouldn't notice the group of tree roots she was herding him toward. Just a bit farther, and they'd be in the right position for her to stumble and stage an accidental kiss.

But keeping his focus was only one of many pieces that had to align for her scheme to work. If Mr. Park didn't react quickly enough, she might end up getting stabbed instead of falling on him. She also had to make sure she didn't tip forward too early; otherwise her mouth wouldn't land on his, and all this would be for naught.

"So, what about you?" she asked. "What made you decide to become a soldier?" Her question was meant to keep him distracted, but she was also genuinely curious. Many sangmin joined the military because it offered the greatest opportunities for advancement.

He blocked her strike, seemingly unaware of the roots at his back. "Joining the military was always meant to be a stepping stone, but when I became a royal guard, I found I enjoyed the position so much I didn't wish to leave it."

Chin Sun's mouth curved downward. "Then what was your original goal?"

"To become a minister in the royal cabinet."

Her sword slipped at his next attack, then fell to the ground unnoticed. "The royal cabinet? But that would mean you're a . . ."

Mr. Park's eyebrows rose. "A yangban? Yeh, I used to be."

She swallowed, throat suddenly thick. "But I thought you said you didn't have any family."

He didn't answer, something wavering in his gaze. Then he broke eye contact and waved at her fallen blade. "Are you going to get that?"

"Ah, yeh." Chin Sun picked up the sword, but her thoughts were so scattered she nearly dropped it again. If Mr. Park was a yangban, he outranked her. How could she have been so stupid! Of course Young Master Kang's friend was a yangban, not a sangmin. And she'd been so arrogant when he'd first arrived.

"If I am to trust you to protect me, I need to know your word means something."

"I apologize for my word choice, but I assumed you knew I wasn't including the Lee family."

"My servants are family. You do not touch them."

Her face flamed up at the memory. She'd been so angry over how he'd treated Pyung Ho, but now his behavior made sense. If he'd grown up in a yangban household, it would have been normal to think of his servants as little more than animals, not people with hopes and dreams much like his own.

But why on earth would a yangban have become a jungin's bodyguard?

Her mind flew back to what he'd said a moment ago. *"A yangban? Yeh, I used to be."*

As in, he wasn't anymore. Did that mean he and his family weren't on good terms? Had his parents cut ties with him?

Her heart swelled with sympathy. To lose your family was one thing; to be abandoned was quite another.

She dipped her head. "Mr. Park, I owe you an apology. Please forgive me for being so disrespectful. I didn't realize you were highborn."

"There's no need to apologize. Like I said, I only used to

be one." The grief in his voice was palpable, calling to her own.

Chin Sun aimed her sword at his chest, but he twisted out of the way and grabbed her outstretched arm, locking her in place. She peered into his eyes—if she wasn't mistaken, they were wet with tears.

It was the first time she'd seen him so open, so vulnerable. Their faces were close now, close enough that she could fall forward and make it look like an accident.

But she was barely thinking about the mission anymore. She was too focused on the wounded man before her, a man who'd undoubtedly been treated worse than he deserved.

"I . . ." Chin Sun swallowed. "I know what it's like to feel alone, to feel lost. It's a pain that can eat you up if you let it. The fact that you haven't says a lot about the kind of man you are."

"And what kind is that?"

"A brave one. One I'd be honored to call a friend." She kept her gaze fixed on him, hoping he could see her sincerity.

The way Mr. Park's eyes widened told her he'd gotten the message, loud and clear. He gave her a small smile. "Thank you, Lady Lee. The honor is all mine."

Chin Sun smiled in return, unable to look away even if she'd wanted to.

But then he pushed her back with a cough, severing the connection between them.

Chin Sun grimaced. She'd meant to distract *him*, not get distracted herself. He was almost in the perfect position. She needed to make the kiss happen now before the moment passed her by.

She swung toward his legs and, just as she'd predicted, Mr. Park swerved to the left, his heel sliding back until it was a hairsbreadth from one of the gnarled roots. He was slightly below her, courtesy of the uneven ground.

He started to move in for another attack, but she rose to her full height, lowering her weapon as though she were tired. "Maybe we should take a break?"

Mr. Park's lips were tight with disapproval, but he sheathed his blade. "Giving up already?"

She ignored the jab and held out her sword. He reached for it, but then she took another step, her foot hitting the edge of the dirt mound she stood on.

She wobbled forward, free hand latching onto Mr. Park's hanbok. His lips parted in surprise as she drew nearer, nearer.

But his reflexes were too quick.

Rather than tumbling to the ground, he managed to plant his right foot, one hand wrapping around her back while the other landed just below her ribs.

Chin Sun hissed as pain shot through her abdomen. She glanced down at the spot where his hand rested—right on top of the wound he'd given her the night he'd swallowed her bead.

It wasn't bleeding anymore—she'd even called Hae Rim back after the fight in the schoolyard to make sure all was well—but she knew her behavior must seem suspicious. Had she just blown her cover?

But Chin Sun's fear melted away as her gaze locked with Mr. Park's, something new sparking between them. She was suddenly very aware of how their bodies were pressed together, her hand splayed across his chest while his gingerly held her in place. He, too, stood frozen, watching her with an unreadable expression.

But beneath her hand, his heart thumped erratically.

Seconds passed, or maybe none at all—Chin Sun didn't

know anymore. All she knew was Mr. Park's nearness, his warm breath on her face, the endless depths of his eyes, the way his touch sent tingles through her skin.

His gaze dropped to her mouth, something smoldering in his dark eyes. Chin Sun's stomach tightened as he leaned in. Her eyelids fluttered closed.

But then she was standing upright on shaky legs while he hovered two steps away, expression neutral. "You really ought to watch your footing," he said hoarsely.

Chin Sun's jaw dropped. Wait, what? She blinked a few times. Had he just—

When he motioned for her to raise her hwando, she grimaced before she could stop herself. Was he trying to pretend like that hadn't just happened?

"Mr. Park, I—"

He swiped forward, forcing Chin Sun to leap to the side to avoid the blow. He raised his eyebrows, then pointed at her weapon again.

She huffed but did as instructed. Fine. He could have it his way.

Mr. Park came at her again, but this time, she side-stepped into a twirl and pressed her blade to his back. "Who needs to watch their footing?"

He turned around with a bright smile. "Nicely done."

"Coming from someone with your skill, that's high praise indeed." She beamed.

The grin fell off Mr. Park's face, and he looked away, almost as if he'd seen something unnerving. Chin Sun glanced behind her, but there was nothing there.

"Mr. Park? Are you all right?"

He slipped his sword back into its scabbard. "Let's stop here for today."

Chin Sun blinked in confusion but didn't argue. It probably was best that they get back. Sang Mi would be wondering what was keeping her. Maybe she could orchestrate another "accident" at their next training session, one that would actually be successful.

"Thank you for letting me use this." She held out the sword she'd borrowed, but the bodyguard didn't take it. "Mr. Park?"

"Promise not to slip again?" His tone was light, teasing.

Chin Sun's face heated with embarrassment, but she boldly met his eye. "Why? Afraid you won't be able to catch me this time?"

He grabbed the sword, expression turning somber. "I'll always catch you."

Before she could process what he'd said, he lumbered off in the direction of the city. She hastened after him, wondering if she'd misheard.

And why her stomach wouldn't stop doing somersaults.

Chapter 15

The Portrait

Hyun Soo shoved a spoonful of rice into his mouth, but he barely tasted it, his head pounding like the ground under a stallion's hooves. He'd left Lady Lee at her chambers an hour ago, but every time he blinked, it was like she was still there, sitting across from him with those haunting honey-brown eyes and pale pink lips he'd almost made the mistake of kissing.

His grip tightened on his spoon. He needed to calm down. It had been one moment of weakness. One.

"I'll always catch you."

He shut his eyes. Make that two. He hadn't had any business making a promise like that. Not when he couldn't possibly back it up. Not when she belonged to someone else.

So, why had he said it in the first place?

Hyun Soo had seen his fair share of beautiful women. There had been pretty yangban girls in Hanyang where he'd grown up, many who had flirted with him until they'd realized he had no interest in anything beyond his studies.

Then, when he'd worked as a royal guard, he'd gotten glimpses of the queen as well as the king's concubines. All stunning enough to make a man's heart stop with a single glance.

Yet none of them had made him feel the way Lady Lee did.

A flush spread up his neck, his mind yanking him back to the moment when he'd caught her in the clearing. At first, he'd thought she was frightened, her face as still as a mountain, but then something had changed in her eyes, beckoning him nearer. And those lips . . .

"Are you a man or an infant?" asked a nasally voice.

Hyun Soo scowled at the cook Na Ri standing in the kitchen entrance. No family name, which was common among lowborns, but that didn't stop the talented ajumma from commanding the rest of the household's respect, from the skittish Pyung Ho all the way up to Lord Lee himself. Na Ri was cantankerous to a fault, but she adored everyone in the house and knew all their favorite foods. She reminded him very much of his grandmother—ornery but loyal.

The only person she didn't care for was Hyun Soo himself.

"I'm not sure what I did to cause offense this time, ajumma, but I'll gladly remedy it if you let me know."

She rolled her eyes before gesturing to his food. He peered down, grimacing when he realized what a mess he'd made. Half his kimchi lay on the floor, and he'd spilled quite a bit of soup onto his tray.

How had he not noticed any of this?

He ducked his head, shame flooding his cheeks. "I apologize. I'll clean it all up right away."

Na Ri glared. "You better, or you won't like the consequences." She spun around and stomped out of the room, grumbling about how she didn't know what young people were learning nowadays.

Hyun Soo bolted to his feet as soon as she was gone. He needed to get out of here, get his head on straight. He tidied up the mess, then headed out to look for leads on Gwishin.

He spent the next few hours going from hut to hut in the poorer areas of Sokju, asking everyone he could find about their experience with the vigilante. The reports he received were very different from what the highborns had said. Just as he'd suspected, most of the sangmin and cheonmin thought Gwishin was a hero, not the villain the police made him out to be. And even with the rumor circulating that he'd murdered that scholar in cold blood, the general consensus among the sangmin was that he'd been slandered.

No one had any information to help identify Gwishin, nor did they know where Hyun Soo might find the elusive criminal.

Leaving him without any more threads to unravel.

Hyun Soo strayed back toward the Lees' home, but a flicker of movement in a nearby alley caught his eye. Someone was watching him.

He took a sharp left, steering the observer away from the Lees. He picked up his pace, then ducked behind a cart full of wood beams. He squatted down, eyes peeled for someone to walk past.

A pair of straw shoes padded by, pausing just beyond the cart. There was a rush of footsteps as the figure darted away.

Hyun Soo emerged from his hiding spot just in time to see the person disappear into a tavern.

A boy? But something felt off about his gait, almost as if the boy wasn't used to his own body.

Hyun Soo hurried after him, but the tavern was so full of customers he lost sight of the child.

"Did you want to order something?" asked a middle-aged woman with her hair wrapped around her head.

Hyun Soo craned his neck, straining to see around a group of drunk men stumbling out to the opposite street.

"Did you want to order something?'" The tavern owner's voice was impatient now.

Hyun Soo turned, realizing he was blocking customers from coming in. With an apologetic bow, he stepped out of the way, allowing the other people to enter and find somewhere to sit.

He ambled off, puzzling over what reason a child would have to follow him. And why even a brief glimpse of the boy's back had made the hair on his arms stand up.

A few minutes later, he caught sight of the Kangs' residence on the next street over and veered toward it. He would let Dol Sam know the sangmin hadn't been helpful. Perhaps his friend would have another idea for tracking down Gwishin.

It wasn't that he was trying to postpone his return to the Lees'. That would have been ridiculous.

When he arrived at the manor, a servant led him to Kang Dol Sam in the courtyard. His friend was bent over a white canvas, putting the final touches on a very lifelike portrait of a woman with bewitching honey-brown eyes. Red spider lilies and mugunghwa flowers surrounded her, and a teasing smile rested on her pretty pink lips.

Hyun Soo looked away, cursing Dol Sam under his breath. He'd gone out to stop the dangerous trajectory of his thoughts. Instead, he'd found yet another reminder of what he was trying not to think about.

Dol Sam glanced over his shoulder, grinning when he saw Hyun Soo. "Ah, what a delightful surprise. I'm glad you took what I said to heart about stopping by for a visit." He set down his paintbrush and swiveled fully around. "What do you think?" He gestured to the canvas. "Is it a good likeness?"

Hyun Soo cast his gaze over the portrait a second time, hating the way his heart skipped. The painted Lady Lee looked straight ahead, boldly meeting the viewer's eye. Her arms hung at her sides, a single mugunghwa blossom clasped in her right hand. A faint light shone around her, almost as if she were the sun itself, bringing life to everything she touched.

Now who was getting poetic?

Hyun Soo pushed the sentiment aside, reminding himself he was looking at Lady Lee through the eyes of a man in love.

Meaning Dol Sam, of course.

His friend had always been a remarkable artist, so it only made sense for Lady Lee to look enchanting. But it was just a picture, not reality. No one could actually be that stunning. . . .

He swallowed. He was in more trouble than he'd thought.

"Well?" Dol Sam prompted. He'd sat down on the veranda outside his private quarters.

Hyun Soo tore his eyes away. "It's beautiful, Dol Sam-ah. You're quite talented."

His friend beamed at the praise, then his forehead creased. "I hope Lady Lee is pleased with it. I haven't been a very attentive fiancé. As soon as I left the two of you the other day, I regretted not escorting her home myself. Was she out of sorts after the attack?"

Hyun Soo took a seat next to his friend. "Not at all. She handled it all so calmly, one might think she was a soldier herself, ready to take on Gwishin single-handedly."

The words sounded funny on his tongue, but they rang with truth. Lady Lee may be a woman, but she bore the heart of a warrior. There weren't many with the courage to stand against a goblin. And the way she'd fought that day—he'd never seen a woman so fierce.

Dol Sam pursed his lips. "My bride to be? Take on Gwishin?" He clapped his friend on the back with a laugh. "You never cease to amuse me, my friend."

Hyun Soo chuckled along with him, but his smile was thin. If Dol Sam had seen how well Lady Lee could fight, he wouldn't find it amusing at all. Hyun Soo considered telling him what had really happened at the school, but if Lady Lee had wanted Dol Sam to know about her sword skills, she would have told him herself.

Besides, he wasn't sure how his friend would react if he knew Hyun Soo had offered to train her. He might think it indecent.

Would that be a false assumption though? an annoying voice in his head asked. *You've certainly been having indecent thoughts about her.*

Not that Hyun Soo could help it, given the circumstances. Being in such close proximity to a beautiful woman would be challenging for any man, not just him.

In a few days, he'd be over it. He'd forget how good it had felt to hold her, how perfectly she'd fit in his arms.

Probably.

"I hope you've not lost your perception since leaving the military," Dol Sam continued, "You always were so good at noticing the things other people didn't. Like that time when we were sparring and I sprained my ankle, but I didn't want you to know. Do you remember?"

Sprained ankle?

Something materialized at the edge of Hyun Soo's consciousness, something he couldn't quite grab hold of. Not about Dol Sam, but about Lady Lee. What was it?

He replayed the moment she'd fallen for the hundredth time. He'd caught her between his hands. One hand had gone to her back, and the other had pressed into her abdomen, somewhere close to her ribcage.

He hadn't paid attention to it at the time, but when he'd grabbed her, she'd let out a sharp breath and glanced down at her chest.

Almost as if she were injured. Right below her ribcage on the left side. Exactly where—

An impossible thought shot through Hyun Soo's mind, like a flaming arrow illuminating the night.

No. It couldn't be. She couldn't be Gwishin.

Images flooded him in quick succession: her lack of fear with the bandits in the alley, her skill with a hwando, her open hostility toward him when they'd first met. Behaviors that were strange on their own, but when put together . . .

He called to mind his run-in with the vigilante, hoping to find something dissimilar between them, something with which he could cast out this suspicion for the absurdity it was.

He'd fought Gwishin under cover of darkness, unable to make out much beyond his opponent's basic shape. How tall had he been? Too tall to be Lady Lee?

But his mind betrayed him, conjuring a figure smaller than himself. Small enough to be a woman in disguise.

But that voice. It had clearly been male. Hadn't it?

The memory of the vigilante's sharp cry of pain filled Hyun Soo's ears, high-pitched and feminine.

"They don't call me the Ghost for nothing. But I'm more curious about you. Did Hong send you? He must be desperate if he's hiring common thugs now."

He'd found the vigilante unbearably cocky, someone who'd needed to be put in his place. But everything changed if he imagined Lady Lee behind the mask. He thought back to the way she'd responded to his taunt during their training session.

"You call this poor technique?"

Her outrage had been so adorable he hadn't been able to hold back a laugh. Now he assessed her words more critically.

Though the pitch had been higher than Gwishin's, the fire had been the same. A bold self-assurance bordering on brazen, especially for a noblewoman.

And then she'd shown him she had *plenty* of reason to be confident in her sword skills.

Hyun Soo bounded back over to the portrait and held his hand over Lady Lee's mouth. A chill went down his spine.

"What is it, Hyun Soo-yah? Did something get on the picture?" Dol Sam came up on the right side. His attention went from the portrait to Hyun Soo.

"It's nothing." Hyun Soo lowered his hand and forced his cheeks into a grin. "Nothing at all."

"Oh, that's a relief. A damaged painting wouldn't make a very good gift."

"Gift?"

Dol Sam clicked his tongue. "Weren't you listening before? I'm planning to give this to Lady Lee." He ran his hand along the edge of the canvas, gaze distant and dreamy.

"So she knows I'm not just marrying her out of duty. I'm marrying her because she's the only woman I want."

Hyun Soo's head jerked toward his friend. "Dol Sam-ah." His voice was weak. He needed to be louder. "I need to tell you—"

"It's so fortunate you came by today." Dol Sam locked eyes with him. "I need to ask another favor."

Chapter 16

The Letter

Chin Sun paced back and forth on the wooden floor, her soft white socks barely making a sound. A slip of paper lay on the low-legged desk nearby, covered in scratched-out ideas. Dinner was already long past and it was almost time to turn in for the night, but sleep was the last thing on the noblewoman's mind.

"It's in your best interest to retrieve the bead in the next eighteen days. Otherwise, you'll be the one getting dragged off to Jeoseung."

The grim reaper's threat loomed, reminding her of how important it was to kiss Mr. Park. Not only was his life at stake but hers as well.

She had nine days left now, having spent the last several trying and failing to convince Mr. Park to train her again. He'd claimed he was too busy, something about needing to search for clues about Gwishin, but she'd gotten the distinct impression he was avoiding her. Especially since he'd asked Pyung Ho or Ah In to come along the few times he'd escorted her into town.

Their almost-kiss in the clearing must have frightened him off. Did he suspect that she'd slipped intentionally?

If he did and was avoiding her because he didn't think of her in that way . . . The thought made something sharp twist in Chin Sun's belly that she couldn't identify.

She'd asked Min Joon if he had any other ideas to reclaim her bead, explaining that it was even more important now since a grim reaper was planning to check up on her, but her friend was just as stumped as she was.

And even if she did come up with a good idea, how was she supposed to execute it if Mr. Park wouldn't be alone with her?

Frustration mounting, Chin Sun balled up her paper and threw it against the wall. She collapsed to the floor in a similar fashion, covering her face with her hands.

"I hope that wasn't important," Sang Mi said as she stepped inside.

"Sang Mi-yah." Chin Sun's smile was tired but genuine. She stood and took her cousin's hand. "I'm sorry I haven't spent as much time with you lately. I've been . . . distracted."

Sang Mi's eyes were sympathetic. "Because of what happened with Gwishin?"

Chin Sun winced. "No, it's—it's not that." She let go of the girl's hand and turned away, wishing she could confide in her like she used to when they were younger. Before all her secrets had come between them. Back when their hearts beat as one.

She knew Sang Mi felt it, too—the distance. She saw it in every downward turn of the girl's mouth, every hitched sigh when Chin Sun refused to give her a straight answer.

But Sang Mi—kind, sweet Sang Mi—never wavered in

her affections. She didn't push. She didn't pry. She just accepted it with a sad smile that broke Chin Sun's heart.

Chin Sun spun back around, meeting her cousin's patient gaze. Perhaps it would be all right to share one small piece of her dilemma. A fresh perspective could be helpful. And Sang Mi did have some experience with this.

"I'm struggling, Sang Mi-yah."

She retrieved her paper and smoothed it out. She offered it to her cousin, cheeks burning.

Sang Mi took the sheet, examining it silently.

Chin Sun didn't watch as she read it over, but the contents danced in her mind's eye.

How to kiss him without him knowing that was my intention:
1. Wait until he's unaware
2. Make it look like an accident
3. Get him drunk - too much potential for embarrassment to even attempt
4. Kiss him while in disguise - too risky
5. ???

Chin Sun was grateful she'd only written "him" at the top; it looked like she was trying to work up the courage to kiss her betrothed, something Sang Mi would heartily approve of.

"Well?" Chin Sun finally asked.

Sang Mi set the paper on the table and grinned. "Unni, I had no idea you were so interested in this. And before your wedding, too."

Chin Sun glared despite the heat in her face. "Are you going to help me or just tease?"

The mischief vanished from Sang Mi's gaze, snuffed out by a confident determination. "Oh, I'm going to help you. And you're going to get your kiss; I guarantee it."

Chin Sun's muscles relaxed. Finally, some good news. "Do you have an idea then?"

Sang Mi nodded, then held up a finger. "But first, I have a question: why are you trying so hard to think of a way to kiss *him*?" When Chin Sun gave her a confused look, she giggled. "What you need to do is get him to kiss *you*."

Chin Sun's eyes went wide, her mouth opening and closing like a fish's. "Wha—you—you think I should—"

She shook her head. No. Mr. Park would never—

Her mind flew back to his arms around her in the clearing. In the split second before he'd set her on her feet, something had flashed in his dark gaze, something that had made her knees go weak and her eyelids close.

She'd thought about it so many times, telling herself it had been her imagination. They'd only just agreed that they were friends. He couldn't have been about to kiss her. He couldn't have. . . .

But no matter how many times she reasoned with herself, she couldn't erase the desire she'd seen in his eyes.

Sang Mi clapped her hands together, startling Chin Sun so much that she jumped. "What perfect timing this is."

Chin Sun pressed a hand to her racing heart. "What do you mean?"

Sang Mi's face was impish. She pulled a letter out from one of her wide sleeves. "I was actually coming here to give you this. It's from Young Master Kang."

Chin Sun's forehead scrunched, but then she remembered Sang Mi thought the kiss was intended for Kang Dol

Sam. She feigned a look somewhere between eagerness and anxiety as she grasped the missive and slowly unfolded it.

My dearest Lady Lee,
I hope this letter finds you well and fully recovered after the vigilante attack. I—

Chin Sun clenched the paper a bit tighter. How many times did she have to say Gwishin hadn't been involved in the murder?

She went back to reading.

—would like to meet with you tomorrow night. I know it's improper, but I have to see you. Park Hyun Soo knows the place and will escort you there safely. Please come.
Kang Dol Sam

Chin Sun's arm fell to her side. He wanted to meet her? Before they were married?

Sang Mi was watching her as if she could barely hold back a squeal. "I told you the timing was perfect."

Chin Sun started to speak, but her cousin cut her off. "I know, I know. I shouldn't have read something so personal, but I couldn't help it." She put her hands over her cheeks. "It's so romantic I could swoon."

"Romantic?" Chin Sun scoffed. "If anyone were to see us, it would be a scandal. His father might even rethink the wedding. I don't understand why he would ask me to do this. . . ."

Sang Mi's expression was incredulous. "How could you

not understand?" She snatched the letter. "It's so obvious. Why else would a man ask to meet a woman secretly except because he's in love with her?"

Chin Sun staggered back a step. "In love? You think that's why? But the letter doesn't say anything of the kind. For all I know, he could want to meet to end things."

Her cousin shook her head as if Chin Sun were stupid. "Trust me, Unni. I'm right about this."

Kang Dol Sam, in love with her? The idea seemed far-fetched at best, even if they were engaged. Marriages between nobles were about establishing connections, expanding power, not about love.

She thought back to the day Young Master Kang had eaten at her family's house, the hurt on his face when she'd tried to reject Mr. Park as a bodyguard.

Had it been love driving his actions? At the time, she'd assumed it was a token of goodwill, a gesture to show he took his responsibilities as a future husband seriously.

But if his feelings toward her were more than that—

Guilt gnawed at her. Kang Dol Sam deserved to love someone who loved him back. Someone who wasn't plotting to do something untoward with his friend.

Sang Mi set down the letter, then waltzed over to Chin Sun's clothing chest and threw it open. "Now, what should one wear for a romantic tryst?"

Chin Sun swallowed. "I'm not going."

Her cousin continued perusing the clothes. "I thought you wanted the chance to kiss him. *This* is that chance."

"I can't. He . . . if what you said is true and he really is in love with me . . . I'm not worthy to be his bride. I . . . Maybe I need to talk with Uncle, call the wedding off."

"What?" Sang Mi's eyebrows flew up. "You can't be serious." She crossed the room and took Chin Sun's hands in her own. Her stare was hard, penetrating, almost angry. "There is no one in all of Joseon worthier than you."

Tears pricked at Chin Sun's eyes, and she pulled out of her cousin's grip. "I wish that were true."

Sang Mi's shoulders drooped. Her expression went vacant for a few seconds before she gave Chin Sun a wicked smirk. "Well, if you don't believe me, I'll just have to get Mr. Park."

"Mr. Park?"

"He's the one who delivered the letter, and the one Young Master Kang asked to escort you. Surely he knows his friend's plans."

Sang Mi moved toward the door.

Chin Sun's hand shot out. "Wait!"

Her cousin turned back, frowning. "What?"

She grimaced, then lowered her hand. She couldn't exactly explain the awkwardness of asking the man she'd tried to kiss about his friend's feelings toward her. The very thought made her neck unbearably warm.

"Don't be embarrassed, Cousin." Sang Mi laughed. "If it makes you feel better, *I'll* do the talking." She slipped out, leaving Chin Sun to wonder if talking to Sang Mi had been a grave mistake.

The hanji doors slid back open a few minutes later, but Chin Sun couldn't look up as her cousin came inside, Park Hyun Soo in tow.

Park Hyun Soo. It was the first time she'd addressed him that way, even in her head.

Chin Sun's eyes widened, her pulse hammering in her ears. All she could think about was their dizzying almost-kiss the other day. His strong grip on her middle, his unnerving gaze, his pounding heartbeat beneath her palm.

"My cousin and I would like to know the meaning

behind this letter." Sang Mi retrieved the note and held it out to Mr. Park.

Chin Sun peeked at him, desperate to know his thoughts. Was Kang Dol Sam truly in love with her? And if so, how did Mr. Park feel about it?

He didn't take the proffered letter and instead addressed Sang Mi. "He wants to meet with Lady Lee tomorrow night. I'm not sure what else you want to know." His posture was rigid, suspicion gleaming in his eyes.

When he turned to Chin Sun, she lowered her gaze.

"What's the purpose of this meeting?" Sang Mi pressed. "My cousin could get into a lot of trouble if anyone saw them. The gossip would be terrible, and Father—well, it wouldn't be good."

"Dol Sam has . . . something to give her, that's all."

"Oh?" Sang Mi tilted her head. "A gift he couldn't send to the house?"

"Yeh."

"I wonder what *that* might be. . . ." There was no mistaking the suggestive note in her voice, let alone the kiss she blew Chin Sun's way.

Chin Sun glared in return, but before she could apologize for her cousin's indecency, Mr. Park turned to her.

"Lady Lee, why did you need to speak to me about this? Are you having second thoughts about marrying Dol Sam?"

His hawk-like stare was searching, nervous, as if he were afraid of her answer.

"I . . ."

What was she supposed to say? If she admitted that she didn't want to marry Young Master Kang, would Mr. Park take it as a sign that she was interested in him instead? Would he give her the kiss she needed?

"You couldn't have wished for a better person to marry."

He'd spoken of Young Master Kang with such admiration—swaying him wouldn't be easy. She'd have to convince him to betray his friend's trust, a thought she hated to consider.

And even if she was successful, what then? She'd have destroyed a friendship and left Mr. Park with nothing.

But if she lied and said she wasn't having second thoughts, would she lose her chance to get the bead back before it stole the rest of Mr. Park's lifeforce? He hadn't been in her life for long, but she'd glimpsed enough of his character to know he didn't deserve such a fate. He may be frustrating and stubborn, but he was also brave, disciplined, self-sacrificing.

And the only man who made her feel capable of anything she set her mind to, even without her powers.

"Of course she isn't," Sang Mi cut in. "She just wanted to know if there was a good reason to put her reputation on the line." She wrapped an arm around her cousin's shoulders. "And a present is certainly a good reason."

Chin Sun watched Mr. Park closely, trying to gauge his reaction. He didn't speak at first, but his jaw tightened, almost like he was holding back anger. But why would he be angry? Because Sang Mi had butted in, or . . . because he wanted Chin Sun to be having second thoughts?

He turned to Chin Sun with a stony expression. "Make sure you're ready tomorrow evening at sunset."

Chapter 17

The Trap

Hyun Soo's hand gripped the pommel of his sword as he snuck Lady Lee through the city streets. Every nerve in his body was on edge, waiting to see if Lady Lee would prove his suspicions true.

He hoped so desperately that she wouldn't.

But whether that hope was for Dol Sam's sake or his own, he couldn't tell. By all rights, any desire he felt for her should have shriveled up the moment she'd become a suspect. It was important for him to be objective, clear-headed, especially when it came to an adversary as dangerous as Gwishin.

Yet even now, her presence was making it difficult to concentrate on the task at hand.

The pair slunk through the shadows, stopping every so often to check for passersby. Most people had already returned to their homes for the night, but they'd come across a few stragglers leaving the tavern near the Lees' residence. It wasn't after curfew yet, but they still couldn't afford to be seen. A single witness was all it took to start a wildfire of rumors. And Hyun Soo knew all too well how powerful rumors could be.

"Is it much farther?" Lady Lee whispered at his side.

Hyun Soo caught sight of people just ahead, so he pulled her close and put his hand over her mouth. He and Lady Lee huddled under the eaves of a yakbang, the local drug store and clinic, still some distance from their destination. An officer stood a few paces away, conversing with a gisaeng whose face was partially concealed by her jeonmo hat. They were laughing, oblivious to Hyun Soo and Lady Lee. A moment later, they strode off together and disappeared into the gisaeng house.

Hyun Soo let out his breath and looked down at his companion. Her eyes were wide, and even in the dying light, he could make out a maroon stain on her cheeks.

He released her with a soft apology and looked away. "Let's keep going. This way."

They weaved through the dim streets, only to be forced to stop once more when a large band of masked men in black appeared out of the shadows, heading south.

Hyun Soo's protective instincts flared, but he steeled himself with the reminder that his job was to protect Lady Lee only.

"They look like they're headed toward the southern district. Aren't you going to do something?" she asked in a strained voice. The judgment in her gaze was unmistakable.

He arched one eyebrow. "If you mean, am I going to abandon you to go after a gang of criminals, the answer is no." He nodded toward the road they needed to turn onto next. "Kang Dol Sam is expecting us."

"But—" Her head swung from him toward the men disappearing around a bend. Her shoulders drooped slightly. "Of course you're right. Only merchants live there, so why would you feel obligated to help them?"

Hyun Soo's lip curled at the jab, but he refused to be swayed.

They'd just resumed course when a new figure in a blue silk robe emerged from a side street, flanked by six officers. Hyun Soo reached for his charge to pull her to the safety of the shadows, but Lady Lee rushed forward.

"Kim Min Joon!"

The lead figure started, then marched over to them, followed by his subordinates.

"Lady Lee, what are you doing here?" Inspector Kim asked, eying Hyun Soo with distrust.

Lady Lee sniffled, transforming from a headstrong noblewoman into the frightened flower Hyun Soo now knew was only a well-practiced act.

"I'm so glad you happened to come by." She placed a hand over her chest, which heaved as though she were just barely keeping her fear in check. She pointed down the road. "There's a group of suspicious men heading toward the southern part of the city. You need to stop them before someone gets hurt."

Hyun Soo grimaced. Although Lady Lee's body language conveyed the perfect mixture of anxiety and relief, there was something distinctly authoritative in her tone. A bit of her domineering nature peeking through.

Hyun Soo scrutinized Inspector Kim's face for any tell-tale signs of indignation. He didn't seem like the sort who enjoyed being ordered around by a civilian.

But concern showed on the inspector's features as he nodded, then addressed his men. "You heard her. Get to the southern district quickly."

The officers bowed and did as directed, scurrying away into the night.

Inspector Kim turned to Hyun Soo. "It's getting late. You should take the lady back to her residence."

"Actually, Inspector, would you escort me home? Mr. Park needs to relay a message for me." Lady Lee smiled at Hyun Soo. "You will give my apologies to Young Master Kang, won't you?"

He peered at her in puzzlement. They could have easily avoided being seen by the inspector and continued on their way to meet Dol Sam. Why had she given away their position? Was it to avoid meeting her fiancé? Or because Hyun Soo had refused to stop the criminals himself?

Her expression hardened for the briefest instant as their eyes met, revealing the anger simmering behind her facade. Ah. So, it was because he'd failed to confront the criminals.

Hyun Soo averted his gaze, chest suddenly tight. He didn't like disappointing her, even if it was for a good reason.

He nodded in acquiescence. "I'll return with haste." He bowed to the inspector before darting off to give Kang Dol Sam the bad news.

As soon as they were alone, Chin Sun dropped the demure noblewoman act. "Thank you, Min Joon-ah. You go ahead, and I'll catch up."

Min Joon frowned. "What are you talking about? I thought you wanted me to take you home."

"You didn't realize I only said that to get rid of my bodyguard?" She laughed, then gestured to her attire. "But I can hardly help you in something this conspicuous. I'll just hurry home and get changed."

Understanding dawned on his face, followed by a quick shake of his head. "Absolutely not. Do you seriously think I'd let you come along?"

Chin Sun crossed her arms. "Since when have I needed your permission to do anything?" When he didn't respond, she added, "Besides, I'm not about to let you have all the fun."

Min Joon squeezed the bridge of his nose, a frustrated sigh escaping his throat. "It's too dangerous without your powers, Chin Sun."

She started to protest, but he grabbed her hands and pinned her with a hard stare. "You're the dearest friend I have. I can't lose you like I lost—" He didn't finish.

Not that Chin Sun needed him to. The only person Min Joon could be referring to was his betrothed, who had died in a terrible accident shortly after he'd returned from Ming. He didn't usually talk about her, preferring to bury his pain behind a quick smile, but occasionally his shattered pieces would rise to the surface and remind Chin Sun that she wasn't the only one scarred by grief.

But she didn't need her powers for this. She'd handled herself just fine swordfighting against Mr. Park the other day, and he was the best opponent she'd ever faced.

That wasn't what Min Joon wanted to hear though, and she had no desire to fight with him, so she gave his hands a comforting squeeze. "I understand. You don't have to worry about me doing anything unwise." She shooed him away. "Now, go on. I don't actually need an escort home, and your men may need backup."

Min Joon smiled and bowed before following his subordinates' path.

Once he was gone, Chin Sun wasted no time in returning home and donning her black hanbok and mask. She just wanted to make sure Min Joon and his men could handle themselves on their own. She'd keep to the shadows and not get involved unless strictly necessary.

She wouldn't do anything stupid, so she wasn't *technically* breaking her word—even though Min Joon wouldn't see it that way if he spotted her.

But he wasn't the only one who worried.

If Chin Sun's hunch was right, the criminals' target was a small neighborhood housing several of the city's wealthiest merchants. Their homes weren't as impressive as the yangban manors, but they boasted plenty of furnishings that would fetch a good price on the black market. And the neighborhood was set far enough from police headquarters that the thieves likely thought they could get away with it.

When she reached her destination, a series of shouts and clanging metal told her she'd been right. She followed the noise to a large gated house and surveyed the area. Smoke rose from one of the outlying pavilions, and the household help ran amok as they tried to douse the flames. Kim Min Joon and his officers engaged a large group of intruders near the courtyard entrance, and a second pair of men battled atop the steps to the main building.

Chin Sun tried to make out the figures on the stairs. Both were dressed in black, and one had a facecloth over his mouth. Had the house's owner gotten involved? She drew closer, then gasped as one man's face became clear.

Mr. Park. He'd joined the fight, after all. Warmth surged through her veins. She'd thought he didn't care, but clearly she'd been wrong. She watched as he skillfully disarmed his opponent, then leveled his hwando at the man's neck.

The man raised his hands in surrender, and Mr. Park's gaze flicked toward the others fighting in the courtyard.

That was when another masked man came up behind him.

Chin Sun flung herself across the courtyard and shoved Mr. Park out of the way. She met the attacker's sword as it plunged down, deflecting the blow meant for her bodyguard's back.

Sweat beaded on her forehead, the man's strength more than she'd anticipated. Mr. Park materialized on her right side, his features more shocked than she'd ever seen.

She dodged her opponent's next move, then knocked the hwando from his hand and struck him on the head. Once he fell unconscious, she turned to her slack-jawed bodyguard, glad her mask hid her smile.

"G-Gwishin?"

She chuckled. His confusion was understandable. With so many masked fighters, any one of them could have been the elusive vigilante.

"What's the matter? Afraid you've seen a ghost?" Part of her knew engaging with him wasn't the wisest move; at any moment, she might slip up and say something that gave away her identity.

But he was simply too fun to tease.

"You . . . saved me," he said incredulously.

"So I did. And I'd appreciate it if you didn't stab me again if you can help it." She winked, then lifted her eyebrows at his sword, which had clattered to the ground when she'd pushed him to safety.

He blinked a few times, still looking a bit dazed, then bent to retrieve his weapon.

Chin Sun bolted behind a pavilion while he was distracted. After a few seconds, she peeked out to check how everyone else was faring. Min Joon had managed to fend off his attackers, but two of his men had fallen in the process. Only a few bandits remained, but they didn't appear to be in any hurry to leave. They moved across the courtyard with purpose, heads sliding from side to side, as if they were looking for something.

A new thug surged toward her, brandishing a long sword. She leaped aside, and the blade cut through the air an inch away from her. She moved into a defensive position. Her opponent was tall and broad-chested with sharp, fearless eyes.

Chin Sun blocked his blows over and over, but each time their swords met, her arms trembled from the sheer force of his attacks. How she missed her gumiho strength.

Another thug approached on her left, shorter than the first, laughter rumbling in his throat. "Finally. We weren't sure you'd show up." He swung at her, and she dove into a roll before springing back to her feet.

She spun around, eying the two men as they fanned out on either side of her. "Show up? What are you talking about?"

The broad-chested man grumbled something to his associate. His voice was so low it took Chin Sun a moment to make sense of his warning to be silent. She'd assumed these were ordinary thieves, but what she'd just heard wasn't Korean. It was Japanese.

She gaped. But that meant—

"You . . ." She whipped forward and brought her sword tip to the short man's neck before he could defend himself. She ripped the mask off his face, noting his foreign features with a sinking dread. "Did Hong send you?" she demanded.

The short man lowered his weapon, glancing nervously between her and his companion. "He—"

The broad-chested man pulled a dagger from his clothes and flung it at his associate's heart. Chin Sun stepped back as the short man collapsed with a grunt, but when she turned to the other thug, he was already fleeing toward the gate.

She threw a dagger of her own, but the shot went wayward when something sliced her leg. An arrow.

Chin Sun yelped and dropped to the ground, narrowly avoiding two more arrows that sailed through the air. Her head swiveled in all directions before homing in on her newest adversary.

A lone archer crouched atop the main pavilion, beady eyes menacing in the moonlight. He nocked another arrow and took aim.

Chin Sun zoomed forward, throwing herself under the shelter of the pavilion's eaves. She listened for footsteps on the tiles above.

A nearby thump told her the archer had dropped to the ground. She gripped her sword against her chest, blood trickling from her leg. Her heart spiked with a heady mixture of fear and adrenaline. Maybe coming here hadn't been a good idea, after all.

The man's dark form appeared at the edge of her vision. She took a deep breath and turned, ready to take on this new assailant.

She froze mid-step.

His hwando was glowing with fire. Blue fire. Chin Sun lifted her eyes, meeting a pair of dark orbs that were all too familiar.

"It's so good to see you again, little fox." The figure approached her slowly, haughtily, as if he had all the time in the world. He swung the long, decorative sword in a wide sweep.

"You're—you're the goblin from the forest."

He laughed, sending a chill down to the marrow of her bones. "Did you think you wouldn't be seeing me again? How amusing you are."

"But the last goblin I fought—"

"Got caught by a grim reaper? He was stupid enough to attack in broad daylight. Though I do understand"—he licked his lips—"his eagerness. It isn't every day a power such as yours is right there in front of us, ripe for the taking. You've done well to keep your human close." He took another step, leaving only a short distance between them. "But you never should have underestimated us goblins. We may have lost one, but our cause is too great to abandon."

Chin Sun gulped, the temptation to flee growing stronger by the second. "What cause? And what does my bead have to do with it?"

The goblin laughed again. "Beat me, and I'll tell you." His sword slammed against hers, sending scorching heat up Chin Sun's arm.

She let out a high-pitched shriek, blade falling from her hand. The burning sensation in her arm vanished, but the goblin kicked away her hwando before she could retrieve it.

"Not so powerful without your abilities, are you? You gumiho always were too confident in yourselves." He clicked his tongue. "Even now, when your numbers are so few."

Chin Sun's eyes flicked to Kim Min Joon for help, but her friend was still engaged in a fight on the other side of the courtyard. She was on her own.

"Why come after me when I don't have the bead?" she asked, hoping to stall him long enough to find an escape. "You certainly seem powerful enough to overcome my—my human on your own." Heat rushed to her cheeks. Calling

Mr. Park hers felt so wrong—yet why did it send a thrill through her blood?

The goblin scoffed. "Like I said, you've hardly let it out of your sight, and you know making a spectacle of ourselves will bring those grim reapers to the human realm faster than I could get away. Your protectiveness has forced my hand."

He waved his palm, and a swath of blue fire flew toward her.

Chin Sun dove out of the way, the flames soaring past before disintegrating midair.

A spectacle would draw grim reapers? That was a wonderful tidbit to know. She didn't want that one from before to find out she still hadn't retrieved her bead, but if it meant scaring the goblin off . . .

She turned and shouted to the others in the courtyard, "Help! It's a goblin! There's a goblin here!"

An officer rounded the corner of another pavilion and rushed over, spear in hand. "What is it?"

Chin Sun grabbed her sword off the ground and directed it at the goblin—

But she found herself pointing at an empty space. She let out a ragged sigh of relief, then glanced down. Good. Now to make sure everyone else was all right.

"False alarm, sir. Please carry on."

The policeman's eyes narrowed in recognition. "Wait, aren't you—"

Chin Sun raced out of sight, then climbed atop one of the pavilions to get a better view. She counted fifteen masked intruders, five household servants, and two police officers, plus Mr. Park and Min Joon. The servants were still trying to put out the fire, but the flames had spread to the building's rafters. The house's residents must have already fled.

Unless . . .

Chin Sun sprinted across the rooftop tiles and jumped off the far side. She landed with a thud, pain shooting through her ankles as they absorbed the impact. When she reached the nearest servant, a thin ahjussi urging the others to move faster, she barked, "Where are your masters?"

The servant turned to her, expression shifting from despair to tremulous hope. "Gwishin, is that you? I'm so glad you're here. They—they couldn't get out in time. Please help!" He gestured to the burning building helplessly.

Chin Sun bit back a curse. The blaze was too great now; the pavilion wouldn't last much longer. Anyone inside was probably unconscious from inhaling all the smoke—if not already dead. She tore around to the back and forced her way through the window, avoiding the flames as best she could.

She was in a woman's quarters. Two men and a woman lay in a heap on the floor, their clothes singed but still intact. Chin Sun grabbed the nearest person and dragged her toward the window. Her muscles strained from the effort, sweat pouring down her back, but she wasn't about to give up. Not when innocent lives were at stake.

Smoke filled her mouth and stung her eyes. Through blurry vision, she shoved the woman through to the other side, then turned to gather the next victim.

She was coughing so much she could barely concentrate on anything but her growing need for air, her surroundings becoming hazier by the second. Licks of flame fell from the ceiling, sending sparks across the floor. Chin Sun pushed one man out and was about to grab the second, but he opened his eyes and stood up with a sneer.

Chin Sun yelped and jumped back as his face shifted from that of a young man to an ahjussi.

"Don't think I'm that easy to get rid of," he growled. "There are a million ways to dispose of a gumiho."

The goblin looked up at the ceiling, which looked on the verge of collapsing, and shoved Chin Sun to the floor. She tried to get up, but he tipped the large clothing chest nearby onto her leg, pinning her down.

She cried out, trying desperately to pull free, but all her strength had left her. She could barely see anything beyond vague shapes, and her mind was getting fuzzy.

The goblin's dark laugh penetrated her swimming thoughts, and she thought she glimpsed a crow disappearing out the open window.

As Chin Sun lay immobile, fighting to stay awake and come up with some way out of this, a large shadow appeared before her. The grim reaper? Had he returned because of the goblin? Or was he here to take her to the land of spirits?

Chin Sun reached forward eagerly, hoping he'd show mercy since she'd died to save the lives of others. The shadow pulled the clothing chest off her leg like the weight was nothing. Then he wrapped her in his arms and carried her out as her eyes closed. A peaceful feeling came over her, along with a wonderful, woody scent.

Chapter 18

The Rescuer

Hazy images filled Chin Sun's vision as she passed in and out of consciousness. Which were dreams and which were real, she couldn't tell. Aunt was there, encouraging her in her needlework, scolding her when she lost her patience. Sang Mi and Sang Ook, too, laughing as they played in the courtyard. Uncle's face beaming with pride as her writing improved.

She tried to hold on to those moments, those happy times when life was simple, peaceful. That was the reality she wanted, the only one that mattered. Except—

Another face crossed her mind, one that tugged at her heart in an entirely different way. It was hard to make out at first; all she caught were fleeting glimpses before darkness swallowed it up again. A distinguished jawline. Thin lips. A faint scar over an eyebrow. Piercing eyes.

A face she didn't want to leave this world without seeing one more time.

Chin Sun came to with a gasp, the faces in her mind fading. She found herself at the back of a dark alley, clay huts on either side of her. A ginkgo tree stood proudly at her back, its fan-shaped leaves stretching toward the stars. She could also hear a faint trickling of water; the river must be close by.

She took in her surroundings in an instant, her focus soon latching on to the alley's other occupant, who was staring at her with crossed arms and a strange, unreadable expression.

Chin Sun's hand went to her face, relief billowing over her when she found her mask still in place. But the movement made her wince, drawing her attention to her hands. The cloth coverings she usually wore on them were gone, exposing tender red flesh beneath. She could feel several bruises forming on her back and legs, but nothing appeared to be broken.

"How are you feeling?" rumbled Mr. Park's voice.

A shiver went through her, though she couldn't tell if it was from fear or . . . something else. "I—I'm fine," she stuttered in the deepest voice she could manage. She rose to her feet and glanced around again. "How did I get here?"

Mr. Park unfolded his arms and strode toward her. "I brought you." His tone was very matter-of-fact, giving away nothing.

"You? Then . . . was that you in the fire?"

He nodded.

Chin Sun's mouth fell open. The black-clothed figure she'd been so certain had been a grim reaper had turned out to be none other than her stalwart bodyguard.

He'd caught her just like he'd promised.

The thought generated a rush of blood in her face, but before she could dwell on it, he said in a gruff tone, "Since you seem to be all right, I better be going." He bowed and turned away.

"Wait a moment," she called, words ending in a cough.

Mr. Park went rigid, but he didn't face her. "What?"

"You're just going to let me go?" She couldn't keep a tremor from her voice. Was this a trick? Were Hong's men waiting around the corner?

He slowly swung around, expression icy. "You saved my life; now I've saved yours. That makes us even."

"Yeh, but aren't you at least going to have me arrested?"

He cocked his head to the side, studying her. "Is that what you want?"

"Of course not," she replied. "It just doesn't make sense why you're doing this."

"Why I'd show honor to a criminal?" he replied in a low, disappointed tone. As if he cared what she thought of him.

"That you wouldn't carry out your duty," she clarified, but she quickly backtracked when she realized that might tip him off about her true identity. "It's no secret around Sokju why you were hired."

The man stepped forward until their chests were almost touching. He scowled down at her. "I was hired to protect Lady Lee from threats. And from what I can tell"—his gaze moved over her—"you're not one."

Chin Sun's heart shuddered, both from his words and the intensity in his eyes. It wasn't just anger radiating off him—it was also something else. Something that reminded her all too much of that moment in the clearing.

Her gaze dropped to his lips before she could stop herself. There was no way she could kiss him right now, not when she was in disguise. The cloth over her mouth was a literal barrier between them.

So, why was she even thinking about it?

A knot rose in her throat as the answer came to her. Her urge to kiss him had nothing to do with the bead and everything to do with the man in front of her.

Park Hyun Soo.

The attraction she felt, this magnetic pull toward him, somehow she'd fooled herself into thinking it was because he was carrying her fox bead. But that didn't explain her burning need to find out what his lips felt like against her own, to run her fingers along his jaw, to lose herself in his embrace.

Such yearning was foreign to her, yet she wasn't so ignorant that she didn't recognize it for what it was. She knew the symptoms of desire.

But he also stirred other feelings within her. Delight each time she saw his smile, guilt for every lie she spun, and worst of all—the strangest urge to shed her disguise and face him openly.

What if this went deeper than physical attraction? What if she'd grown too fond of their game of cat and mouse and something unseemly had sprung up in her heart?

Chin Sun went cold.

That couldn't happen. She was about to marry Young Master Kang, for heaven's sake. And what about her family? They were counting on Chin Sun to uphold the Lee name, to open doors of opportunity for Sang Mi and Sang Ook. She couldn't let them down.

And yet . . .

She lifted her gaze to her bodyguard, meeting his fierce, probing stare that seemed to see through her facade, right down to her very soul.

He'd said he didn't think Gwishin was a threat to Lady Lee's safety, but what *did* he think of her, of this vigilante he'd tried so hard to eliminate and had somehow ended up saving?

Her mouth moved with a will of its own. "Then what am I?"

He hesitated, eyes roaming over her again. "I haven't figured that out yet," he admitted, so quietly he seemed to be speaking to himself. He lifted his hand slowly, fingers reaching for her mask.

Chin Sun's brain screamed at her to move, draw the dagger out of her clothes, do *something*, but she found herself paralyzed, waiting to see if he'd keep going. Wanting him to.

He hesitated, searching her gaze like he wanted to make sure he had permission before he touched her, before he unveiled her secret once and for all.

Hyun Soo's fingers grazed the top of her cheek, pausing on her skin. A shock ran through her, stoking the fire growing in her belly. She leaned into his touch, eyes still locked on his.

His lips parted as he drew in a sharp breath. His hand drifted toward the knot holding her mask in place.

A rush of footfalls sounded nearby, and Chin Sun jumped back, head swerving toward the main road. Had the pirates caught up with them? Or perhaps some patrolmen passing by? Either way, she couldn't afford to be seen. Chin Sun gave Hyun Soo one final glance, then stole away into the darkness.

Hyun Soo was relieved when the vigilante slipped out of sight, identity still unconfirmed. Part of him hadn't wanted to unmask Gwishin. Not when he was sure he'd find Lady Lee staring up at him.

That had been several hours ago, and now he stood in his room with his back to the door, the first light of dawn peeking in through his open window. He pressed his hands to his forehead and groaned in frustration. He'd barely gotten a wink of sleep. This mission had seemed so simple when he'd first accepted it. If he'd known it would make him question everything, he'd have declined Dol Sam's offer.

Gwishin had been a thorn in his side for weeks, yet when he'd seen the masked figure trapped inside the burning building, he hadn't hesitated to jump into the inferno. Protecting Lady Lee was his top priority, but what if all his instincts were wrong and Gwishin wasn't his mistress in disguise? Had he just sabotaged himself?

Except . . . Gwishin had saved his life.

What kind of criminal would risk their neck for someone who'd tried to kill them?

He called to mind the charges stacked against the elusive vigilante: assault, robbery, murder, destruction of property. Could they all have come from trying to protect the lowborn?

Hyun Soo was guilty of just as much, yet the law didn't condemn him because he'd done it all for the throne's sake.

He lowered his hands and stared out at the pink sky, wishing it could give him the answers he sought. Or better yet, that he could turn to his father. The sage minister had always been generous with his counsel, earning Hyun Soo's respect and admiration from a young age. He hadn't realized until years later just how important his father was, for he was none other than Byeongjo Panseo, Minister of National Defense.

And Hyun Soo was his greatest joy.

Until someone found a series of letters in Hyun Soo's

quarters that detailed the palace's weapons arsenal and guard assignments. That was when everything changed. Hyun Soo was searched, questioned, and eventually arrested on suspicion of selling country secrets. He had no idea how the messages had gotten into his satchel, nor whom they were for. He couldn't even read them since they were in Japanese. But all his cries of innocence fell on deaf ears.

When his father heard what happened, his influence kept Hyun Soo from standing trial, but the young guard's reputation and position were lost.

Hyun Soo's relationship with his father disappeared next, for a son branded as a traitor was an embarrassment for a man who'd lived his entire life seeking to bring honor to his country.

"I would have thought my message clear. You are not welcome here any longer," Father declared when he finally exited his chambers. He stood several paces away on the veranda, but his booming voice easily reached Hyun Soo's ears where he bowed with his face to the ground.

Hyun Soo didn't move from his position, but he couldn't hold back the tears streaming down his face. He'd been kneeling in the family courtyard for hours, unwilling to move until he'd gained an audience.

"And where shall I go? Without you and Mother, without the Park name, I am nothing."

"You should have thought of that before you betrayed this great nation. If it weren't for my influence, you'd be behind bars right now."

Hyun Soo's head snapped up, eyes locking with his father's. "I am innocent. Why can't you believe me?"

Father turned his back on him, and Hyun Soo's hurt spilled over. "You spoke often of the importance of loyalty, that the bonds of family were stronger than any other," Hyun Soo said. "Were those just words you could toss aside when things got hard?"

Father whipped around, teeth bared. "An archer has no use for a broken arrow." He strode down the stairs to Hyun Soo and wrenched his son's sword from the scabbard, his tiered gauze hat making him appear as tall as a grim reaper.

When Father raised the sword, Hyun Soo stretched his neck forward and shut his eyes, ready to accept his fate. If there was nothing he could do to change Father's mind, perhaps this was best. If he could restore the Park family name with his death, so be it.

He waited for the sword to fall, but when it did, it stopped short, slicing his braid rather than his skin.

Hyun Soo let out a weak cry, then peered at the sheared hair in confusion. Had Father changed his mind about killing him? Was this mercy?

Minister Park turned his back on him once more, chest heaving. "Just as that is severed, so is our family bond. We are of no relation henceforth."

The servants had thrown Hyun Soo out shortly after, and Dol Sam found him passed out in a tavern that evening. He would only later realize the finality of his father's dismissal. The audience Minister Park had granted him that day would be the last gift his father bestowed.

Hyun Soo was eternally grateful he'd had Dol Sam around to bolster his morale in the past few months. . . .

Dol Sam!

Hyun Soo's hands fell to his sides, panic setting in at the realization that he'd left his friend waiting last night. He burst out of his room, startling a servant so badly that she dropped her linens. Muttering an apology, he retrieved the linens and pressed them into her hands before continuing on, not stopping again until he'd reached the Kang residence.

He rapped his knuckles against the gate, smiling when a young man answered. "Please let Kang Dol Sam know his friend Hyun Soo is here."

"Ah, he's been expecting you," the servant replied, and he stepped back to allow him in.

When Hyun Soo arrived at Dol Sam's quarters, the young lord was writing a letter at his desk, calligraphy brush in hand. He looked up at Hyun Soo, eyes widening with relief. "Hyun Soo, you're here. I must admit I was worried."

Hyun Soo bowed and sat down across from him. "I apologize for not meeting you last night, my friend. There was . . . an incident."

Dol Sam stiffened. "Is Lady Lee injured?"

"No, she's fine. But while we were en route to the bridge, we came across a group of bandits. Luckily, an inspector was in the area, so he sent his officers after them. I was going to come to you, but the bandits attacked a merchant's house and started a fire. I couldn't leave without first doing my part to help. And then Gwishin showed up."

Dol Sam blinked a few times. "Gwishin was out in the open after what he did to that scholar? He's even more arrogant than I thought. And he was working with the bandits, you say?"

Hyun Soo shook his head. "No, that's not it. He had nothing to do with the bandits. He was there to stop them."

"Stop them? That doesn't make sense. Are you certain?"

"Yeh. In fact, while I was fighting one, Gwishin jumped in and helped me."

His friend sucked his teeth. "Now I know you're making this up. Very funny, Hyun Soo-yah. You almost fooled me."

"But, hyung, I mean it. Gwishin saved my life."

Dol Sam held up a finger, anger overtaking his normally cheerful face. "You mean to tell me the best swordsman in Joseon—and the only friend I trust with my most prized possession—had to be rescued by a murderer? Because that sounds an awful lot like you're telling me you're incompetent."

Hyun Soo drew back at the man's sudden shift in demeanor. "Of course I'm not saying that. I—"

"When I hired you to serve Lady Lee, I didn't think I was hiring someone incompetent. If you're not up for the task of protecting her, say so now, and I'll gladly give the job to someone else."

"No, I want the job," he exclaimed a bit too hastily.

"Good." Dol Sam nodded once, calming down a bit. "I can't afford to have anything less than the best for my fiancée. You understand, right?"

Hyun Soo gave him a pinched smile, still rather shaken up by his friend's outburst. Dol Sam had always been level-headed; even when he'd been under the assassin's knife at their first meeting, Dol Sam had barely flinched.

Surely he could be reasoned with.

Hyun Soo tried again. "Hyung, what if the vigilante isn't the person you think?"

Dol Sam's brow furrowed. "What do you mean? Did you figure out his true identity?"

Hyun Soo dropped his head, unsure how to respond. He didn't want to drive a wedge between Dol Sam and Lady Lee if she was innocent. But what if she was the vigilante and his friend was about to marry a criminal?

A criminal Hyun Soo just might be falling in love with.

But Hyun Soo's allegiance had to be to his friend, no matter his feelings for Lady Lee. Dol Sam had been there for him when no one else had. He deserved to know the truth.

Hyun Soo opened his mouth, ready to divulge the vigilante's identity—until he saw the bloodlust in his friend's eyes.

He swallowed the words on his tongue. Whatever Dol Sam had against Gwishin, it seemed to go beyond simply protecting Lady Lee. This was something personal, perhaps even irrational.

What would happen if that wrath were directed at Lady Lee?

"No," Hyun Soo lied, "I've just been trying to consider all the possibilities. Gwishin could be anyone, even a member of the police bureau."

"Nonsense. No one with any sense of morality—even a twisted one like some of the men on the force have—is capable of such heinous crimes." Dol Sam paused. "I know I told you before to stop him by any means necessary, but I've changed my mind. If it's within your power, bring him to me—alive. Gwishin is the worst thing that's ever happened to Sokju. He needs to be made an example of." His lips peeled back in an unpleasant smile. "And I know just how to do it."

Chapter 19

The Plan

Chin Sun scurried back to her quarters, heart galloping like a horse. She couldn't believe she'd nearly given away her secret. What had she been thinking?

She hadn't been. Clearly, she'd been caught up in a moment of desire, hypnotized by Mr. Park's delicate touch. She could still feel the effects of it now, that hint of longing buried in her chest.

She tried to pry it out so she could extinguish it, but the ache refused to budge, burrowing deeper like an eaglet in its nest. What *was* this?

Now that she was away from Mr. Park, it should have been easy to stamp out this feeling and clear her head. Why couldn't she?

Chin Sun removed her outer layer of clothes and got onto her sleeping mat, but sleep didn't come easily. Every time she shut her eyes, Mr. Park's peered back at her.

"What are you doing here?" Kim Min Joon hissed through his teeth. He checked over her shoulder, then pulled her into one of the police bureau's empty rooms.

Inside was a long table with tall chairs, a place for the officers to share updates and strategize before leaving for their individual assignments. Chin Sun had never been inside the police bureau before; when she and Min Joon had become allies, they'd agreed not to meet in public unless it was an emergency.

The night she'd just had definitely constituted an emergency.

She'd calmly told the officer at the entrance that she had information for the inspector's ears only, but at the sight of her friend, all her composure shriveled up like a persimmon. She collapsed in one of the chairs and rubbed circles into her throbbing temples.

"There's so much I need to tell you, but I don't know where to start," she murmured.

Her friend's warm hand on her shoulder was comforting, but it also made her throat constrict. She swallowed a few times, then confessed, "You were right to tell me to stay home last night."

Min Joon's hand slid away, and he sat down in the seat beside her. "You came anyway." It wasn't a question. His voice was soft, controlled, yet it carried an undercurrent of anger that cut to Chin Sun's core.

He pulled her hand away from her face, urging her to look him in the eye. "What happened?"

She started with the easiest part: fighting the bandits and discovering they were more than they seemed.

Min Joon slammed his hand on the table. "You mean Magistrate Hong hired them? Why would he—" His eyes widened with sudden clarity, and he slumped into his chair. "That sniveling little rat. I knew he wanted to catch you, but I didn't think he'd stoop so low as to harm innocent people."

"There's more," Chin Sun revealed. "One of the bandits wasn't part of Hong's group. He was a goblin."

"A goblin?" Min Joon leaned a little closer, one eyebrow raised. "Are you sure?"

She nodded. "The same one who tried to take my bead in the forest." She filled him in on the rest of the details, stopping after the part about Hyun Soo rescuing her from the fire. Min Joon didn't need to know that she'd almost revealed her identity.

Her friend stayed silent for a long moment. "Then it's only thanks to Mr. Park that you're alive today."

Chin Sun dropped her gaze to the table, accepting his words with a heavy heart. She couldn't help but think back to when Hyun Soo had snapped at her in the schoolyard.

"How am I supposed to protect you if you have no sense of self-preservation? Is jumping into fights you can't win a habit of yours?"

"It sounds to me like I've made a grave mistake in judgment," Min Joon continued.

Chin Sun's head snapped up. Was that amusement in his voice?

A touch of a smile played on his lips. "This Mr. Park is much better alive than dead, even if he did try to kill you. I suppose I shouldn't fault him for that, considering I tried to do the same once."

"I think you're focused on the wrong thing. I came to you because I need your help figuring out how to stop this goblin."

"On the contrary, I believe I'm focused on exactly the right thing. The goblin has beaten you twice, yet both times, you've managed to get away. Why is that?" He snapped his fingers. "Mr. Park."

Chin Sun started to protest, but Min Joon held up his hand. "I'm not saying I doubt your abilities. The first time the goblin overpowered you, you were already injured. The second time, you didn't have your bead. I've seen what you're capable of, Chin Sun-ah. I'm willing to bet that if you were at your full strength, you could take that monster down."

"But I'm not."

"*And* that's where it comes back to Mr. Park. If you want to defeat the goblin, you're going to need every weapon you've got."

Chin Sun turned away, something unpleasant pressing on her chest. "I've tried to get my bead back. You know that."

"I do. And I know how much is at stake. That's why I'm willing to do whatever it takes to help you. Even if it means I lose my job."

Chin Sun shifted around with a look of surprise. Surely he couldn't mean that.

But Min Joon's face held such sincerity, tears of gratitude stung her eyes.

"Here's what I'm thinking: I'll call him in to ask him some questions about what he witnessed at the merchant's house last night. You'll be waiting just outside. I'll knock him out when he's not looking, and then you can sneak in and kiss him. You'll get your bead back, and your reputation will still be spotless." He grinned like he was so proud of what he'd come up with, but his mouth was too tight, his smile too broad.

Chin Sun shook her head. "Thank you, my friend, but I can't ask you to do that. I know how much this position means to you."

"But—"

She shook her head again, resolve flooding her veins in the wake of his unwavering loyalty. She wouldn't allow him to sacrifice himself, not for her. A plan began to form in her mind. It was terribly risky, but with Min Joon about to jump into the flames to save her, she couldn't afford to wait any longer.

Especially when there were only seven days left until the bead absorbed the last of Hyun Soo's lifeforce.

"This is my problem to fix," she stated. "I've tried using subterfuge, and that hasn't gotten me anywhere. It's time for a more direct approach."

Min Joon covered his mouth, eyes wide with disbelief. "You don't mean you're going to just do it openly?"

"That's exactly what I mean."

"But what about Kang Dol Sam?"

"I'm going to call off the betrothal. My uncle will be upset, but it can't be helped. Mr. Park is a good man, too good to keep such a betrayal from his friend, and I won't delude myself into thinking Kang Dol Sam could still want me after he finds out what I've done."

"Are you sure that's what you want to do?"

"Yeh, it's for the best. With time, perhaps my reputation will recover enough that someone will be willing to marry me, and my cousins will find good matches for themselves."

"Wait, you're not going to tell Mr. Park you're a gumiho though, right?"

Chin Sun scowled. "I don't have a death wish, Kim Min Joon."

Her friend let out a chuckle, but it was a dull, lifeless sound. "So, what *are* you going to tell him?"

"I . . ." Chin Sun cringed. She hadn't thought that far ahead, but there was only one thing she could say besides the truth about her bead. "I'll just tell him I have feelings for him." She shrugged like it was no big deal, but inside, her heart was hammering against her ribs, demanding to be heard.

Min Joon crossed his arms. "Do you think you can lie that convincingly? I know you're good at acting, but that's— Chin Sun? What's wrong?"

She tilted her head to the side, then felt what he must have already noticed on her eyelashes: tears.

She sniffled, hating her body for betraying her like this. She was supposed to be strong, to show no weaknesses, but when it came to Park Hyun Soo, she became as emotional as any other lovestruck maiden.

Min Joon still waited for an answer, his forehead creased in concern.

Chin Sun licked her lips and gave him a wan, self-deprecating smile. "Who's to say it's a lie?"

His jaw fell open. "What? Lee Chin Sun, are you serious?"

She closed her eyes but nodded. "I know it's dangerous and utterly foolish, but I just . . . I just . . ."

Min Joon grabbed her hand, and when she opened her eyes, her friend's expression was full of compassion. "You don't need to explain." He swiped a tear off her cheek. "Who can truly know the ways of the heart?"

Chin Sun's mouth widened into a real smile. She hoped Min Joon knew just how much she appreciated his tenderness. If their roles had been reversed, she would have chided him for letting his heart run away from him.

"Do you think . . ." She took a deep breath, gathering her courage. "Do you think there's any possibility he could feel the same?"

A spark of mischief lit up Min Joon's face, as if he knew something she didn't. "If the way he acted when we first met is any indicator, I'd say there's a *strong* possibility."

"What do you mean?" Her brow furrowed as she tried to conjure up the memory. "How did he act?"

Min Joon waggled his eyebrows. "Like he was so jealous he wanted to choke me."

What? Mr. Park, jealous? Fire blazed down the back of Chin Sun's neck, but try as she might, she couldn't stop grinning. Up until now, she hadn't allowed herself to dream he might reciprocate her feelings. But if Min Joon was right . . .

She dipped her head in a quick bow, suddenly eager to return home. "I better go."

Chapter 20

The Confession

Hyun Soo had been waiting outside Lady Lee's quarters for almost an hour now, and to say he was anxious was an understatement. None of the servants had seen her this morning, but they'd given him judgmental looks when he'd asked after her whereabouts. What good was a bodyguard who couldn't keep track of the mistress he'd sworn to protect?

His palms were slick with sweat, a host of possible reasons for her absence trickling through his mind. What if she'd been more injured last night than he'd thought? What if she'd been captured or—

A swish of floral orange skirts announced Lady Lee's arrival, and when she noticed him in the hallway, she gave him a shaky grin. "Mr. Park!"

Hyun Soo bounded over and clasped her hands between his. "Lady Lee, are you all right?"

His mistress didn't speak at first, a soft blush coming over her cheeks. "Yeh, of . . . of course. I'm sorry I didn't tell you I was going out, but I had an urgent matter to attend to."

Hyun Soo's brow wrinkled. Why wasn't she meeting his eye?

"What sort of matter was so urgent that you wouldn't bring your bodyguard along?"

The rosy color in her cheeks deepened, and he followed her line of sight down to their joined hands.

He pulled away with a gasp. "I'm sorry, Lady Lee. I didn't realize—"

"Please don't apologize," she whispered.

"What?" Hyun Soo looked up in confusion, but his mistress was already sashaying into her quarters.

"Wait here," she called, so he planted himself outside the door. A few minutes later, she returned with folded parchment in hand.

"I'd like you to escort me somewhere today. . . . And don't ask Pyung Ho or Ah In to come with us. Please."

Her voice hitched at the end, halting the refusal on his tongue. Had he upset her by not spending as much time with her lately? He hadn't meant to. But he couldn't exactly explain that he didn't trust himself to be alone with her anymore. Not after the clearing. And certainly not after his debacle last night.

A delicious shiver went down his spine at the memory. The more he'd turned it over in his mind, the more confident he'd grown. Gwishin could *only* be Lady Lee. Their demeanors, fighting styles, even the feel of them in his arms —all identical.

And the way she'd leaned into his touch . . .

Hyun Soo cleared his throat, trying to shift his thoughts to safer subjects. He'd tell Lady Lee he couldn't escort her, and that was that.

Except, where did she go?

Chin Sun resisted the urge to glance over her shoulder and check if Hyun Soo was following. She'd given Pyung Ho the letters for Uncle and Young Master Kang, then loudly made her way out of the courtyard to ensure her bodyguard found her. Now her insides were trembling like the tail of a salmusa snake as she made her way down the road. At this rate, she might accidentally blurt out her confession before they'd even reached a secluded area.

Soft footfalls behind her made her pulse quicken with anticipation. He'd caught up with her. Good. Or maybe terrible. She wouldn't know if she was making the biggest mistake of her life until she heard his response. Chin Sun wasn't used to situations where she didn't have any sense of control. It was . . . disorienting, but also a little exhilarating at the same time.

Focus, Chin Sun. She made a right turn onto a path out of the city, her heart in her throat. If he hadn't yet realized she was leading him to the clearing, there could be no doubt of it now. Would he turn back, or continue on with her to find out why she was taking him there?

She lifted her chin, defying the anxiety charging through her. If this didn't go the way she hoped, she was still going to maintain her dignity. She'd just reached the tree line when Hyun Soo said, "Lady Lee, stop."

She flinched but called back, "Just a bit farther," and carried on. She didn't wait for him to reply, terrified of what he might say. All she had to do was get to the clearing. That was all.

When the woods opened up to the familiar space, the weight on her chest eased. Until she turned to Hyun Soo.

He averted his gaze guiltily, then drew his mouth into a thin, straight line. "We shouldn't be here."

Chin Sun bit her lip. This wasn't going the way she'd planned. "I need to tell you something." She swallowed. "Mr. Park . . ." she trailed off, eyes drifting to his shoes. Why was this so hard!

She tried again, blood rushing through her ears. She needed to stop trying to get this perfect and just do it. "In the time we've spent together, you've become more than a bodyguard to me. You're someone I deeply respect and consider a friend."

"As are you," he said quietly, setting her heart ablaze. "What—"

"But that's not all," she added. She squeezed her eyes shut, unsure if she could get this next part out. "I see you as a man, too."

There. She'd said it. She waited for the ground to open up and swallow her, but her feet remained steady despite her frayed nerves. Had he heard her? Why wasn't he saying anything?

Did she dare look up?

When the silence became unbearable, Chin Sun peeked at her mute companion. His body was shifted slightly away from her, eyebrows pressed together like she'd just given him the worst news imaginable.

"Mr. Park?"

His eyes zoomed to hers, so full of anguish she nearly looked away. But he hadn't given her a response. He owed her that much.

"Lady Lee, I . . . Dol Sam—" He broke off, one hand

clenched into a fist. He turned around as if he couldn't bear to look at her.

Chin Sun wilted like a mungunghwa flower, but she fought against the tears threatening to drench her cheeks. How could she have been so foolish!

She took a deep breath. "I understand. I don't want to come between you and Young Master Kang. But you should know"—her voice dropped to a mumble—"I've decided to break off my engagement."

"What did you just say?" Hyun Soo spun back so fast Chin Sun barely registered the movement before he was an arm's length away, devastating her with the intensity of his gaze. There was something dangerous about it, and desperate.

Yet she couldn't look away.

"I'm not going to marry Kang Dol Sam," she said, more confidently this time. "I want to be with you. Do you—do you want that, too?"

Hyun Soo cocked his head to the side, a playful smile tugging at his lips. "That's a very bold question, my lady."

Chin Sun frowned even as her stomach fluttered with hope. What did *that* mean?

She waited, but when he didn't say more, she put her hands on her hips and gave him the most withering look she could manage. "Well? Are you going to give me an answer or not? I'm not in the mood for teasing, not about . . . this." Her face flamed up, ruining the angry front she was going for.

"Oh, but isn't it only fair after everything you've put me through"—he seized her chin between his index finger and thumb—"Gwishin?"

She jerked away, whipping out a hidden dagger before he could blink. "You knew about that?"

Hyun Soo glanced at her weapon and laughed, a deep, rich sound that made her want to let down her defenses.

But he *knew*.

"There's no need to be afraid," he said softly, stepping closer. "I'm not going to betray your secret."

She wanted to believe him, but fear urged her to run, to hide, to strike him down before he could harm her. She shook her head to dislodge the thoughts, but she couldn't bring herself to lower the blade. "How can I trust your word?"

He covered her hand with his own, then guided the dagger to his heart. "Because if you carved this out, you'd find your name written upon it. Take it if you don't believe me, but that is the truth. A truth I've tried to deny for so long, not only for fear of hurting my friend, but also because I didn't think you could possibly feel the same."

He released her hand but didn't move away, waiting for her to answer. Or to strike a killing blow. Knowing her secret identity made him a terrible threat. If he told the authorities, she'd be forced to flee for her life.

Yet he hadn't. Instead he'd quite literally placed his life in her hands, knowing full well how easily she could end it.

What room was left for doubt when he had such faith in her? Chin Sun tossed the knife aside, lips twisting into a smirk. "There's no need to be so dramatic."

Hyun Soo laughed again, then his expression shifted, all traces of humor stripped away to reveal something that sparked a fire in her veins. He bent forward slowly, as if waiting to see if she'd retreat again.

When she didn't, his gaze dropped to her lips, his intentions quite clear.

Chin Sun raised an eyebrow at his hesitation. "Don't tell me you're not brave enough to follow through. Again."

Hyun Soo's mouth crashed into hers like swords on a battlefield, stealing her breath and overwhelming her senses. Surprised by his fervor but not about to be outdone, she responded to his kiss hungrily. Two could play at this game.

He smiled against her mouth and deepened the kiss, hands sliding around her back and crushing her against him. Chin Sun gripped his shoulders, pleasure radiating through her as their lips fought for dominance.

She felt her fox bead rise in his chest and happily accepted it into her mouth, a shot of power bursting through her at its safe return. Yet there was a new energy humming within it unlike anything she'd ever experienced. It tasted of sunshine and sweat, betrayal and desire, hardship and joy. Was this what it felt like to consume human lifeforce?

The taste was almost as intoxicating as Hyun Soo's kisses. But not quite. Chin Sun would have to figure out all the effects of the additional lifeforce later. That could wait until after they were done kissing.

But Hyun Soo stilled in her arms. He pulled back. "Lady Lee, what—" Something flashed in his eyes, and he stepped out of her embrace.

"Mr. Park? What's wrong?"

He pressed his fingers to his mouth, forehead wrinkled. "I . . . What did you just do?"

Guilt rapped at the door of her heart, but she refused it entrance. "What are you talking about?"

"You . . . you did something to me. I—" His eyes rolled back into his head, and he slumped forward.

Chin Sun caught him as he fell, holding him up easily with her gumiho strength restored. "Mr. Park?" She patted his cheek, panic building in her chest. "Park Hyun Soo!"

It couldn't be. There was still time.

She forced her bead back up into her mouth and spat it into her hand. It was cool to the touch, as small as a robin's egg. But its glowing blue light was so blinding she almost couldn't look at it. Full of human lifeforce.

"No . . ."

The grim reaper said Hyun Soo had eighteen days, and it had only been eleven. Hyun Soo had to be all right. He had to—

"Finally decided to take back your bead, I see," came a deep voice.

Chin Sun whirled around, tensing at the sight of the grim reaper himself, smirking on the other side of the clearing. His black robes fluttered in the breeze, the only indicator that this specter was still flesh and blood.

"Nauri, what's—what's wrong with him? He should still have some time left."

The grim reaper vanished, then reappeared directly in front of her, crossing the clearing in a span of seconds. He squinted at Hyun Soo, then shook his head. "I'm no expert on fox beads. Perhaps I miscalculated how long he had."

His words were nonchalant, but then his face darkened, cold eyes locking on to hers. "But you better hope he just passed out from the energy transfer." He grabbed Hyun Soo's wrist. "His pulse is very weak."

"Can you help me? Please," she pleaded. She knew she sounded pathetic, but maintaining her dignity no longer mattered. All she cared about was saving Hyun Soo.

The grim reaper clucked his tongue, as if offended that she would even ask. "That's not my job."

He was gone a second later, but his voice carried on the wind. "I'll be watching to make sure you keep him breathing though."

Chin Sun screamed, half of her terrified and the other half enraged. What a heartless creature!

She returned her attention to Hyun Soo, touching his temple with the back of her hand. Burning up with fever.

Was there any way to return the lifeforce she'd collected? She glanced at her bead, but it gave no answer besides a derisive shimmer.

She swallowed it once more. If she couldn't give back what she'd stolen, she'd use her speed to get help.

"I'll be back soon," she promised, then dove into the wood, unable to avoid an ominous sense of déjà vu. She'd made that same promise to Aunt, and it had been the last thing she'd ever said to her.

Chapter 21

The Mistake

Chin Sun flew to the police station, feet moving faster than they ever had in her life. She didn't bother concealing herself from passersby; she wasn't about to waste what precious little time Hyun Soo had left. To most, she must have looked like a vaguely human blur, gone before they could fully grasp what they were seeing.

When she arrived, a great crowd had gathered to watch a public interrogation in the inner courtyard. An officer sneered as he stood over the accused, who lay on the ground with a straw mat wrapped around his body. Two more officers hovered behind him, clubs raised. Magistrate Hong sat in a chair at the edge of the main pavilion, watching the proceedings with sadistic pleasure. Judging by the tears and bruises on the accused's face, the police had already begun torturing him.

Chin Sun's ribs tightened as they always did when she witnessed such injustice, but she curbed the flow of anger inside her. That was a fight for another day. Right now, she had to get Hyun Soo the help he needed. She pushed her way past the spectators and stopped in front of an officer coming out of one of the side rooms.

"Where's the damo Hae Rim?" she demanded.

The officer started at her abrasive tone, then pointed toward the bureau kitchen. Chin Sun burst inside, setting off a chorus of high-pitched screams from the group of damos working within. She marched past the clay hearth to the medicine cabinet, where Hae Rim was in the midst of sorting herbs.

"You need to come with me—now."

Hae Rim's mouth opened like she was about to protest, but something in Chin Sun's expression must have caught her eye. She nodded and grabbed a small bag. "Where are we going?"

Chin Sun grabbed the girl's hand and yanked her out of the kitchen. Since those outside were focused on the officers' brutal display of power, no one batted an eyelash when the two of them disappeared in a blur of movement.

Chin Sun bolted back to the clearing with a frightened Hae Rim in her arms. When they reached Hyun Soo, she set the nurse down, then knelt at her beloved's side.

"Can you save him?"

Hae Rim pressed her fingers against her forehead like she was trying to fight off a wave of dizziness.

"Hae Rim!" Chin Sun shouted, impatience getting the better of her. Hyun Soo was barely breathing.

The damo seemed to come back to her senses and bent to grab Hyun Soo's wrist. She frowned, then scanned his unconscious body. She turned to Chin Sun. "What happened to him?"

"He . . ." Chin Sun trailed off. "Is there anything you can do to help him?"

"Not until I know what brought him to this state," Hae

Rim said sharply. "I see no signs of physical trauma, yet his heart struggles to beat. Are you going to tell me the truth, or did you bring me here to watch him die?"

Chin Sun internally winced at the woman's insensitive remark. In normal circumstances, Hae Rim would be absolutely right. Except, what use would it be to tell her what happened? It wasn't like Hae Rim knew anything about gumiho or fox beads.

"I don't know. He just passed out all of a sudden."

The angry glint in Hae Rim's eyes made it obvious she didn't believe that for a second, but she turned back to her patient and opened her bag. She withdrew a small herbal pouch with a sweet, earthy scent. Ginseng, if Chin Sun wasn't mistaken.

"I don't suppose you have a way to brew tea here, do you?" At Chin Sun's grimace, she huffed. "I didn't think so. Well, the first thing we need to do is get him somewhere I can treat him. Do you think you can . . . ?"

Chin Sun caught her meaning and threw the man over her shoulder with ease. "I'll take him back to his room at my family's residence. Then I'll return to get you."

Hae Rim held up her hand. "Wait, that's all right. I can get there on my own." Her face was pinched and pale, as if the thought of being carried again made her feel sick.

"Do you have any idea where we are?"

"Uhhh . . ." Hae Rim surveyed the clearing, eyes wide with uncertainty.

"I'll be back soon." Chin Sun darted off. Hyun Soo's warmth was comforting, reminding her the body she carried still had life pulsing within it. But for how much longer?

She vaulted over the wall into the family courtyard and deposited him on his bed mat before any of the servants noticed her. She tucked him under the blanket and stepped back.

From this vantage point, he looked like he was in the midst of a peaceful sleep. That grim reaper better have been right, or she'd make sure he regretted his mistake.

A gasp sounded behind her. "Lady Lee!"

Chin Sun whirled around to a startled Pyung Ho. "Mr. Park is ill. Watch after him for me until the nurse arrives."

The servant nodded his assent, so she stepped around him and hurried back down the servants' corridor. She retrieved Hae Rim and brought her home, this time entering through the front gate.

"Agasshi?" Ye Seul approached from the back of the house with a tub of water, eyebrows drawn together in concern.

"Mr. Park has fallen ill. I've brought Hae Rim to treat him."

"A damo? Shouldn't he be treated by a male physician?"

"She is the only one I trust." Chin Sun's voice left no room for argument. She turned to Hae Rim. "Let her know what you'll need."

Once the damo had rattled off a few items, the servant bustled away to prepare them, water sloshing from her basin.

Chin Sun brought Hae Rim to Hyun Soo's room, where Pyung Ho waited anxiously. She thanked the young man for his diligence before dismissing him so he could return to his duties. Ye Seul appeared not long after with the tea, setting it down on a tray before excusing herself.

"Let me see if I can get him to drink this," Hae Rim said once they were alone, voice uncharacteristically gentle. She placed one hand under the bodyguard's head, and with the other, she grasped a cup of tea. "Mr. Park, I need you to drink this."

The man's eyelids fluttered but did not open. Hae Rim pressed the cup to his mouth and got Hyun Soo to swallow a sip of the warm liquid before he fell unconscious again. The nurse lowered his head and checked his pulse again. A beat later, she turned, her features mirroring the relief spreading through Chin Sun's chest.

"His heart is still weak, but the fact that I was able to get some tea into him is encouraging," Hae Rim said. "I'll remain here and see if I can get him to drink the rest. You don't have to stay."

"I want to," Chin Sun insisted. "He's . . ." She watched the slight rise and fall of Hyun Soo's hanbok, heart clenching painfully in her chest. "He's important to me."

"Important enough to expose your true identity?"

Chin Sun's pulse leaped, but she forced her body to relax. She let out a fake laugh. "True identity? Hmm? Whatever are you talking about?"

Hae Rim rolled her eyes. She glanced at the door, as if to make sure no one was listening, then leaned close. "No woman could do what you just did. No human woman, that is."

Chin Sun sucked her cheeks in, debating how to respond. Her fingers itched for the knife she only then remembered she'd left behind in the clearing. "What is it you want?"

Hae Rim held up empty hands. "Nothing, except that you don't treat me like a fool."

Chin Sun examined the damo carefully. "You're not curious what I am?"

Hae Rim met her eye with a blank expression. "Your

secrets are your own, mistress. I have no right to demand you share them."

What a strange answer. She showed neither interest nor fear in the face of Chin Sun's otherness. Chin Sun had often wondered what it would be like if others found out she was gumiho, but she'd never imagined a reaction like this. Or rather, the lack of one.

Shouldn't Hae Rim be terrified right now, begging Chin Sun to spare her life? Or perhaps fleeing to alert the police bureau? She'd been prepared to threaten or bribe the girl into silence, but this . . . this was disconcerting.

It couldn't be that Hae Rim already knew what she was, right?

"Lady Lee," Hyun Soo whispered.

The women broke off from staring each other down and turned to the bodyguard, whose eyes opened wide with alarm. He glanced from Hae Rim to Chin Sun, then around the room.

"What happened?" He directed the question to Chin Sun. "The last thing I remember . . ." His cheeks filled with color.

"You passed out," she explained. "I called Hae Rim to help you."

Hyun Soo nodded, accepting her answer, but then his eyebrows stitched together. "How did I get here?"

"Pyung Ho carried you back," Chin Sun lied. "Are you feeling all right now?"

"A little dizzy, but it's bearable."

"Here, drink more of this then." She gave him some tea, blushing when her fingers grazed his stubble.

"It seems my presence is no longer needed," Hae Rim stated. She dipped her head and rose to her feet. "Make sure he finishes that tea, and send for me if you need anything else."

Chin Sun almost stopped her, but she didn't want to raise Hyun Soo's suspicions, so she gave the damo a glare that said, *Don't you dare betray me.*

Hae Rim smiled sweetly and swept out of the room, but as she passed, something snagged Chin Sun's attention. The ring on the damo's index finger. Or more specifically, the symbol engraved into it: a pearl surrounded by flames.

She'd thought it peculiar before, but now a heavy feeling settled in her gut. She'd seen that symbol recently.

On the goblin's sword.

Chin Sun chewed her lower lip. Could she have been mistaken?

No, the image of that symbol surrounded by the glow of blue fire was seared into her memory. There was no mistake. Hae Rim's ring matched the design on the goblin's blade.

But why? The symbol was too unusual to be a coincidence. Was Hae Rim connected to the goblins somehow?

"Lady Lee?"

She turned to Hyun Soo with a loving grin, hiding the fear clawing at her chest. "Yeh?"

Hyun Soo opened his mouth, then closed it again as if he was struggling with whether or not to ask something. Finally, he said, "Was it really Pyung Ho who brought me here?"

"Yeh, that's right. Who else could it have been?"

"I must have dreamed it, but I had the strangest thought that you were the one who carried me back."

Chin Sun forced herself to chuckle. "I may be strong, but that's way too far for me to carry you by myself."

"That's true. Anyway, I want to say thank you. You

saved me . . . again." He smiled at her with such open adoration she had to look away; otherwise, her heart might crumble under her guilt.

She was lying to protect him. If he knew she was gumiho, that would put him in even more danger. If the public ever found out her true identity and then learned he'd concealed it, he'd be executed alongside her.

Chin Sun pulled at the sleeve of her jeogori. "I guess you owe me again."

"Yeh, I suppose so. Well, since I now know jumping into danger *is* a habit of yours, I'm sure I'll be able to return the favor soon." Amusement danced in his voice, the pair returning to their normal rhythm of banter. It was easier that way, comfortable, especially in light of their weighty confessions earlier.

"Only once you're feeling better." She shook her finger at him, but his hand snaked out and grabbed hers.

"And then we can pick up where we left off."

"Where we . . . ?" Chin Sun pulled away and threw her hands over her blazing cheeks.

Hyun Soo raised a teasing eyebrow. "Figuring out our future, of course. What did you think I was talking about?"

"I . . ." Her tongue stuck to the roof of her mouth, unable to form words in the wake of her embarrassment.

He laughed at that, a great belly laugh, but the movement brought on a coughing fit. "You must stop looking so adorable, Lady Lee. Until I'm better, that is."

Chin Sun scowled through her blush, though inwardly she was squealing that he thought her adorable. "And you must stop calling me Lady Lee if your intentions are what you're implying."

Hyun Soo pursed his lips. "Then what should I call you?"

In a burst of courage, Chin Sun grabbed his hand and placed it against her jaw. "When we're alone, you can call me Chin Sun, and I shall call you Hyun Soo. Is that fair?"

"Chin Sun?" called a voice behind her.

She dropped Hyun Soo's hand and whirled around, all the blood leaving her face.

Uncle stood in the corridor, mouth open, paper clasped in his right hand. He looked from his niece to Hyun Soo and back, eyes rounder than the moon. "Chin Sun, what are you . . . ?"

Chapter 22

The Rift

Chin Sun snapped up like a string breaking from a geomungo. "Samchon, this—this—" She glanced down at Hyun Soo, who had gone stiffer than stone.

Uncle's expression hardened, shock overcome by outrage. His hands went slack, the parchment he'd been holding fluttering to the ground.

"You!" Samchon glowered at the bodyguard. "You seduced my niece?!"

"Uncle, no!" Chin Sun tried to block Samchon's view, but he ripped her away from her beloved. She crashed against a wooden pillar with a grunt, then pushed off, distraught at the disaster her carelessness had wrought. If Uncle wouldn't listen to her, what could she do?

Samchon wrenched Hyun Soo to his feet, breath coming out in a hiss. "I brought you under my roof because I believed you were a man of character, sworn to uphold virtue and truth, but you have proven yourself a servant of darkness, eager to swallow up the light of this house."

"Nauri, you're mistaken," Hyun Soo insisted. "My intentions toward your niece are entirely honorable."

"There is no honor in stealing what belongs to another."

"I assure you, I've stolen nothing. It was only after Lady Lee explained she'd decided not to marry Kang Dol Sam that I made my feelings known."

"A-a-after . . . Chin Sun!" Samchon's stuttering turned to a roar, his eyes locking on to his niece's with such ferocity that fear shot through her heart. He grabbed the letters he'd dropped and shoved them in her face.

She didn't need to read them. She knew exactly what they were. The messages she'd hastily scrawled a few hours ago, expressing her decision to end her engagement. One had been for Uncle and the other had been for Young Master Kang himself. Neither explained the reason behind her decision, only her sincere apology.

Uncle must have intercepted Kang Dol Sam's before it could get to him.

"Did Mr. Park pressure you to write these?" Samchon demanded. "Did he ask you to break off your betrothal?"

Chin Sun lowered her gaze. "He didn't ask me to. It was my idea."

Footsteps approached, followed by a startled gasp. "Father, what's going on?" Sang Mi asked. She looked from Uncle to Chin Sun to Hyun Soo, eyebrows knit in confusion.

The heat of Samchon's stare rippled over Chin Sun's shoulders. Without a word, he crumpled the letters in his fist and tossed them aside. Finally, he said, "You *will* marry Young Master Kang."

Defiance flooded Chin Sun's belly. She didn't meet Uncle's eye, but her voice rang clear as she replied, "I will not."

The back of Samchon's hand collided with her cheek. "Curse you and your infernal stubbornness, child. Don't you understand what will happen if you don't follow through with this marriage?"

Chin Sun covered her burning cheek and lifted her gaze. She said nothing, but the resolve in her eyes was answer enough: neither reprimand nor physical punishment would change her mind.

As that realization dawned on Uncle's face, his nostrils flared. "If you won't do it for the family's sake, then do it for his." He gestured to Hyun Soo. "Otherwise, I will see him flogged for this."

Chin Sun's breath whooshed out of her lungs. "You wouldn't. Samchon, with the state he's in, you'd be sending him to his death."

Defiling an innocent maiden was no minor offense. A penalty of one hundred lashes awaited any man foolish enough to get caught.

Conflict shimmered in Uncle's eyes, but he lifted his chin. "If that's what it takes to preserve this family, so be it."

"But, Uncle—"

"Choose."

Chin Sun didn't hesitate. She lowered her entire body to the floor and conceded, "I will do as you say. I'll marry Young Master Kang."

"Lady Lee, don't—"

"You don't get to speak," Samchon snarled at Hyun Soo. "My niece has made her decision. Now get out of here before my patience runs out."

Chin Sun peeked up and locked eyes with Hyun Soo, hoping he'd understand her silent message: *Don't worry about me. I'll be fine.*

His face crumpled, and he shook his head.

Uncle stepped in between them. "You better hurry up. If I hear you're still in Sokju come tomorrow . . ."

Hyun Soo stumbled down the corridor without glancing back, and Chin Sun couldn't help but wonder if this would be the last time she'd ever see him. With Samchon so opposed to them being together, what future could they have? As much as she wished otherwise, she wielded no power as an unmarried jungin woman. Samchon's word was law, and she had no choice but to abide by it.

She swallowed the lump in her throat. She wouldn't allow Uncle to see her cry.

"Sang Mi," Samchon said once Hyun Soo was gone, "escort Chin Sun to her chambers so she can reflect on her sins."

Sang Mi pulled Chin Sun to her feet and gave her a small, sympathetic smile. Chin Sun looked away and started toward her room.

As she passed her uncle, he grabbed her face and turned it toward his. His grip was gentle, but trembling. As if it was taking all his willpower not to squeeze until she screamed for mercy.

She would have preferred that to the heart-wrenching grief on his face. "Samchon?"

His eyes clouded over. "You were so headstrong as a child. Always insisting on doing things on your own. So angry anytime you saw something you deemed unfair." He let out a bitter laugh. "Your aunt thought I needed to temper you, that all that spirit would only lead to trouble. But I told her she didn't see what I saw. A peony among the weeds . . . destined for something wonderful." His eyes sparked with pride as they came back into focus, and he rubbed his thumb over her cheek.

But as quickly as it had appeared, the flame flickered out, leaving ash and regret. "Now I realize how blind I was; what I thought was a flower really was a weed all along."

He released her, a single tear sliding down his face.

Hurt swelled in Chin Sun's chest, and she stomped off to her room, slamming the hanji doors behind her.

"Unni?" came a soft, soothing voice.

Chin Sun didn't respond, instead staring at the flock of cranes on her folding screen. How could Samchon say that? She'd always put the family before herself. Always. Why did wanting something for herself make her lose all worth in his eyes?

Sang Mi's touch was warm on her shoulder, but she shrugged it off. "Get away from me."

"Unni, everything is going to—"

"*Don't* say it's going to work out, Sang Mi." Chin Sun bared her teeth. "You have no idea what I've lost today. How could you when all you do is waste your time at home, daydreaming about boys you hardly know?"

Her words were like arrows, striking her wide-eyed target with vicious precision. Did she mean them? Chin Sun wasn't sure, only that it felt good to say them after the onslaught she'd just received from her uncle.

"Let me tell you something," she continued. "Real life is not like your silly novels. It's messy and complicated and overwhelming, and everyone doesn't find happiness in the end."

"Chin Sun, I didn't—" Sang Mi tried to interject, but Chin Sun spoke over her.

"You're lucky Samchon loves you more than he does me, because you can get away with things I'll never be able to. So enjoy it while it lasts. Just know that as soon as your pretty smile isn't enough to hide your uselessness anymore, you'll find yourself married off to whomever Uncle sees fit. Then you'll have to grow up and stop waiting for others to take care of you because you'll be the one responsible for getting everything done."

Sang Mi flinched like she'd been struck, lips trembling with unspoken words. She took a shaky breath, but then a great sob burst out of her, and she dashed out of the room.

Chin Sun threw her hands over her face and screamed.

Hyun Soo tramped down the road toward the Kang residence, heart even heavier than his steps. How was he going to tell Dol Sam what had transpired? His friend would see this as a betrayal of the worst sort, no matter how Hyun Soo tried to defend himself.

But it wasn't like he could just omit the fact that Lord Lee had cast him out. Dol Sam had hired him to protect Lady Lee, and now he couldn't fulfill his duty. He'd failed, so utterly it was almost laughable, and now he would reap the consequences. Lord Lee's rage had been great, but it was probably nothing compared to what awaited him.

Still, he kept going. Dol Sam would be the one to decide whether their friendship could withstand the truth. Hyun Soo was almost panting by the time he reached the estate, his body not fully recovered from the strange ailment that struck him earlier. He banged his fist against the gate until a servant opened it and, with a surprised look, motioned for him to follow.

They arrived at Kang Dol Sam's room just as a nobleman in a wide-brimmed hat exited. He didn't stop to greet Hyun Soo, instead brushing past in what appeared to be a terrible hurry.

"My lord, you have a guest," the servant announced.

"Send him in," Dol Sam replied with an impatient huff. "I've already had several disappointments today, so what's one more?"

Hyun Soo stepped inside, gawked at the papers strewn all over the desk, then bowed.

Dol Sam was seated at his desk with his bamboo screen hanging from the ceiling, but as soon as he glanced at the threshold, he leaped to his feet. "Hyun Soo!" He rounded the screen and grabbed Hyun Soo's arm, gaze full of concern. "My friend, I've been meaning to find you."

Hyun Soo clasped his arm in return. "Hyung . . ." His eyes drifted back to the messy desk, mouth running dry. For all his courage on the battlefield, the thought of losing the only friend he had left had his gut clenching uncontrollably.

He opened his mouth to confess, but Kang Dol Sam spoke up first.

"I received a letter from a friend in the capital this morning. I'm so sorry about your father."

"My father? Did something happen to him?"

"Wait, you didn't—but then what were you . . ." Dol Sam's eyes widened. "You better sit down. You're whiter than a bowl of kongguksu." He guided Hyun Soo to the seat across from him at the desk, then called for some tea.

Hyun Soo sat with perfect stillness, dread pooling in his middle. "What's going on, Dol Sam?"

His friend grimaced. A servant appeared with refreshments, and Dol Sam gestured to the honey cookies. "Please help yourself, Hyun Soo."

Hyun Soo ignored the offer. "Hyung, stop stalling and just tell me."

His friend swallowed the tea in his mouth, then let out a resigned sigh. "He passed away three days ago."

Chapter 23

The Heir

The world went dead quiet, save for Hyun Soo's pulse thudding in his ears. Father—gone? That couldn't be right, couldn't be real. He'd been in excellent health when Hyun Soo had left him.

Hyun Soo's throat constricted, but he stammered, "Are —are you sure?"

Kang Dol Sam nodded gravely and shared what he'd learned from an associate in the capital. Minister Park Ha Kyun had taken ill with a cough, which worsened over the next several days despite the best efforts of the city's doctors. He'd passed into the next life three mornings ago.

Hyun Soo tried to focus on breathing, blinking, swallowing, anything to keep from crumbling as this new reality sank its claws into the future he'd been fighting for. Reconciliation with his father had always been a lofty goal, but it had still been within reach. Now . . .

"I saw him recently, actually," Dol Sam said, drawing Hyun Soo back into the conversation. "It's so hard to believe he's not here anymore. Did you know—"

"Wait, you saw him? Why?" he asked, clinging on to his

friend's words like they were the only thing keeping him from tumbling off a precipice.

Dol Sam steepled his fingers, expression thoughtful. "I had a proposition for him. About you. He seemed very open to it."

"What was it?" It came out demanding, but Hyun Soo didn't care. He needed something to hold on to, something to ease the weight bearing down on his chest.

Dol Sam flinched away from his intensity, but then his eyes flooded with understanding. "Hyun Soo, now isn't the time to discuss such matters. You need to return home."

"But—"

Dol Sam's hand came down on his arm in a consoling squeeze. "I'll let Lady Lee know what happened, don't worry. And I'll come to see you in Hanseong soon. I promise."

Hyun Soo bit the inside of his cheek but didn't press further. His friend cared too much about him to let him run away from his problems, even though that was what he desperately wanted to do.

And Dol Sam was right. He had to face this, whether he was ready to or not. He rose shakily to his feet and dipped his head in a brief motion. "In that case, I'll await your visit. Until then."

A letter arrived from Young Master Kang late in the evening, explaining that Park Hyun Soo had departed Sokju suddenly on account of his father's passing. When Chin Sun read the message, she didn't know whether to laugh or sob. It had given Hyun Soo the perfect excuse to leave the Lee residence without revealing that Uncle had already thrown him out. But the relief she felt at benefiting from such a tragedy made her thoroughly disgusted with herself.

How must Hyun Soo be feeling right now?

His moist eyes when he'd admitted he used to be a yangban were still so vivid, so heart-wrenching. She wished she knew the story behind his pain, but even without it, she was sure his father's passing couldn't be easy. Grief never was.

He'd said he didn't have much in the way of family. She wasn't the best when it came to offering comfort, but she hated the thought that he might be suffering alone. There had to be something she could do. . . .

An idea struck her like a hammer against iron, and she wasted no time in retrieving paper from the lacquered cabinet in her room. With a bamboo calligraphy brush in hand, she wrote out two missives, then called for Ah In to deliver them. The first went to the city blacksmith, while the second was a reply to Young Master Kang.

Once Chin Sun was alone again in the quiet of her room, she wrung her hands. Now all she could do was wait —and hope her fiancé wouldn't see through her.

According to Confucianism, Minister Park Ha Kyun's firstborn son should have become the sangju, or chief mourner, and handled all the affairs of the funeral. But a body could only wait for so long, and by the time Hyun Soo's horse arrived in Hanseong, his relatives had completed the funeral rites without him. His paternal uncle and cousins had taken care of all the arrangements, and when Hyun Soo finally strode onto the estate, exhausted and sore from riding harder than ever before, his uncle took him to Father's quarters to speak privately.

"Uncle," Hyun Soo stammered, "when I heard the news, I got here as fast as I—"

Samchon held up a hand, silencing Hyun Soo's excuses. The man's judgmental gaze was like an icy wind settling into his bones, and he ducked his head to avoid the full brunt of it. Uncle, along with the rest of his family, had supported Father's decision to cut Hyun Soo off and hadn't spoken a word to him since his privileged life as a yangban had disintegrated.

"It seems your father's integrity was compromised."

Hyun Soo's heart dropped, various scenarios flicking through his mind, each more unbelievable than the last. Father had always been the epitome of morality, a strict follower of Confucian values. Where could he have possibly fallen short?

"What do you mean?"

Uncle crossed the room to Father's lacquered cabinet and retrieved a document. He unfolded the paper, eyed it for a moment, then shook his head in disgust. "Rather than disowning you as he led everyone to believe, his final wishes were for you to inherit his estate."

Hyun Soo blinked. "What . . .?" A mixture of emotions swirled in his gut, incredulity being the primary one. "Let me see that," he demanded, closing the distance between them in two strides.

Samchon passed the document to him with a sneer, mumbling about how he didn't know how he could respect a brother whose word meant so little.

But Hyun Soo barely registered his uncle's grievance,

his gaze locked on the script written in Father's elegant hand. The message was short and direct, bequeathing the entirety of Father's property and possessions to Hyun Soo and indicating that if any dispute should arise, this document should be brought to the appropriate government office to be used as legal validation of Hyun Soo's claim.

Hyun Soo's hands shook, the weight of the implications pressing down on him. This had to have been written a long time ago, and Father simply hadn't remembered to update it to reflect their change in relationship.

But then he glanced at the date. A mere two months ago.

He collapsed onto one of the floor mats, unable to support himself in the wake of such a revelation. He let out a deep groan, tears cascading down his cheeks as the tangled emotions he'd been trying to suppress broke free.

Relief hit him first, for the paper proved he hadn't lost nearly as much as he'd believed. Even after everything, in the end, Father had still seen him as his son, his heir.

But quick on its heels came anger, bright and scalding. If Father's love hadn't dried up, why had he hidden it? Were pride and social standing truly so important that he couldn't have been honest, at least with him? Their separation could have ended, they could have parted on good terms, if Father had only allowed it.

Uncle left at some point while Hyun Soo tried—and failed—to sort through his confused feelings, but he didn't notice until he looked up hours later, after the sun had dipped low in the sky and his throat had long since gone raw. Shadows stretched across a room that was at once too small, the memories it held pressing too tightly.

Hyun Soo fled to his old quarters in the hopes of a reprieve, whereupon he found a tray of food and drink. He tried to get down some soup, knowing he needed the nourishment, but after the first swallow, he spat it all back up. He wiped his mouth on his sleeve and dragged himself to the already-prepared bed mat. He'd barely slept in the past two days, instead forcing his body and horse almost to their breaking point so he could get home sooner.

He closed his eyes and drifted off, not sure if he even wanted to wake back up.

Chapter 24

The Gift

Hyun Soo turned his mind to more practical matters. His momentary lapse of control was just that—momentary. Father's affairs still needed to be put in order, leaving no more time for useless things like grief. Hyun Soo threw himself into this purpose with such abandon that the servants had to remind him to eat, to drink, to rest; otherwise, he might wind up in an early grave, too.

But grief had a way of haunting Hyun Soo's steps no matter how diligently he distracted himself, clinging to him like the hemp mourning clothes he wore. Occasionally he'd find his cheeks wet with tears or feel a lump forming in his throat, but each time, he fought the sorrow back, fearing if he allowed himself to succumb again, he might never find his way back out. He wished he could chase the feelings away with alcohol, but doing so would violate Confucian dictates, and despite the anger he felt toward his father, he didn't want to shame the Park family further.

His dogged focus had been legendary when he was part of the palace guard. When he set his mind to something, nothing could shake him. He would win this fight, too. He had to.

Except . . . it wasn't just memories of his father that he was trying to push away. It was also memories of *her*. And she had a way of sliding past his defenses like no one else could.

He'd be eating a meal and suddenly wonder if she was eating well, too. Or sharpening his weapons and start wishing he could spar with her again. One time, he asked a servant her name and then realized he never used to care about such things.

But the worst time was in that breath between sleeping and waking, when dreams hover at the edges of memory, whispering wishes that could never be reality. The best mental shield in the world couldn't help him there. Each morning, he woke with a sharp pain in his chest, as if his heart had been pierced during the night.

He chuckled bitterly anytime he thought about it, for how could his heart be pierced when he'd left it behind in Sokju?

One afternoon, Hyun Soo was in his quarters, reading through a list of some of his father's assets, when a knock sounded at the door. He frowned. It wasn't the time the servants normally brought him a meal.

A wide-brimmed black hat entered the room, followed by elegant eyebrows pinched together in concern. The visitor clucked his tongue. "Hyun Soo-yah, what's become of you?"

Hyun Soo's gaze cleared, alertness flooding his limbs. "Dol Sam?"

His friend smiled softly, though a touch of sadness remained in his eyes. "I told you I was coming, didn't I?" He glanced around the disheveled surroundings and wrinkled his nose. "And by the state of this room, not a moment too soon. Why don't we talk outside? You look like you could use some fresh air."

Hyun Soo rose to his feet, hope and strength returning to him. Dol Sam had drawn him out of his melancholy before; surely he could do it again.

As the pair circled the courtyard, they exchanged a few words about the events of the past week. Dol Sam was courteous and thoughtful, allowing Hyun Soo to lead the discussion instead of pushing him to share more than he was comfortable with. Hyun Soo wasn't a very forthcoming person, but it felt good to get a few things off his chest, namely the cold reception he'd received from his relatives and his bewilderment over his unexpected inheritance.

Dol Sam offered his sympathies and encouragement, but his eyes widened as they passed the estate's stable. "Oh! I almost forgot."

He hastened inside and returned a few moments later with a large item wrapped in cloth. A sword of some kind. He held it out expectantly. "When Lady Lee heard about Minister Park, she felt so bad she had this made to express her condolences."

Hyun Soo stumbled, pain flaring in his chest as a pair of honey-brown eyes skittered across his thoughts.

"Are you all right?"

He waved away his friend's concern and took the proffered gift. "Yeh, nothing to worry about." He forced himself to smile, relieved when the pain subsided to a dull ache.

"Well?" Dol Sam prompted.

Hyun Soo waited for a beat, not understanding the man's meaning.

Dol Sam dipped his chin at the sword. "Aren't you going to look at it?"

Hyun Soo reluctantly peered down and removed the cloth, revealing a beautiful hwando. Of similar make to his own, but the craftsmanship was more ornate than anything he had ever seen. Lightweight with a hand guard of blackened brass and a blade of the finest steel. There was no doubt such a weapon would cut down anyone foolish enough to oppose its wielder.

"This sword looks like it's taken quite a beating in your care. You should get it replaced."

Hyun Soo swallowed a lump in his throat. She'd said that to him the day they'd sparred in the clearing, the day he'd very nearly kissed her.

"She had this made for me?" His voice trembled with more emotion than he intended.

"Yeh, she's so generous, isn't she? I continue to fall more in love with her the longer I know her," Dol Sam said dreamily. "I'm actually planning to see her as soon as I return so I can give her—"

"I'm very interested in hearing more about your conversation with my father," Hyun Soo interrupted, hanging the sword at his hip. It was rude to cut his friend off, but his heart couldn't handle any more torture right now.

Besides, he was genuinely curious to hear about Dol Sam's proposition. If it was something within his power, he wanted to do it. For his father's sake.

His friend stiffened momentarily. Then he nodded and said, "Of course. But let's head back inside. What I'm about to tell you is for your ears only."

Once the two were seated in the sangbang and had refreshments, Dol Sam began, his expression grave. "I'm sure you've noticed the unrest in Sokju. There's always been some, but in the last year and a half, the sangmin and cheonmin have become more rebellious than ever. I fear we may be on the brink of an uprising."

Hyun Soo took in this information with a somber nod. So, his friend wanted help preventing a revolt. Familiarity settled over his shoulders. Assessing and removing threats was his specialty. "Why do you think things have become worse lately?"

"It's all that vigilante's fault," Dol Sam snarled.

At the mention of Gwishin, Hyun Soo schooled his expression into one of detached concern despite the way his pulse roared in his ears. "Is that why you've been so determined to capture him?"

When Dol Sam's eyebrows rose, he coughed and added, "Besides your desire to protect Lady Lee, of course."

Dol Sam rolled his lips, frustration etched into his features. "Gwishin has thwarted my attempts to better this city, stirring up the commoners with dreams of grandeur. Before he was here, they knew their proper place. Now they're questioning the systems this city depends upon. More and more are refusing to pay their taxes—the taxes we yangban use to serve them—which has forced the police to crack down harder on lawbreakers. There's even been talk of a rebel camp in the mountains, but so far, no one can prove it's more than a rumor. It all puts me in a difficult position. I want to be understanding and merciful—these people have children to take care of. But how can I let it go when my fellow nobles are so angry they're about to start forcing sangmin into slavery until they can pay off their debts?"

"So, what solution have you come up with?"

Dol Sam's face brightened. "Magistrate Hong and I have been working closely for the past several months to gather enough firepower to silence this resistance once and for all."

"Firepower? You mean, you intend to put rifles in the hands of the police?"

Dol Sam shook his head, a smug twinkle in his eye. "Not the police, though Hong doesn't know that yet." He pulled a document out of his sleeve and handed it to Hyun Soo. Correspondence between himself and a commander by the name of Song Seo Jun.

"I've been amassing an army, and according to this, it's ready to move on my command."

Hyun Soo nearly dropped the paper, nausea building in his stomach. "What? Dol Sam, you know keeping private armies was outlawed years ago. If anyone were to find out—"

"Who's going to stop me?" The nobleman chuckled dryly. "The magistrate? He's the one who helped make it possible. If I go down, he'll go down with me."

Hyun Soo didn't answer, trying to process what he was hearing. Dol Sam had always advocated for following the law, not taking it into his own hands.

His friend cocked his head to the side, curiosity flickering in his eyes. "This is something your father approved of."

Hyun Soo stared at him in disbelief. "My father supported your army taking over Sokju?"

"Yeh, he did, my friend"—Dol Sam drew the words out, slow and deliberate—"especially when I told him you would be the one to lead it."

Hyun Soo gulped down some more soju, disappointed when he realized he'd completely drained his bottle. "Jumo!" he called to the tavern owner.

An older woman bustled over, but at the sight of his raised drinking bowl, she snapped, "Not until you pay for it."

Hyun Soo reached into his sleeve and withdrew a small bag of rice. He handed it to the woman, who shook her head.

"This will only cover what you've already had." She held out an open hand.

Hyun Soo sucked his teeth, alcohol fanning his annoyance into a flame. "What do you mean, it's not enough? That's robbery, woman."

The ajumma put her hands on her wide hips. "What choice do I have when ingredients cost so much? If you don't like it, you can go complain to someone else, you ungrateful boy."

"Boy?" Hyun Soo blinked until his double vision subsided. "I'll have you know . . . I'm the son of the Minister of National Defense."

The tavern owner snorted. "And I'm the king's favorite concubine. Now, get out of here so someone else can have your spot."

Hyun Soo sullenly rose to his feet, faltered a few times, then made his way to the street, not caring which way he went. Twilight was falling over Sokju, painting the city an ever-deepening blue. How long had he been in there?

Dol Sam's proposition still had his head reeling, or maybe that was the soju—he wasn't sure anymore. Had he given his friend an answer?

Hyun Soo pressed the heel of his hand into his forehead, forcing up the memory.

"That's quite the undertaking. May I have some time to think it over?"

Dol Sam's mouth twisted with disapproval. "What's there to think about? Go to the base and look over the recruits. If you're satisfied with them, return to Sokju and we can make a plan of assault. You always were such a brilliant strategist, thoroughly wasted in your position as a guard. Now's your chance to show the world who you really are."

Hyun Soo swallowed. "I still have a few things to finish up here. . . ."

Dol Sam looked skeptical, but he asked, "How long do you need?"

"Just a week, hyung. Then I'll go to the base and make my assessment."

"Agreed, but not a day more. Sokju can't afford to wait much longer."

Hyun Soo grimaced. All he'd done was buy himself some time, and for what? To dishonor his father by drinking himself to oblivion rather than solving his predicament? Even now, he was tempted to wander into the next tavern he found, just like he had when his father had thrown him out.

Except this time, he wouldn't have Dol Sam to drag him out of his despair. Not when his friend was the reason for it.

Hyun Soo kept walking, his heart more torn than ever. How was he to know what to do without any direction? He'd always had someone to lead him down the right path. First, he'd looked to his father, a great mountain of wisdom and strength. When that relationship had crumbled, he'd turned to his friend, clinging on like his life depended on it.

Now he had no one. He was a ship at sea with neither map nor compass, watching brewing storm clouds with no idea how to proceed. Should he face the tempest head-on? Should he avoid it at all costs?

And then there was the matter of his father supposedly approving of the scheme. Had his friend lied about that? Or had Father actually believed oppression was justified if it meant maintaining order?

Hyun Soo had seen enough to know the lowborn of Sokju struggled under a heavy yoke. It was no wonder some were resisting. But to add guns into the mix . . . How many would die needlessly before Dol Sam felt like the people were properly subdued?

Then there was the worst question of all: what guarantee was there that Dol Sam would return that power to the police once he'd succeeded in his plan? Dol Sam had always been ambitious; Hyun Soo wanted to believe his friend wasn't in this for his own gain, but lately it was difficult to tell. Like Gwishin, perhaps Dol Sam wasn't the person Hyun Soo had thought he was.

"Sir?" called a male voice.

Hyun Soo spun toward it, throwing his arms out to steady himself when the world began to tilt.

A large man in worn-out hanbok stood at his side, hand outstretched as if to catch Hyun Soo should he slip.

Hyun Soo squinted, but the man was completely unfamiliar. "Who . . . ?"

The stranger bowed and extended his arm, a sword clasped in his hand. "You left this in the tavern."

Hyun Soo peered at the weapon. Ah. Right. He thanked the man for returning it and started walking again, the blade heavier than he remembered. He unsheathed it, wondering if it would be better to just sell the sword and be done with it. How could he forget about Chin Sun with this serving as a constant reminder?

Sunlight reflected off the steel, blinding him for a moment. What was that engraved on the blade?

Hyun Soo moved it closer. A ginkgo tree. The symbol of resilience and strength in the face of adversity. How had he not noticed this before? Hyun Soo traced the image, then flipped the hwando over. On the back was an inscription that read, "Brave enough to stand alone."

Hyun Soo's mouth fell open, the past filling his mind's eye.

"I know what it's like to feel alone, to feel lost. It's a pain that can eat you up if you let it. The fact that you haven't says a lot about the kind of man you are."

Curiosity stirred in Hyun Soo's belly, taking hold of his tongue before he could stop it. "And what kind is that?"

"A brave one. One I'd be honored to call a friend."

Hyun Soo's grip tightened, a spark of clarity chasing away the haze of alcohol. What was he doing, ambling about like a fool when people were in danger? He didn't need someone to tell him what was right; he just needed the courage to do it.

Even though it meant turning on his dearest friend.

Hyun Soo whirled around and marched back toward the Park estate with determined steps. If he was going to succeed, he needed to be prepared. Chin Sun already believed in him. It was time to prove her faith hadn't been misplaced.

Chapter 25

The Declaration

Once Chin Sun had sent out her letters, she tried to resume the old routines she'd lived by prior to Hyun Soo's intrusion: taking care of the household and preparing for her wedding by day, and guarding Sokju's downtrodden citizens by night.

But to her surprise, those rhythms, once energizing and fulfilling, now evoked a strange sense of futility. How could she protect others when she wasn't strong enough to protect her own heart?

Anytime that feeling arose in her mind, she quickly silenced it, reminding herself that she was strong. Not only was she gumiho but she was also about to marry Kang Dol Sam, the most powerful nobleman in the province. That would give her more influence than any other woman in Sokju. That should be enough for her. It had to be.

And yet, the more time passed, the less she believed it. Bitterness and cynicism took root in her heart, making her increasingly difficult to be around. Uncle, for his part, stopped punishing her with his absence after a few days, but whenever he tried to engage with her, her responses were so terse he would soon give up and turn his attention elsewhere. Sang Ook was met with similar results, and more often than not, he left her quarters with tears in his eyes. Sang Mi didn't even bother trying, and whenever Chin Sun approached her with household duties, Sang Mi would stiffen and make an excuse that kept them from spending any time alone together. The servants also began giving Chin Sun a wide berth, knowing she was liable to shout at them if they made even the tiniest mistake.

Her relationship with Kim Min Joon was slightly less volatile, for she was able to release some of her pent-up anger through sparring, though he also took care in the topics he chose to discuss. Hyun Soo was completely off-limits, as was any talk of Chin Sun's wedding plans. The goblin threat was a point of contention as well, for there had been no sign of the goblin ahjussi who'd been so bent on stealing her bead since the night of the fire. Min Joon did give her regular updates on the damo Hae Rim, but so far, her only unusual activity was taking leave to visit her ailing sister.

When the Chuseok holiday finally arrived, Na Ri prepared a grand feast that filled everyone's belly nearly to bursting, but what should have been a cheerful occasion was shrouded in crackling tension. Uncle tried to lighten the mood by asking Chin Sun to play the danso, but she blew into the instrument so forcefully that everyone covered their ears and begged her to stop. She set the danso down with an apology that sounded sincere enough, but Samchon's sharp hiss made it clear he suspected she'd done it on purpose.

Which was indeed true, for how could she be expected to celebrate when there was nothing to be thankful for?

One evening, Chin Sun received word that Kang Dol

Sam wished to present a betrothal gift to her at the bridge, so she asked Uncle for permission to meet him. He agreed with great eagerness, with one condition: Sang Mi had to come along as a chaperone.

The bridge was a popular rendezvous location for young couples because of a group of zelkova trees by the river's shore. Their saw-shaped leaves turned a burning orange in the fall, and it was said that anyone who declared their love under the trees' branches was destined to have a happy marriage. Chin Sun didn't believe in such things, but perhaps Young Master Kang was more superstitious than she was.

Normally, Sang Mi would have been giggling at Chin Sun's side about how romantic this all was, but today she lagged behind with vacant eyes and shuffling steps. Her skin seemed paler than usual, and Chin Sun almost asked if she'd been eating enough, but she stopped herself at the last second.

She and Sang Mi didn't have that sort of relationship anymore. She doubted Sang Mi would even give her an honest answer if she asked. Not that Chin Sun blamed her after all the horrible things she'd said.

An apology rose in Chin Sun's throat, but she swallowed it down. The brokenness between them had been inevitable, and she needed to accept that. Trying to repair it would be like trying to repair shattered glass: useless and likely to cause even more damage.

When the pair arrived at the bridge, Young Master Kang stood directly under one of the zelkova trees, its lush leaves sheltering him in their shade. He kept one arm behind his back, concealing a large item beneath a cloth. His handsome appearance was like something out of a fairytale, his deep sapphire blue robes with silver embroidery reminiscent of those worn by the crown prince himself. Coupled with the fierceness of his gaze and the hard set to his jaw, it was obvious how important this moment was to him.

But as Chin Sun moved toward her betrothed, the man she envisioned was none other than her former bodyguard, his dark eyes teasing.

Chin Sun started, one hand sliding over her mouth as she fought to hold back a gasp. The vision lasted only a second, but in its echo, a deep ache spread through her chest. Kang Dol Sam was thoughtful and generous, but he was no Park Hyun Soo.

She lowered her hand and pulled back her shoulders, determined to follow through with this. She had to marry Kang Dol Sam if she was going to regain any semblance of control in her life. Her heart would get over it. She resumed her approach, stopping directly in front of Young Master Kang with a small grin.

She bowed. "Good morning, nauri. I was told you wanted to see me."

He bowed in return, first to her, then to Sang Mi, who stood a few paces back, giving them enough privacy not to be overheard. His countenance softened as he turned to Chin Sun. "Indeed, Lady Lee, though 'wanted' doesn't feel like a strong enough word."

He ducked his head, cheeks going pink, then raised it again, pressing his lips together. "I know this union is something our families arranged, but I believe it's only right for you to know *I* was the one who brought it up to my father."

Chin Sun's brow furrowed. "You did? But . . . why? I don't understand."

Hurt flashed across his face before he masked it behind a weak smile. "Perhaps this will give you the answer. . . ."

He withdrew the item behind his back and slid the cloth off, revealing a beautiful portrait of a noblewoman encircled by flowers. Her.

Chin Sun froze, taking in each intricate detail. From the lovely mugunghwa blossoms and spider lilies, whose delicate petals looked so realistic she nearly reached out to touch them, to the soft curve of her lips, to the folds of the silk chima, everything about the painting was absolutely exquisite. Masterful.

Yet she took no pleasure in it.

For every brushstroke told the same story, one that should have been a warm embrace but instead slammed against her like a cold slap. It was as she'd feared: Kang Dol Sam was in love with her.

Chin Sun peeked up at him, saw the expectant look in his eyes, and turned away. Before she knew what she was doing, she'd stepped over to her cousin and grabbed her hands.

"Sang Mi-yah," she said helplessly, voice cracking, "what do I do? I don't want him." She trembled under the weight of her confession, of her weakness. She couldn't bear to meet her cousin's gaze, afraid of the rejection she'd find staring back at her. She'd been so cruel; how could she ask for support now?

But Sang Mi squeezed her hands, drawing Chin Sun's eyes to hers. And in those inky black depths, there was no judgment, no resentment, only a question.

"Are you asking me what I think you should do?" Sang Mi's voice shook, not with fear but with hope.

Chin Sun gripped her cousin's hands tighter, longing coursing through her veins. Had she not lost Sang Mi, after all?

"Yeh, I am."

Sang Mi smiled, and in that heartbeat, all was restored, their souls knitting together as though they'd never been apart. Chin Sun felt it in the deepest part of her being, the tears welling up in her eyes identical to the ones in Sang Mi's own. This was her cousin, her sister, and she'd been stupid to think her anger was strong enough to sever the bond they shared.

"I'm sorry, Sang Mi-yah. I'm so sorry," she whimpered.

Sang Mi stroked her cheek. "I know, Unni." She withdrew her hand and let out a relieved laugh. "Now, let's get back to what you were asking before."

Chin Sun's stomach sank as she shot a glance at Kang Dol Sam, who was watching them with a patient, puzzled frown. "Yeh. I . . . I don't know if I can go through with this."

Sang Mi leaned forward and whispered in her ear, "Then don't."

Chin Sun stepped back, heart screeching in alarm. "But, Samchon—"

Sang Mi gently shook her head, mouth tugging up into a sad half-smile. "It's time you were true to yourself, Unni. Even if Father never understands it, even if no one understands it, I will stand by that—and by you—until the world ends."

Chin Sun sniffed, tears brimming over, and wrapped her in a tight hug. "Thank you," she whispered against her cousin's hair. This was the truth she'd needed, the one her heart had been yearning for all this time, but she'd never allowed herself to believe. Being true to herself had always seemed like a luxury she couldn't afford, but now she knew better.

She couldn't gain control of her own life by hiding herself; for that, she'd have to be honest.

And when she pulled back, a new strength rose within her, one that defied anyone who would tell her differently.

Chin Sun waltzed over to Kang Dol Sam, and her voice rang steady and pure as she declared, "Young Master Kang, I cannot marry you."

Chapter 26

The Spy

Kang Dol Sam stared at her slack-jawed, as if he couldn't comprehend the words that had just come out of her mouth. "What?" he finally stammered.

Chin Sun's heart swelled with sympathy—and no small amount of guilt. He'd been nothing but good to her. She hoped he'd find someone else who could love him better. "I'm sorry, it's just that I'm—"

Footsteps interrupted her confession, and the two turned as a middle-aged servant hurried up to them.

The man bowed, body quivering all over. "Master, I need to speak with you."

"Couldn't you have waited until I returned?" Dol Sam barked, his voice harsher than Chin Sun had ever heard it.

The servant kept his gaze on the ground. "My apologies, Master, but you'll want to see this."

Young Master Kang huffed, but he motioned for the servant to come closer. He snatched the missive from the frightened servant's grip. His expression darkened as he read the message, the muscles in his jaw straining.

Finally, his head snapped to Chin Sun, and she resisted the urge to flinch at the maelstrom swirling in his gaze. She'd never seen him so enraged.

"We'll discuss this more later," he stated, his sharp tone leaving no room for argument. Without waiting for a reply, he dipped his head and strode off, his servant scuttling after him.

Sang Mi strutted over to her cousin and gathered her in a warm embrace. "I'm so proud of you, Unni. What did Young Master Kang say?"

Chin Sun pulled back and shook her head. "He didn't really get a chance to answer before his servant interrupted him."

Sang Mi's forehead bunched together. "I wonder what could have been so urgent that he'd leave in the middle of such an important conversation."

Chin Sun glanced up the road at Young Master Kang's retreating form, his blue robes billowing behind him like rain clouds. She bit her bottom lip, an unmistakable dread pulling at her core. "So do I."

Sang Mi looped her arm with Chin Sun's. "Well, let's go home and see if we can come up with a good excuse for you to visit the capital."

Chin Sun's cheeks swam with heat. "What are you imply—"

Her cousin silenced her with a perfectly arched eyebrow.

Chin Sun swallowed, then gave her a sheepish smile. "Yeh, that sounds good."

The pair made their way back to the Lee manor, but upon reaching Chin Sun's quarters, they stopped short.

Someone in a blue uniform was waiting inside.

"K-Kim Min Joon?" Chin Sun managed.

The police inspector rose to his feet and gave a quick bow, then addressed Chin Sun. "I apologize for the intrusion, Lady Lee, but I need to speak with you *alone*."

Sang Mi gasped, hands fluttering at her sides. "Chin Sun, did something happen?"

Chin Sun shook her head, flabbergasted. Min Joon hadn't come to her home before, not since he'd returned from Ming, at least. She peered at her friend, noting the anxiety etched into his face. "Sang Mi, leave us please."

Her cousin didn't answer, so Chin Sun spun around and gave her a sharp nod. Sang Mi looked torn, but after glancing at Kim Min Joon one more time, she excused herself and sashayed down the corridor.

Once she was certain they wouldn't be overheard, Chin Sun turned to her friend. "What's going on?"

Min Joon relaxed his stance, but his mouth remained tight. "I just received word of an army stationed a few days' walk north of here."

Chin Sun's eyes bulged. "An army? For what purpose?"

"Supposedly it's to restore order to Sokju because the police haven't been doing their jobs properly."

Chin Sun didn't answer at first, simply gestured for him to sit back down while she took the seat across from him behind her low-legged table.

Once they were both situated, she placed her hands on the table and leaned forward. "Tell me everything."

Min Joon's tone was grave as he explained what he'd learned this morning from an informant. Apparently, the yangban had lost the last of their faith in the police and Magistrate Hong after the fire in the merchant neighborhood last week. Everyone knew Gwishin had been there, and the common sentiment among the yangban was that the vigilante was behind the destruction.

But that wasn't the only reason the nobles were angry. The magistrate's methods of suppressing resistance hadn't just failed—they'd made things worse. The commoners were more rebellious than ever, and there was even a rumor circulating that some of them had fled to start a colony in the mountains.

This was nothing new to Chin Sun; she'd heard that same rumor, though she didn't know how much truth there was to it. And she'd witnessed firsthand the sangmin's growing anger toward the governing authorities. This year, there had been more attacks on patrolmen, as well as accounts of peasants refusing to pay their taxes, than ever before.

But she hadn't realized it was bad enough to warrant usurping the magistrate.

"And that's not the worst part," Min Joon continued, dragging his hand down his face. "My informant tells me Kang Dol Sam is the one who commissioned the army."

Chin Sun went cold. "What? Why would he—are you sure it wasn't his father, Lord Kang Ki Yong? That sounds like something he would do. He's been trying to take control of Sokju for years now." Desperation colored her tone, but she couldn't help it. She may not love Kang Dol Sam, but she knew him well enough to believe he wasn't capable of something like that. It had to be his father. "All those police bribes and the extortion—you know we've nearly caught him a dozen times. If only his influence didn't go so far, he'd have been executed already."

Min Joon shook his head sadly. "I have spies watching the Kang estate, and there hasn't been anything to suggest Lord Kang is involved in something like this. His son, on the other hand . . . He's left the city many times over the past several months, and no one seems to know where he's been going. I have a strong suspicion Kang Dol Sam has been using his father as a smokescreen, and the villain we've been fighting all this time has been your future husband."

"He's not my future husband," Chin Sun snapped. "I broke the betrothal off today."

Her friend's eyes widened, then a slight smile formed on his face. "Oh, well, good. I'm glad to hear it." He rubbed the back of his neck sheepishly.

Chin Sun put her elbows on the table and folded her hands together, thinking back through the many run-ins she'd had with Lord Kang's men. She didn't want to believe Min Joon was right, but she had to admit it was possible. How well did she really know Young Master Kang?

Kim Min Joon watched her intently, a question burning in his eyes. He opened his mouth, then seemed to change his mind and shut it again.

"Is there more I should know?"

He dropped his head and fidgeted with the string of beads on his hat. "Yeh. Even though the army is ready, Kang Dol Sam hasn't yet finalized how and when to have it march on Sokju. This works in our favor because my source has also written to the governor to inform him of the situation. If luck is on our side, the governor's forces will reach the army before Kang Dol Sam has a chance to mobilize it."

A wave of relief came over Chin Sun, but something about the way her friend continued playing with his beads felt . . . off. Why was he nervous if everything was taken care of? And why had he felt the need to tell her about this? Normally, he only shared information when he needed her help. Was it just because of Kang Dol Sam's involvement?

Somehow, that didn't seem like the right answer.

"Min Joon-ah," she said gently, "are you hiding something from me?"

He grimaced, then reluctantly met her eye. "My informant is planning to observe the army for now, though he also stated he'll be looking for opportunities to infiltrate the base and sabotage its operations."

Chin Sun frowned. Why would that be something he didn't want to tell her? If the spy could get inside the base undetected and steal weapons or burn supplies, that would lessen the risk of an attack on Sokju. The only downside was that the spy might get caught.

And it wasn't like she knew the spy personally. . . .

"What's your informant's name?"

Min Joon blanched, then closed his eyes with a deep sigh. When he opened them again, he said softly, "That's why I came to tell you. The letter I received this morning was from Park Hyun Soo."

Chin Sun's heart dropped to the floor. "But that would mean he's spying on his friend's . . ."

Min Joon nodded. "I was shocked when I read the letter, too. I wouldn't have expected him to turn Kang Dol Sam in like this."

Tears pricked at Chin Sun's eyelids. She sat quietly for a moment, then whispered, "But he would if it was the right thing to do."

Min Joon didn't argue with her, simply took in her words with a somber look. She'd known Hyun Soo was a good man, but to choose justice over loyalty to his friend . . .

Her fingers dug into the fabric of her chima, anchoring her in the wake of emotions flooding over her soul. Heartache for what Hyun Soo must be feeling, anger for Kang Dol Sam putting him in such a position, shame for not recognizing her betrothed's true character sooner . . .

But the strongest emotion that came, the one that overwhelmed her senses, was the love burning in her chest. A love that went beyond fear, and distance, and even self-preservation.

Her head swiveled to Kim Min Joon. "Did his letter tell you exactly where to find the base?"

"Yeh, I've got it right here."

As soon as he pulled the paper out of his sleeve, Chin Sun swiped it from his hand. She scanned the letter, homing in on the part where it stated the base's location.

"What are you planning to do?" Min Joon asked, voice full of suspicion.

A ghost of a smile passed over Chin Sun's face as she stood. "Do you even need to ask?"

Min Joon jumped up, head shaking. "Chin Sun, this is a military base with trained soldiers. If they spot you, you might not make it out of there."

"That applies to Park Hyun Soo, too," she pointed out.

"But—"

"If you'd had a chance to save your betrothed's life, would you have taken it?"

Min Joon looked away, crestfallen, but when she tried to walk past, he blocked her exit.

She scowled. "Get out of my way, Min Joon."

Her friend gave her a wry smile, his dark eyes twinkling as they often did when he'd done something he knew got on her nerves.

Before she lost her temper though, he said, "You may be a gumiho, but that doesn't mean I'm letting you go alone."

Chapter 27

The Mission

"**O**ver here, men! I think I saw something near those trees," shouted a sentry.

Heavy footsteps crashed through the undergrowth toward Hyun Soo, but he remained crouched in the tall pine tree he'd retreated to, silently observing as a line of troops in light armor stomped below, torches held aloft. What the guard had seen was actually a moon bear, but Hyun Soo wasn't about to correct him. After about thirty seconds, the sounds of the soldiers faded, leaving him alone.

For the time being.

After following the map Dol Sam had provided, Hyun Soo had found something much worse than the simple encampment he'd envisioned. The mist-covered mountains above Sokju weren't sheltering a small band of soldiers; they concealed a fortress.

The enclosure itself was massive, with high stone walls and watchtowers at both ends. The main gate had guard platforms on either side, where sentinels monitored the surrounding area like hawks in their perches, and troops also patrolled the perimeter every hour. Hyun Soo couldn't be certain how many men were stationed within, but from the rumble of voices each morning during drills, he guessed at least sixty. Enough to be a solid challenge for the police—even without considering the distinct advantage of rifles over bows and spears. If these men marched against the city of Sokju, there was no question who would be victorious.

Was this what Sokju's taxes had been paying for? A fort like this must have taken years to construct. How had Dol Sam gotten enough manpower and kept it secret all this time?

Hyun Soo had done his best to gather intel since arriving, but progress had been painfully slow. All he'd managed to do so far was listen in on some interesting conversations between the guards. From the sounds of it, Commander Song was not an easy man to get along with. Brash, controlling, and strangely temperamental, the commander would compliment the men on their drill performance in the morning, but then he would fly into a rage that same afternoon, claiming the troops were nowhere near ready for battle.

He was also apparently growing impatient as he awaited Kang Dol Sam's "expert strategist," and the general consensus among the guards was that if Hyun Soo didn't arrive soon, Commander Song was going to march on Sokju without him.

When Hyun Soo wasn't scoping out the base, he was in the woods, foraging roots and berries or resting on a thick tree limb for short spans of time. A mountain stream supplied him with plenty of fresh water, which he'd been overjoyed to find the day after his canteen had run dry. Birds, deer, and gorals roamed freely through the forest, and he'd even spotted a lynx the third day he'd been here. So far, the wildlife hadn't bothered him much, but he was always careful not to startle them in case the commotion drew unwanted attention. He needed to stay alive if he was going to help when the authorities arrived.

But what if the governor didn't send anyone? That was a very real possibility, and with each new sunrise, Hyun Soo's fears grew stronger. He'd hoped Governor Choi was a man of honor, ready to do what was needed in the face of injustice. But the entire province held the Kang family in high esteem, and even the most compelling evidence in the world might not be enough to embolden a governor known more for his diplomacy than his fairness.

Good thing Hyun Soo had a backup plan.

He'd been ruminating on it for days, uncertain if it was even a viable option at such a well-guarded garrison. He preferred to consider all scenarios before acting, making sure he eliminated as many risks as possible.

But the governor had to have received his message by now—and the guards in the woods weren't going to chase that moon bear forever.

Hyun Soo pulled his mask over his nose, then clambered down the pine tree like a marten. With the ground-level guards out of the way, the only eyes he'd have to watch out for were those on the western wall. And with the overcast night sky obscuring everything, he couldn't have asked for a more opportune time to sneak inside.

He slunk toward the fortress, gaze darting about in case more soldiers appeared. During his surveillance, he'd discovered a high ridge protruding from the face of the mountain. It was close enough to the fortress that if he could just climb to the top, he could drop onto the western walkway. Then he could make his way to the armory and destroy their firearms.

When he reached the treeline, he paused, checking for the guard he knew would be patrolling the parapet. But to his shock, the wall was completely empty—was it time for guard rotations?

Hyun Soo barreled toward the ridge and began his ascent, no seconds to waste during the brief interim between sentry shifts. The torturous climb up the ridge was concealed from view, but he kept a brisk pace, not knowing when the soldiers guarding the perimeter would return from the forest and spot him. More than once his foot slipped and he nearly tumbled down. But he managed to grab a foothold each time, and despite his aching muscles, he wasn't about to give up.

Finally, he heaved his body onto the semi-flat surface of the ridge, ducked behind a boulder, and allowed himself a few minutes to catch his breath. Once he'd stopped panting, he peeked around the rock, noting the sentry approaching from the opposite end of the parapet.

Hyun Soo pulled a knife out of his clothes and landed on the unsuspecting guard's head. The man went down with a dull thud, and before he could cry out, Hyun Soo plunged his knife into the man's kidney, silencing him once and for all.

Hyun Soo retrieved the blade from his victim and shuffled past a hwacha—a fire cart he'd heard about but never seen in the flesh—to the inner side of the wall. His heart quivered at the sight of the barracks, which housed an even bigger force than he'd thought. He wouldn't be surprised if there were at least a hundred men stationed here.

At that moment, two truths became abundantly clear. The first was that destroying the army's firepower wouldn't be enough to save the people of Sokju. The second was that it would take a miracle to leave this place alive.

Hyun Soo stepped back from the edge, a strange hollow feeling settling into his chest. When he'd become a soldier, he'd known the risks and accepted them without hesitation. To die in the service of one's country was a great honor, a sacrifice he was proud to give.

But now . . . all he could think about was the woman he was leaving behind.

Would Chin Sun mourn his passing, or had she already smothered her feelings as she prepared to marry Dol Sam? What would happen to her when the truth of Dol Sam's crimes came to light? Would she be dragged down with him?

Hyun Soo shook his head. Now wasn't the time for woolgathering. He had a mission to carry out. And if it meant forfeiting his life, he would take as many soldiers with him as he could.

Hyun Soo swung back to the hwacha. With several rows of iron-fletched arrows propelled by gunpowder, a weapon like this could obliterate one's enemy from a distance. It was overkill to have one here, where there was little chance of an enemy attack, but perhaps the army intended to take it to Sokju as added intimidation or . . .

Hyun Soo swallowed as a dark thought filled his mind. Could Dol Sam's plans extend beyond taking control of Sokju? With a force this large, he could do much more than subdue a single city.

All the more reason for Hyun Soo to try to incapacitate the base while he had the chance. He bent down and grabbed the dead sentry's torch, then wheeled the fire cart around. Now it wasn't aimed outward to defend against approaching enemies but instead inward, right at a large building that looked like the armory.

Hyun Soo lit the fuses and stepped back, watching with a mixture of fascination and horror as the arrows launched into the night, whistling through the air until they collided with their target in a blast of fire and smoke. Almost immediately came a second, larger explosion that made his ears ring as the armory collapsed in a shower of debris.

A chorus of shouts and thundering feet followed the blasts, jarring Hyun Soo to his senses. He had to move. He abandoned the hwacha and charged across the parapet back in the direction he'd come.

Guards came up the inner stairs, cutting off his exit. He spun around to go back, but more soldiers appeared on the other side. He backstepped, searching for another way out. Torches flickered at the ground outside the fortress—the troops must have returned from the forest.

There was only one thing left to do. With a deep breath, he flung himself off the wall toward the fortress interior, rolling forward as he fell. He winced but maintained his form as he hit the ground, legs going over his head as the momentum carried him back up onto his feet.

But he came up in the midst of a second group of soldiers, their spears raised. They surrounded him, barring any further attempts to escape.

"Surrender," barked a tall man as he joined the group. The other soldiers gave way as he came up between them, a hideous sneer on his face. From the authoritative air about him, this must be Commander Song. He held an ornately decorated sword, which he pointed at Hyun Soo's throat.

They obviously wanted to extract information; otherwise, Hyun Soo would already be dead.

He opened his palms, but as soon as one of the soldiers

started to withdraw his spear, Hyun Soo twisted to the left and rammed his shoulder into the unsuspecting man's nose.

The injured spearman yelped, but Hyun Soo was already gone, flying toward the main entrance like a raven. Flames blazed at his back as his feet pounded against the dirt. When he reached the entrance, ten more soldiers met him, this time armed with swords.

Hyun Soo's shoulder ached, both from the fall and from smacking into the spearman, but he unsheathed his hwando and took stock of his new opponents. Hardened, stocky men who looked like they could take on a tiger with their bare hands. Nothing he couldn't handle.

An arrow whizzed through the air, grazing his cheek just before it plunged into the earth. Hyun Soo ducked behind one of the barracks to keep out of range, but he could only hide for so long. Between the swordsmen, the archer, and Commander Song, capture was inevitable. And once the commander realized he couldn't torture information out of him, death would swiftly follow.

Hyun Soo's face sagged. Up until now, he'd carried a sliver of hope that, even amid such terrible odds, somehow he'd find a way through. He needed to survive to warn Sokju just how bad this threat truly was.

But determination would only get him so far when he was this outnumbered. From what he'd seen, at least thirty men were actively pursuing him. Where the other troops were, he had no idea, but that hardly mattered. Thirty was still too great a number for a single man to overcome.

A crash grabbed his attention, and he whirled toward it. A body lay on the ground between the building he was crouched by and the next one over. Had the governor come through, after all?

Hyun Soo called to his would-be rescuer. "Identify yourself. Did Governor Choi send you?"

"Not exactly," replied a voice from above.

Hyun Soo's lungs shuddered as he stepped away from the safety of the barracks to get a glimpse of the speaker. That voice. It couldn't be.

But atop the roof of the adjacent building stood a black-clothed figure with a familiar mask and topknot.

Chapter 28

The Reunion

Chin Sun tramped up the mountain, rolling her eyes when she glanced over her shoulder and saw how far behind Min Joon had fallen.

"Do you need me to carry you? We could get there a lot faster," she mocked.

Her friend grumbled under his breath but didn't take the bait, climbing at the same, steady pace he'd maintained for most of their journey. They'd been doing this for the past few days, stopping to eat and rest when Min Joon grew too exhausted, then picking back up where they'd left off as soon as he was ready. Much to Chin Sun's frustration. With her gumiho powers restored, her speed and stamina far outweighed her friend's, meaning she spent a lot of time waiting, waiting, waiting.

She'd nearly left him several times, but whenever she was ready to succumb to the temptation, Hyun Soo's scolding voice would pop into her thoughts. *"Going into a fight unprepared is the quickest way to lose your life."*

Even though it tested her patience, bringing Min Joon along was smarter than going alone. He was a skilled negotiator, fighter, and held a certain level of authority as a police inspector. Besides, Gwishin couldn't testify about this illegal operation, whereas Kang Min Joon's word held significant weight since he belonged to one of the most powerful yangban families in the region.

During her waiting stints, Chin Sun often shifted into her nine-tailed fox form, which allowed her to scout ahead and circle back with greater speed than her human legs afforded. She'd ached to walk on four paws again, become part of the forest in a way humans could never understand. Her senses picked up so much more this way, including the faint tracks leading up the mountain. They had to be Hyun Soo's; they just had to be.

It was evening when their path evened out. They must be getting close now. Chin Sun stopped and leaned back against a thick tree to give Min Joon time to catch up. She examined her nails, willing them to transform into claws, then shorten again.

Agh, why were humans so slow?

When Min Joon finally appeared, she took a breath to speak, but he gave her a dark look as if to say, *Don't you dare.*

Chin Sun shut her mouth but didn't try to hide her amusement.

Min Joon grumbled some more as he passed, but he didn't engage with her.

She placed her hands behind her head and shut her eyes with a satisfied grin. Having an advantage over her friend again felt good.

"Get up here. I can see the base," Min Joon called.

Chin Sun's eyes flew open, and she pushed off from the tree. She came up on her friend's right as he gaped at a large fortress tucked into the side of the mountain. Torches illuminated the tops of the walls and watchtowers, evidence of the enemies lurking within.

Chin Sun had to stop herself from gaping, too. "That's not something for overtaking a city," she pointed out, ignoring the fear shooting down her spine.

"Indeed it's not," Min Joon said vaguely.

What in the world was it for? Protection against Jurchen attacks? Relations between Joseon and its northern neighbors were complicated, with frequent skirmishes occurring near the border despite Joseon's best efforts to end the bloodshed. Or perhaps it was meant to be a place to hole up in the event of a Japanese invasion?

Chin Sun turned to Min Joon. "The first thing we need to do is locate Hyun Soo. He can tell us what we're dealing with here."

"Agreed. Except . . ." Her friend's head swiveled, one eyebrow raised. "Hyun Soo's safety isn't our first priority. Protecting the people of Sokju is. If it comes down to it, can I count on you to make the hard call?"

Heat blossomed in Chin Sun's cheeks, but she met Min Joon's eye steadily. "I haven't lost sight of our objective. And I won't let the people down."

He nodded, satisfied, then his lips twisted into a wry grin. "Then let's go find your bodyguard."

The pair split up when they reached the treeline; Min Joon would explore the southern wall while Chin Sun explored the west, then they'd regroup in an hour.

Clouds shifted in front of the moon, casting the world into deeper darkness. Chin Sun summoned her fox eyes, checking for guards. One on the nearby watchtower and another patrolling the wall. Hmm. No sign of Hyun Soo yet. If she could get up to the watchtower roof, perhaps she'd be able to spot him from there.

She stayed under the shelter of the trees until she was directly across from the tower, then darted over to its base and ran her fingers over the stone. There were no places to grab on and even her superior jumping abilities were no match for something this tall.

Chin Sun held back a curse. She'd thought getting her powers back would mean the end of problems like these, but as soon as she really needed them, her gumiho abilities couldn't help her. Pathetic.

She turned away from the tower, searching for another spot that offered a good view. A nearby ridge looked promising, so she veered in that direction.

Sudden explosions thundered in her ears, drawing her attention back to the fortress. Smoke billowed in the air, followed by angry voices and rumbling feet. Was Min Joon attacking the base?

No, he wouldn't do something like that when they'd only just gotten here. He would have reconvened with her first. But if not him . . . ?

Chin Sun sprinted to the ridge, chills running through her body. She clambered to the top, hoping against hope that she'd reach Hyun Soo in time. From her new position, she could see a slew of warriors running to and fro inside the base. Some were dealing with the impact of the explosion, which had started multiple fires and collapsed an entire building. Others swarmed the ground near the western wall, where a dark silhouette stood surrounded.

Chin Sun's fox eyes zoomed in on the masked figure, taking in his broad shoulders, muscular physique, and hair tied at the back of his head. She gasped, heat radiating through her chest.

Hyun Soo. He was alive.

But not for long. The soldiers had completely encircled

him, and a tall officer stood in the center with a hwando at Hyun Soo's throat.

"Surrender," the officer ordered. Something about him niggled at the back of Chin Sun's mind, but she couldn't quite put her finger on it.

Hyun Soo raised his hands, but before Chin Sun realized what was happening, he slammed his shoulder into a spearman's face and created an opening in the circle. He dashed toward the fortress gate, the angry soldiers trailing behind him.

Chin Sun smiled, pride surging through her. That was the man she knew. She'd worried needlessly. Still . . .

She dropped from the ridge onto the western wall, grateful the guards were too distracted by the spectacle to notice her. She crept past a few, then leaped onto the roof of a nearby barracks.

Hyun Soo was facing off against a large group of swordsmen now, looking as cocky as he had the night they'd fought on the streets. He slowly pulled out his sword, and even though his mouth was covered, she was certain he was smiling in anticipation.

It was a feeling she experienced each time she donned her mask. A heady mixture of fear and exhilaration as her sword clashed with her opponent's. Not the desire to kill, but the thrill of the fight itself, of grappling against an adversary and finding out who would come out on top.

And based on Hyun Soo's confident stance, it was safe to say he didn't doubt whom the victor would be.

Chin Sun scowled. No one had the right to look that good in a life-or-death situation. He was supposed to be struggling—just a little bit—then she could swoop in and rescue him. She sat down at the edge of the roof, slightly disappointed, and let her feet dangle over the side. Perhaps she should go check on Min Joon since Hyun Soo clearly didn't need her help.

An arrow zipped through the air, slicing Hyun Soo's cheek before he ran for cover.

Chin Sun was on her feet in a heartbeat, swinging toward the source of the unexpected attack. A stocky man on the roof next to hers was in the midst of nocking another arrow.

She whistled, startling the archer so greatly that his next shot flew straight up into the air. He whirled around, eyes narrowing as they landed on her.

"Looks like you need to work on your aim," she said. "Want to practice on a moving target?"

The archer reached for his next arrow, but by the time he'd grabbed it, Chin Sun was already an arm's length away from him, hwando raised. His face paled, and he turned to flee, but she didn't give him the chance.

With a quick slash to the throat, he tumbled backward, plummeting to the ground with a thud.

Hyun Soo's deep voice reached her ears. "Identify yourself. Did Governor Choi send you?"

Chin Sun's heart gave a joyous flutter, impatient to reunite with the one she loved and declare her feelings. "Not exactly," she called down.

Hyun Soo stepped out from the shadow of the barracks beside the one she stood atop. Recognition flooded his eyes, followed by a warmth that made Chin Sun's knees go weak.

Keep it together, Chin Sun. You can't let yourself come undone with a simple look. At least wait until he tells you how much he missed you. She sheathed her hwando and jumped down, landing gracefully at his side.

Hyun Soo grabbed her hand and yanked her under the shelter of the barracks. Once he'd checked that no one had seen them, he turned to her, the warmth gone from his eyes. "What are you doing here?" he asked gruffly.

Annoyance sparked in Chin Sun's chest. She'd come all this way, and *this* was the welcome she received? Had she been wrong in thinking he'd be glad to see her? Had his feelings for her vanished that quickly?

Chin Sun inclined her head toward the man she'd just dispatched. "Isn't it obvious? I came to help you. But perhaps I shouldn't have since you don't seem to want me here."

She sighed and shook her head, irritation turning inward. That wasn't what she'd wanted to say, what she'd been dying to say ever since she'd realized it back in Sokju. Maybe he didn't feel the same way anymore, but she needed to get this out. "I have to tell you—"

Footsteps cut off her confession, and Hyun Soo ushered her around the back of the barracks, where they stood motionless until the sounds of soldiers faded. Rain began to fall, splattering against the dirt.

Hyun Soo turned to her. "We need to get out of here."

"Yeh, but—"

"But what?" he snapped.

Heat rushed to her cheeks. She felt silly now, wanting to confess when they were in such a dire situation. But perhaps that was what made it all the more important—this might be her last chance to tell him.

"Before I left Sokju, I ended things with Kang Dol Sam. Officially. I know I told my uncle I would marry him, but I . . . I just couldn't do it. Not when I'm in love with you. Maybe you don't feel the same way anymore, but I just wanted you to know."

Hyun Soo drew in a sharp breath and pulled her to his chest, one hand cradling her head while his sword arm wrapped around her shoulders. Something cracked inside her, and she melted into him like wax, molding to his form like she'd been made for it. Tears welled up in her eyes, her irritation fizzling away. She'd known she'd missed him, but this—this was like coming up for air when you didn't even realize you were drowning.

He pulled back and stared down at her, rubbing his thumb over her cheek. The fierceness in his gaze made her stomach tighten. "Chin Sun . . ."

Her heart shuddered. It was the first time he'd used her given name rather than "Lady Lee" or "agasshi." For him to speak it now, as if it was so precious it could only be whispered, was almost dreamlike. How many times had she longed to hear it pass over his lips, only to remember bitterly that she'd lost her chance when she'd allowed Samchon to send him away?

"You never have to doubt my love for you," he whispered. "Never."

Though his words were soft, he spoke them firmly, reverently, both a promise and a hope. Despite all the forces working against them, they *would* create a future together—it was a truth she could rest securely in, no matter what.

Chin Sun wrapped her arms around Hyun Soo again, completely overcome.

After a moment, Hyun Soo forced himself to step away, torturous though it was, and tried to refocus on what was most important right now. What was it again?

Getting Chin Sun to safety. That was it.

His eyes flicked back to his companion, then he realized

he was still standing too close. He took another step back, fighting the desire raging inside that demanded he give in to his feelings, rip that mask off her face, and kiss her until daybreak.

Hyun Soo stifled a groan, then spun away so he wasn't looking at her anymore. That helped him clear his head a bit. "We should get going."

A small hand on his shoulder made him freeze, his flimsy defenses threatening to collapse. Her voice was low, gentle, and uncharacteristically vulnerable as she said, "Hyun Soo, why didn't you tell me your plans? Why did you try to do this on your own?"

He slowly turned, shuffling back to keep some distance between them. "I was just following your advice," he said stiffly, afraid to meet her eye.

"What advice?"

He waved the hwando in front of her, the engraving on full display: "Brave enough to stand alone."

Lady Lee put her hands on her hips, indignant. "Are you serious? That's not what I meant when I had that made for you! I—"

He chuckled before he could stop himself. He'd missed getting under her skin. To placate her, he admitted, "The truth is, I didn't want to put you in harm's way. I swore I would protect you, remember?"

"You also swore you'd kill Gwishin the moment you saw him. And we all know how that turned out." Chin Sun huffed so dramatically he wasn't sure if she was joking or not.

Hyun Soo rubbed the back of his neck, guilt rising in his chest. "Yeh, that is something I've been meaning to—"

"But like you said, we better go," she interrupted. "Kim

Min Joon is probably already waiting for us at the rendezvous point."

"He's here, too?"

"Of course. Unlike *some* people, I knew better than to come alone," she said dryly.

"I can't tell if you're angry with me right now."

"Oh, I'm always angry with you. But"—

A sultry tone slipped into her voice, and she leaned forward until their facecloths were nearly touching.

—"when all this is over and we don't need these masks anymore, I'll be happy to show you just how . . . *angry* . . . you've made me. Until then, follow me."

Hyun Soo sputtered, a dizzying current racing through him. Was she implying what he thought she was?

Before he could form a reply, Chin Sun bolted into the rain, and it was all he could do just to keep up.

With unmitigated confidence, she zigzagged through the camp toward the main gate. She acted as if she had an extra sense as she moved, ducking around corners before he'd even heard footsteps or signaling for him to wait just in time to avoid a passing guard. Once, he even thought she sniffed the air, but the moment was over too quickly to be sure, then they were off again, following some invisible route only Chin Sun seemed to know.

In the madness of their retreat, Hyun Soo only caught snippets of what the soldiers themselves were doing, but it seemed most were dealing with the aftereffects of the explosion rather than continuing their search for the mysterious intruder. The damage Hyun Soo had done with the fire cart was extensive, and he was relieved to spy broken weapons amongst the rubble. He'd blown up the right building, after all.

When they finally reached the main gate, Hyun Soo

deflated at the sight of the ten swordsmen from earlier. But Chin Sun didn't seem to mind. She darted forward, so rapidly Hyun Soo almost couldn't make out her movements, and cut down three of them in seconds.

Hyun Soo eyed his companion with a mixture of disbelief and admiration. Since when was she that fast?

The remaining men lifted their swords, nervous but ready to defend themselves. The rain continued to fall, seeping through Hyun Soo's hanbok and chilling him to his core. They needed to get this done quickly; otherwise, more soldiers were bound to notice them and join the fight.

"Think you can handle that one?" Chin Sun nodded at the swordsman on the far left, a lanky fellow who was swiping his hwando back and forth in a challenge.

Hyun Soo balked, unable to keep a hint of skepticism from his voice. "And what, leave the rest to you?"

Chin Sun gave him a wink that pulled at his insides. "If you can keep up, I suppose we could split them." She skated over to the nearest swordsman and swung her blade, nearly cleaving the man in two with each successive strike.

Hyun Soo blinked a few times, marveling at her impossible strength, then approached the swordsman she'd suggested as the others crowded around Chin Sun. With a single twist of his sword, he knocked his opponent's weapon away, then leaped forward and pierced the man's chest. By the time he'd turned to attack the next one, only Chin Sun was left standing, her eyes glistening with satisfaction.

"Have you been practicing since the last time I saw you?" he asked.

She inclined her head to the no-longer-guarded gate. "We can talk about it later," she said cryptically.

The pair hurtled through the gate, blurry pine trees visible in the distance. They were going to make it. The rain began to ease up, a splinter of the pearly moon coming into view.

"I think I see Kim Min Joon." Chin Sun pointed at a vague shape in the woods, so small Hyun Soo could barely see it.

"Not so fast," rasped a deep voice that prickled the back of Hyun Soo's neck. A hint of familiarity stole through him. Where had he heard that voice before?

He and Chin Sun swung toward the source, only to find Commander Song a few paces to their right. Someone was just behind him, and the commander sidestepped to allow the second man to come forward.

Kang Dol Sam.

Chapter 29

The Murderer

Chin Sun hardly noticed her former fiancé. How could she when the enemy she feared most was only a few paces away? The human guise he wore now was masterful, but she'd known the truth the moment she'd gotten a good glimpse of his sword.

How had the goblin found her here?

She turned to Hyun Soo, who stood stiffly, except he wasn't paying attention to the real threat. He was too busy watching the decoy, the one the goblin wanted them to focus on.

Chin Sun swiveled back to the shapeshifter. He looked exactly like a high-ranking soldier, his hat and hanbok of noticeably better quality than that of the other troops'. A quiver of arrows was slung over his shoulder, with a bow attached to his front. Even the way he carried himself was perfect, like a man used to being in charge.

It was a flawless facade, if not for the beautiful hwando in his hand. The symbol upon it seemed to almost glow in the darkness, taunting her.

The goblin met Chin Sun's eye in a challenge. No, he

wasn't trying to deceive her. His smirk indicated the exact opposite. He wanted her to know it was him. Hyun Soo and Kang Dol Sam were the ones he wanted to fool.

Chin Sun longed to run him straight through after all he'd done to her, but she kept her anger in check. While the goblin's deception was likely to prevent any grim reapers from showing up, she could work this in her favor. Pretending to be human meant the goblin would be slower to reveal his powers, thereby giving them a greater chance of making it out of here in one piece.

It rankled her, but she tore her gaze from the goblin and instead turned to Kang Dol Sam. She gave him a mocking bow. "To what do we owe the pleasure?"

"Gwishin." The word passed over Kang Dol Sam's lips like a curse, his jaw clenched. This wasn't the young master she'd met four days ago. Gone was the warmth, the affection, the very humanity she was so used to seeing in the man she'd once hoped to marry. In their place lurked a cold, ruthless hatred that looked willing to destroy anything and anyone who got in Dol Sam's way.

And Gwishin had gotten in the way for too long.

"When I heard a masked man had infiltrated the base, I suspected it was you." He sneered. "You always have enjoyed ruining my plans." He unsheathed the hwando at his hip. Triumph flared in his eyes. "But you're not getting away this time. Tonight, I swear I'm going to kill you."

"I can't let you do that, hyung." Hyun Soo pulled down his mask and moved forward. Time seemed to slow, each of his footsteps pounding in time with the steady thrum of Chin Sun's heart. His hwando glinted in the moonlight, flecks of blood spattered on the blade. When his eyes found hers, they softened ever so slightly, and he dipped his head in a quick nod.

Kang Dol Sam's face crumpled, first with disbelief, then with horrified betrayal. "Hyun Soo? You're here? What . . . what are you doing?" His voice was broken, pleading, as though he couldn't accept the reality in front of him without falling apart.

Hyun Soo positioned himself in front of Chin Sun, weapon raised. His stance was confident, steady, leaving no doubt of his loyalties. Just as he'd once sworn, he was ready to defend her, no matter the cost.

"Gwishin isn't behind the attack on your base. I am," Hyun Soo declared. "What you're doing here is wrong. You must call it off. Find another way to deal with the unrest in Sokju. I'll help you." His words, though soaked with regret, also bore a thread of hope, a final attempt to end this before it was too late.

Kang Dol Sam's upper lip curled back in a snarl. "Why would I accept help from someone without honor? You shame yourself further with such an offer." He lifted his hwando and swung it at his friend's head.

Hyun Soo blocked the blow, the two blades slamming together before they pulled away. Hyun Soo made the next move, thrusting his sword at Dol Sam's exposed stomach. Dol Sam sidestepped, but Hyun Soo struck again, faster this time, then Dol Sam went on the offensive. As the fight continued, the men's movements changed from hesitant and uncertain to resolute, as if they both realized at the same time that the other wasn't going to back down.

"I believe you and I have a score of our own to settle," came an unwelcome voice.

Chin Sun shifted to the right, hwando raised. The goblin hovered at the forest's edge, several paces from where he'd stood only seconds before. He smirked at her quick intake of breath, relishing the fear she couldn't conceal fast enough.

Chin Sun dashed over to him, stopping a few steps away. "You're right," she agreed. She steeled herself, then sheathed her hwando. "But I want answers, not blood."

The goblin regarded her warily, his expression unreadable. "I'm not in the business of explaining myself to my prey."

"Then you will make an exception." When he started to shake his head, she added, "I am owed that much for my sacrifice."

His eyes widened in recognition, the echo of his first words to her stretching between them. *"Thank you for your sacrifice."*

When goblin pressed his lips together in a tight grimace, Chin Sun knew she'd swayed him. For despite the animosity between them, he still recognized the value of the life he was taking.

"Ask your questions."

"First, I want to know what you're doing here. Did you follow me?"

The goblin sneered. "As much as I want your bead, I have other reasons for being here. Your arrival was simply a happy coincidence."

Chin Sun's eyebrows drew together. "Then you're part of this scheme to take over my city? This"—she gestured to his attire—"wasn't a ploy to get into the fort unnoticed? You're truly acting as the army's commander?"

He widened his stance, chest puffing up with pride. "When it suits me."

What? Did that mean there was a real Commander Song somewhere and the goblin just impersonated him whenever he felt like it? That sounded like the goblin mischief she'd heard of in stories.

But she doubted he was doing this on a whim. Every move he made felt like a calculated decision, like tiny stitches that would eventually come together to form something magnificent. Or terrible. He'd spoken of a cause before—did taking over Sokju somehow play into it?

"Stop with the riddles. Just tell me what I want to know."

The monster gave her a knowing look, blue fire flaring in his eyes. "Ah, in that case, I shall answer the question you asked the last time we met, for that is what you wish to know more than anything else."

"What are you—"

"The reason your bead is so important, so . . . desirable," he explained.

Chin Sun's hands clenched into fists. She hated the hunger in his voice, how it made her skin crawl. Her fox bead was hers, *hers*, and no matter how much he wanted it, she was never going to let him have it.

But perhaps if she knew why, she could persuade him to find something else that would satisfy him.

"And that reason is?"

He paused, making her wait until she almost couldn't bear it any longer. "It will give the goblins the strength we need to overcome our enemy and take back what belongs to us."

Chin Sun blinked a few times, catching a quick glimpse of something in the distance before she returned her gaze to the goblin. "Your enemy? Who?"

"The reapers, of course."

"And how can my fox bead accomplish that? It takes life; it doesn't give it."

The goblin snorted. "Do you think you can fool me with a lie like that when you're drinking in all that human life-force as we speak?"

Guilt pricked at Chin Sun's conscience. He was right. Hyun Soo's lifeforce swam through her veins, flooding her with strength.

"Now, I've done my part. It's your turn." He held out his hand. "Give me the bead willingly, and I'll make your death painless."

"But you're not gumiho," Chin Sun pointed out. "Swallowing my bead would only drain you." Just as it had drained Hyun Soo.

"What is this? More attempts at trickery? Fox beads can give life to anyone, so long as you know how to open them."

"Open them? What . . . ?" Chin Sun's forehead creased. Was that how she'd gained Hyun Soo's lifeforce? When she'd kissed him and taken back her bead, it had been so instinctual she hadn't paid attention to what she was doing. But now that she thought about it, she *had* felt the bead open just before her powers had reemerged.

The goblin tilted his head, confusion etched into his face. "Why are you so surprised? Don't you know anythi—" He broke off, understanding dawning in his eyes. "Ah. But you wouldn't know, would you? How could you when you didn't have parents to teach you?"

Chin Sun's heart skipped. "How do you know that?"

Laughter rumbled in the goblin's throat. "Because we wiped out the last two gumiho in Sokju eighteen years ago. No one's been back since then. Well, not until a rumor started circulating that a vigilante was giving the humans all kinds of trouble. A vigilante too fast to catch." He dipped his head toward her middle, where her fox bead lay hidden, radiating with power.

Chin Sun froze, struggling to grasp the full meaning of his words. The goblins killed the last gumiho in Sokju? Two of them. Eighteen years ago . . .

Her chest seized up, phantom hands squeezing her windpipe. She'd never known her parents, never known what it was to be their child. But she'd thought about it endlessly, wondering what it would have been like to be known completely, to not have to hide a part of herself for fear of being cast aside. To see her features in another's face.

Aunt and Uncle had loved her as well as they were able, and she loved them in return, but they'd never filled the hole deep inside herself, the one that whispered to her in the dead of night, making her chest cave in and her eyes swim with tears. The empty longing for that which had been stolen from her.

But now she knew who was to blame.

Rage flooded Chin Sun's body, an animalistic scream tearing from her throat. Claws emerged at her fingertips, bloodlust blurring the edges of her vision until all she saw was the figure in front of her.

Murderer.

Maybe he wasn't the one who'd ended her parents' lives, but he *was* guilty. And now, he would pay.

She whistled.

Min Joon leaped from his hiding place in the nearby brush, sword raised. The goblin turned to defend himself, but Chin Sun's hand whipped out and slashed at his face.

The goblin swerved to the side, narrowly avoiding her claws while also blocking Min Joon's attack. Their swords collided in a burst of blue fire, which sent Min Joon flying backward with a cry of pain.

Chin Sun drew her hwando, slicing at the goblin's back while he was turned away. The strike created a long diagonal slash from the goblin's shoulder down to the edge of his torso. Her sword came away flecked with silver blood.

The goblin spun around with a howl, sweeping his flaming sword at her. Chin Sun leaped out of the way, tucking herself into a roll. She came back up as the goblin swiveled toward her, but before he could get in another swing, Min Joon was there, stabbing him in the stomach.

The goblin threw a burst of blue flame at Min Joon's face, forcing him to fall back. The monster grabbed at the wound in his stomach, blood dripping onto his hand.

Chin Sun came in for another attack, but he summoned a fiery barrier around himself, holding her at bay. She circled the enclosure but found no openings, no weaknesses.

She hissed. Did he think a little fire was going to keep her out? She reached inside herself, drawing on as much power as she could until she hit it. That wall. The one she'd fought over and over, the one that had kept her from defeating Hyun Soo in their first fight.

She examined it more closely, determining what it was. It wasn't weakness—no, it was something much worse than that.

Fear. Fear that the humans would harm her once they learned the truth of what she was. Gumiho. Monster. Other.

"What do we do now?" Min Joon asked from her side.

Chin Sun looked at her friend. A bloody cut marred his cheek, and several bruises were forming along his neck and face. But he peered at her steadily, with all the confidence in the world. Despite knowing what she was.

Or maybe, just maybe, because of it. A human couldn't win this fight. The goblin was simply too strong. But perhaps a gumiho could.

Sang Mi's voice brushed at her thoughts. *"It's time you were true to yourself, Unni."*

Chin Sun felt something inside herself snap, and suddenly, she knew what she needed to do. "Stand back, Min Joon." She took a deep breath and stepped up to the flames.

She shifted into fox form and leaped through, howling as fur and flesh began to burn.

But the power she'd been unable to access before flowed freely now, allowing her to tap into a well deeper than she'd ever imagined. Was *this* what it was to be gumiho? This overwhelming strength that seemed almost infinite? She felt her wounds knitting themselves back together, repairing themselves in seconds.

When she opened her eyes, the fire had died away and there stood the goblin, shaking his head even as blood continued to gush from his abdomen. "H-how . . . ?"

Chin Sun returned to human form and gripped his hanbok, lifting him into the air. She drew back her arm, ready to end this, but he whimpered. "Wait."

She paused, heat roaring through her veins. "Why should I?"

Sweat beaded on the goblin's forehead, but then his eyes locked on something behind her. His lips twitched. "Because if you don't, you won't have time to save him."

Chin Sun followed his line of sight. In the distance stood Hyun Soo and Dol Sam. Hyun Soo's weapon lay on the ground while Dol Sam's hovered in the air, aimed for Hyun Soo's torso.

Chin Sun's heart shattered like glass.

Even at her top speed, there was no way she could cross that distance before Dol Sam's blade struck its target. No way to stop what was about to happen. Unless—

Chin Sun sprinted across the mountain, shifting into fox form as she ran. Her body slammed into Dol Sam's, knocking him to the ground. She landed on his stomach with a groan, relieved to find him unconscious. She pushed herself up and turned to Hyun Soo.

His eyes widened as they took her in, first with shock, then with something that made Chin Sun's insides go cold. A burst of breath flew from his lips, and he collapsed, Dol Sam's sword lodged in his chest.

Chapter 30

The Revelation

Chin Sun returned to human form in an instant. She rolled Hyun Soo over onto his back. His eyes were slightly open but unfocused, as if he were already far away from here. The blade had pierced deep into the left side of his chest. There wasn't much blood yet, but she knew as soon as she pulled the sword out, he would—

She ground her teeth, fighting against the panic gnawing at her insides. He would be fine. He had to be. "Hyun Soo?"

The bodyguard dragged his eyes to hers, a relieved smile stretching over his face. "Chin Sun," he wheezed, "you're here. I was so worried . . . when you disappeared. . . . So worried that something had happened to you."

"Shhh, don't talk," she cooed, cradling the back of his head. The rain had stopped several minutes ago, but it had been enough to turn the dirt beneath them into slick mud. A thin layer of it coated Hyun Soo's clothes, spreading to Chin Sun's as she held him.

"Where did you go? I thought"—he gasped, the sound

sending icicles through Chin Sun's heart—"I thought I saw a goblin. Did . . . did it hurt you?"

Chin Sun shook her head, tears brimming in her eyes. This stupid man, worrying about her when he was the one who was dying. Why did he have to be so frustrating!

"I'm fine. I'm completely fine," she choked out.

Hyun Soo's eyelids fluttered. "Good. That's good." He started to drift off, then jerked, eyes widening. "I saw a gumiho. Did you see it, too?"

Chin Sun held back the sob climbing up her throat. "Yeh, I saw it." She paused. "What did you think of it? Was it frightening?"

She waited for his answer with bated breath.

"No," he murmured, shutting his eyes. "It was beautiful. I saved one once. Did I ever tell you that?"

She laughed, the sound almost a whimper. Beautiful? She'd thought countless times about what he would say when he found out, but she'd never imagined that response. Had all her worry over his rejection been for nothing?

Except . . . a tiger was beautiful. That didn't mean you were brave enough to embrace it.

Chin Sun set her jaw. She'd promised herself she was going to be honest, at least with the people who mattered. She'd meant to tell him of her true nature after they'd gotten out of this mess, but now it seemed she wouldn't have the chance. It was time for Hyun Soo to know everything.

"Actually," she began, "you didn't just save her once. You saved her many times. From goblins"—she ran her thumb down his cheek—"from bandits"—she slid her finger to his lips—"from her own stupidity." She sniffled. "But in the end, all I did was steal from you. Do you think you could forgive me?"

Awareness flashed in Hyun Soo's eyes, but before she

could determine how he felt about her confession, his eyes closed and he slumped in her arms.

Chin Sun pressed her ear to his chest, sighing when she found a faint heartbeat. He was still alive. Still alive.

Pounding feet approached from behind. Chin Sun checked over her shoulder, relieved to discover it was Kim Min Joon. He blanched as he took in Hyun Soo's wounded form. "Is he . . . ?"

"Don't say it," Chin Sun snapped. She turned back to her beloved bodyguard. She brushed a few strands of hair away from his face. He almost looked peaceful, like he was just sleeping. "He's going to be fine."

Min Joon's lack of response told her how much he believed that. She felt his gaze on her as he squatted down, but she refused to meet his eye for fear of losing her last slip of control.

"Impossible . . ." he whispered.

"What?" She swung toward him, voice sharper than she intended.

Min Joon was staring in amazement, not at Hyun Soo but at her. He stretched his hand toward her face. "Chin Sun, your burns . . . they're gone."

She looked away. What did it matter that she'd healed herself when Hyun Soo was fading away in her arms?

She laid her head on Hyun Soo's shoulder. "Stay with me," she said. "You're not allowed to do anything else, do you hear?" She tried to sound authoritative, but it came out more like begging.

"It was your fox bead, wasn't it?" Min Joon pressed.

She didn't answer, couldn't answer, not when everything was crashing down around her. Hyun Soo couldn't die. He had to live. He had to be with her. She needed him too much. How could she breathe if he wasn't at her side?

Min Joon shook her arm so hard it hurt. "Chin Sun, what are you doing? Didn't you hear what the goblin said about fox beads giving life?"

She went rigid, his words tickling something in her subconscious. What was it?

She tore her attention from Hyun Soo back to her friend, struggling against the sea of grief she'd started drowning in. "What did you just say?"

Min Joon released an exasperated groan. "Open your bead and kiss him," he ordered, his tone leaving no room for argument. "Now, before it's too late."

Chin Sun still didn't fully understand, but she heard the urgency in his voice and brought the bead up into her mouth. With a flick of her tongue, it opened, then she pulled down her mask. She leaned forward and pressed her mouth to Hyun Soo's.

Before she could tell if anything happened, a flurry of footsteps neared. Soldiers charged toward them, armed with swords and bows. Meanwhile, Kang Dol Sam was starting to stir.

"We'll have a better chance if we split up," Min Joon hissed. "Get him out of here."

Chin Sun retrieved her bead, hoping it had had enough time to work its magic, then lifted Hyun Soo in her arms and sped off.

Hyun Soo ran his fingers over a white mugunghwa flower, marveling at its intricate details. The bottom of each petal was blood red, stretching out in thin tendrils like veins, while the very center of the flower held a cluster of pollen so light it almost looked like snow. Surrounding him was a field of mugunghwa flowers and spider lilies, so large it stretched all the way to the orange horizon. He meandered through the field, without worry or care, his steps leading him toward the setting sun.

A tinkling laugh stirred something in his chest, overwhelming him with a feeling he couldn't name.

His breath hitched at the sight of a young woman sitting on the ground a short distance away. She was absolutely exquisite, with a smooth, round face and eyes like honey. She didn't seem to know he was there, for she was completely enraptured with the companion sleeping at her side: a small white fox with nine tails.

Without warning, the woman stood and turned Hyun Soo's way, but when their gazes met, he found himself staring into slanted pupils.

Hyun Soo gasped, shocked at her fox-like appearance. He lowered his eyes to the ground, searching for the gumiho, but the white fox had disappeared, leaving himself and the woman alone in the field. She peered at him curiously, almost as if she were waiting for something.

After a moment, her expression saddened, and she pressed her palm over her mouth. When she moved her hand away, there in her palm rested a small orb, glowing blue in the dying light.

Hyun Soo looked from the orb to the woman, trying to understand. She smiled warmly, holding the orb out like she wanted him to take it. Hyun Soo reached forward, but then he spied the blood at the corners of her mouth. Her smile widened as fangs descended, and her fingernails transformed into claws.

A scream tore from his throat as he awoke, the nightmare ending and reality closing in on him. Pain returned, scorching hot in his chest. It was night, not sunset, and he was not in a field—he lay on a mountain, dying to protect the woman he loved.

But if he was dying, why was the pain fading? Instead of growing weaker, energy began coursing through him, spreading from his stomach toward his extremities. Hyun Soo felt new and whole, ready to fight off a hundred foes without even breaking a sweat.

What was happening?

A canopy of leaves hung above him. He'd been just outside the fortress when he'd passed out. How had he wound up in the forest? He pushed himself into a sitting position, trying to get his bearings.

Chin Sun sat beside him, mask at her neck and hands over her face as tears flowed down her cheeks. A sword lay on the ground nearby, covered in blood. Dol Sam's sword? He glanced down at his chest, expecting to see a hwando sticking out but finding only torn fabric.

"Chin Sun?"

She gasped, countenance going from stricken to elated in half a second. She threw her arms around his neck, nearly knocking him off balance. The sweet scent of flowers tickled his nose as his companion sobbed against his chest, dampening his hanbok with her tears. "It worked. You're all right."

Faint alarm bells rang in his mind, but there were other matters to attend to first. He gently pried Chin Sun off him and scanned their periphery. Empty forest in all directions. "Are we safe?"

She nodded. "Yeh. There's no need to worry."

"How did we get here?"

Chin Sun paled. "I . . . carried you."

Her answer was so ridiculous Hyun Soo almost

laughed, yet something about the way she dropped her gaze and started fingering her jeogori gave him pause. "You're serious." When she didn't say anything, he pressed on. "But that's impossible, Chin Sun. There's no way you could carry me so far. I can't even see the fortress. How could you—"

Dread rose in his gut, and though he couldn't quite pinpoint what he was so afraid of, it was almost strong enough to stop him from asking his next question. Almost.

"What are you hiding from me?"

Chin Sun went completely still, as if all the life had been sucked out of her. She didn't speak for so long, he started to reach for her hand.

When she lifted her gaze, his hand froze mid-air. The shame in her eyes was raw, palpable, and suddenly Hyun Soo couldn't breathe. A single tear slid down her cheek.

"I'm sorry, Hyun Soo."

She opened her mouth, revealing a small blue bead inside.

Chapter 31

The Monster

At first, Hyun Soo didn't understand what he was looking at, but then bewilderment gave way to clarity. That wasn't just any bead. That was a fox bead. A gumiho's bead. But that meant—

He lurched backward, everything he'd thought he'd known collapsing in the blink of an eye. Lee Chin Sun, the woman he'd fought his dearest friend for, was . . . was . . .

Chin Sun's expression withered at his retreat, but she didn't speak, didn't move, just waited. Watching with those honey-brown eyes that sent his blood racing even as the hairs on his arms stood on end.

He swallowed thickly, trying to wrap his head around it. He'd seen a gumiho earlier and written it off as the hallucination of a dying man. But it had been her?

Hyun Soo couldn't believe it. He *knew* Chin Sun. Loved her. Didn't he?

"The gumiho who attacked Dol Sam—that was . . . ?" He trailed off, the rest of his question dying in his throat.

She grimaced, understanding what he couldn't bring himself to say.

He waited for her to deny it, to tell him he was mistaken. The Chin Sun he knew would never lie to him about this. After everything he'd lost, she was the one person he could count on, the one person he could trust.

But the word that left her lovely lips drained the life out of him in a single breath.

"Me." Her voice was small, weak, like a defenseless creature fearing for its life.

Hyun Soo recoiled, shaking all over. He felt like the ground had been ripped out from under him, and he was just left to fall endlessly. He shut his eyes and pressed the heels of his hands to his forehead, trying to stop the wave of dizziness.

Small fingers brushed the back of his hand. "Hyun Soo?"

In a motion so fast it was almost a blur, he pulled a knife out of his pocket and pressed it to the monster's throat.

Chin Sun froze, the steel like a brand against her skin. She looked up into Hyun Soo's eyes, drinking in all the fear, betrayal, and distrust leaking from his gaze. She'd known this would happen once he learned the truth about her, yet she'd dreamed of something different, something better. Her voice came out in a broken whisper. "You would kill the woman you love?"

Hyun Soo's eyes widened, going from her to the knife, then down to the ground. His hand trembled against her collarbone, his chest heaving with anguish.

Finally, he lowered the blade and dragged his gaze back

to hers, eyes wet with tears. "Are you the woman I love," he choked, "or are you a monster?"

Chin Sun's heart rent in two. "Can I not be both?"

A whimper escaped Hyun Soo's lips, and he closed his eyes like he was on the verge of falling apart. He took a shaky breath, steadying himself.

When he reopened his eyes, they were guarded, wary. The eyes of a man regarding his enemy. The dagger was still clenched in his hand, ready to be used at the first sign of danger. "No, you can't," he said coldly. "Now, explain what you did to me, gumiho."

"I used my bead to heal you."

"But I thought fox beads only—" He broke off, nostrils flaring. "Are you lying to me again?"

Chin Sun flinched, hating that he needed to ask that. "No, I'm telling the truth. Fox beads can give life and take it away. If I hadn't given it to you, Dol Sam's sword would have killed you."

He seemed to accept her words, expression turning pensive. "But this isn't the first time I've had your fox bead, is it? That day in the clearing . . ."

He didn't have to finish for her to know what he was referring to. The memory of their first kiss brushed over her like a winter wind, chilling and bitter. What had once been something she cherished was now achingly hollow, the echoes of a love dying away.

When Hyun Soo's face darkened, she could tell he was thinking the same.

Chin Sun took a deep breath, forcing herself to push through the pain. "Yeh, that was when I retrieved my bead from you the first time. You'd swallowed it on accident the night you nearly killed me and the goblin tried to steal it."

He nodded with a kind of sad resignation, as if he'd

known this already but hated to hear her say it aloud. "Then . . . is that why you did all this?"

"Did all what?"

He let out a dry laugh bordering on a sob. "All *this* . . ." He motioned between the two of them with the dagger. "Getting close to me, acting like you cared, was it just a ploy to get back your bead?"

Chin Sun's mouth fell open. "What? No. *No.*" Her voice cracked with despair. "Well, maybe in the beginning," she admitted, "but after you saved me from the fire, I realized how much you meant to me. I love you, more than I could have ever imagined. Please, Hyun Soo . . ."

She reached toward his cheek, but he leaned away, raising his knife. "Don't touch me! After everything you did, how could you say you love me? You don't. You're not capable of it."

His words sliced her open more than that dagger ever could. They were painfully familiar, drawing her back into a past she longed to forget. *"Don't touch me! Do you still not understand? I'm not your aunt. You're not even human. And now I'm going to die and your horrible face will be the last thing I see."*

"Put down your weapon," called a new voice.

Hyun Soo and Chin Sun whirled around. A few paces away, nearly invisible in the darkness, stood a solitary figure dressed in black. He held a hwando in his right hand, which was pointed at Hyun Soo.

"The grim reaper," Chin Sun breathed. He'd returned. But why?

The newcomer stepped forward, gaze fixed on Hyun Soo. "I said, 'Put down your weapon.'" His eyes narrowed, making his austere face even more frightening. "I don't like repeating myself."

Hyun Soo lowered his dagger and moved in front of Chin Sun. "Who are you?"

"My name is Eun Mook." The reaper's voice was cool yet rippled with unmistakable firmness. "And you're both under arrest."

Terror seized Chin Sun's entire being, locking her in place. "Both of us? For what? We didn't—"

A beastly growl tore from Hyun Soo's throat, and he surged forward with impossible speed, hwando aimed for Eun Mook's heart.

"Hyun Soo, don't—"

Her plea died on her lips as the grim reaper reached into his robe and drew out a handful of shimmering red dust. He blew it toward Hyun Soo, who stopped cold as a red cloud struck his face. The bodyguard crashed to his knees with a gasp, then fell limply onto his side.

Unconscious or—

No, that had to be it. After all they'd just gone through, Chin Sun *refused* to consider the alternative. He would be fine once he woke up.

If she got him out of here.

Driven by a desperation emanating from deep within her, she sprang forward. She didn't know how she would overcome Death himself, but she had no choice. Not with Hyun Soo's life on the line.

Eun Mook's sword met hers with a great crack, snapping her hwando in two. She barely had time to register it, though, for the reaper was already reaching back into his hanbok. By the time she thought to duck, scarlet dust was already entering her nostrils, turning her world on its end.

Hyun Soo's still form was the last thing she saw before everything turned to darkness.

Epilogue

"Halmeoni?" called little Hyun Soo one particularly stormy night. "Halmeoni?"

Feet shuffled down the hall just before the hanji doors to his bedroom slid open. A wizened face peeked inside, expression softening when it landed on him. "Yeh, Grandson?"

Thunder rumbled outside, making the boy so scared he nearly hid beneath his blanket. But he was much too old for that now. He was nearly eight, after all. "Would . . ." He cleared his throat to get rid of the squeak in it and put on his bravest face. "Would you tell me a story?"

His grandmother smiled and hobbled into the room. She sat cross-legged beside his bed mat, wrinkled hands folded in her lap. "What would you like to hear about tonight? I know a good story about an unlucky haetae."

Hyun Soo shook his head. "No, I want to hear what happens to people who swallow fox beads."

Halmeoni frowned. "I told you before that gumiho take back their beads once they're satisfied with the amount of lifeforce absorbed. When that happens, the human will either grow sick or, if all his lifeforce has been consumed, he'll die."

The little boy shook his head again. "But what about the clever ones who kill the gumiho? What happens to the beads inside them? Will the bead still kill them if the gumiho is dead?"

The old woman pursed her lips, thinking it over. Suddenly, she clapped her hands, startling Hyun Soo so much he jumped. "Ah! I did hear a story once about a gumiho who was outsmarted by the human she gave her fox bead to." Grandmother leaned closer, her countenance bright as she recalled the tale. "He tricked her into opening it, and once she had, he scooped the bead up and ate it. As soon as he did, the bead released its power, giving him abilities no human could ever dream of."

The boy's eyes widened. "What kind of abilities?"

Halmeoni ruffled Hyun Soo's hair with a wistful laugh and pushed herself to her feet. Another peal of thunder shook the house, but Hyun Soo barely noticed. He tugged at his grandmother's clothes, urging her to give him an answer.

But she shook her head sadly. "I'm sorry, dear one. I wish I could remember. . . ."

General Terms

Agasshi - Title for a young, unmarried woman.

Aigoo - Exclamation of surprise or dismay, similar to "Oh, dear."

Ajumma - Term for an older woman.

Ahjussi - Term for an older man.

Bongsunghwa - Balsam flower.

Chima - Skirt.

Chuseok - A three-day holiday to celebrate the harvest.

Damo - A female nurse who works for the police bureau. This job is not desirable and is given as a punishment for low grades. Damos are useful for entering areas where men are not allowed as well as examining female corpses.

Danso - A traditional Korean woodwind instrument resembling a flute.

Dongsaeng - Term for one's younger sibling or cousin. Denotes intimacy.

Euihon - Marriage negotiations.

Eunjangdo - A silver knife worn by men and women.

Gayageum - A traditional Korean zither with twelve strings.

Gisaengs - Female entertainers of the lowest social class. Owned by the state.

Gwishin - Ghost.

Halmeoni - Grandmother.

Hanbok - General term for clothing.

Hanja - Classical Chinese.

Haetae - A creature from Korean folklore with the physical features of a lion, goat, and unicorn.

Hwacha - A fire cart.

Hwando - A traditional Korean sword.

Hyung - Term a younger male uses for an older male that indicates a brotherly bond.

Janggukbap - A dish made with white rice, beef broth, and soy sauce.

Jangseung - Korean totem poles meant to act as village guardians that ward off evil spirits.

Jeogori - Jacket.

Jeongjugan - A large room between the kitchen and the main part of the house.

Jeonmo - An umbrella-shaped hat worn by gisaengs.

Jumo - Female owner of a tavern.

Jurchen - The language of the Jurchen people who lived in eastern Manchuria.

Kongguksu - Soy milk noodle soup.

Ming - Ruling dynasty of China from 1368 to 1644.

Mugunghwa - A type of hibiscus flower that is native to Korea.

Nauri - Lord.

Noona - Term younger boys and men use for an older female that indicates a close bond, such as that of an older sister and a younger brother.

Samchon - Uncle, the brother of one's father.

Sangbang - The main area in a house.

Sangju - Chief mourner and organizer of a funeral.

Soju - A Korean alcoholic beverage.

Sokgot - General term for undergarments.

Sokjeogori - Underjacket.

Sungmo - Aunt, the wife of one's father's brother.

Uinyeo - Female nurse.

Unni - Term a younger female uses for an older female that indicates a sisterly bond.

Wokou - Japanese pirates who raided the coastlines of Korea and China from the 1400s to the 1800s.

Yakbang - Drug store and clinic.

Acknowledgments

My biggest thank you always goes to God for the creativity, energy, time, and passion needed to complete this project. He placed this story in my heart that has allowed me to share a small piece of the beauty of Korean culture, and I am so grateful.

I want to say thank you to my incredible alpha reader, Tiffany Goldman. Your enthusiasm and comments were not just encouraging—they also elevated this story into something I'm so proud of. You are a treasure to know!

I also want to express my gratitude to Amber Lambda for editing the manuscript. Thank you for strengthening my prose with so much grace and insight! You're awesome.

Thank you to my family, especially my husband, who endured question after question over the past several months as this story came together. Contrary to what he would say, more death and fighting isn't always the answer, but I appreciate him helping me brainstorm and pointing out trouble spots in the story. Chin Sun did need to be standing higher than Hyun Soo for that "accidental fall" to work out like I wanted it to.

Thank you to my wonderful ARC team, which included but was not limited to Praise Abraham, Aubrey Ann, Emma Bahnmiller, Jasmine Blakemore, Becky Briggs, Allison Burkhart, Tanvi Chandra, Liz Chapman, Divya, Elizabeth Ervin, Tiffany Ewald, Ebimobo-ere Faith, Kiana Gerhart, Natalia Gonzalez, Melanie Hafer, Ami Jacobs,

Xenobia Mustafa Khan, Kaitlyn Kerns, Samantha Krager, Kristen, Lucy's Library Reviews, Martelize, Pat Martin, Iris Maya, Lindsay Michelle, Patty Moony, Morgan, Iyanu-Oluwa Olorode, Aubrey Ozolins, River Seabrook, Julia Serwaa Owusu gyawu, Storm Shultz, Ridaa Z. Sultan, Susan Thomas, Alice Wang, Candice Yamnitz, and Kitana Zamora.

And thank you to everyone who supported the Kickstarter campaign, which allowed the book to become so much more than it would have been otherwise. This included but was not limited to Amsel, Ashley, Abigail B., Melissa B., Amanda Balter, Kailey Bechtel, Christine Boatwright, Elisabeth Brown, Bryce, Dana C., Gianna Christopher, CopperKettle, Lorien Cord, Alexandra Corrsin, Anna Crockett, Gail Cu, Ash D., Ty Davies, Regina Dawn, Stephanie De Luna, Jes Drew, Amber E., Shae Eckhardt, Sarah Everest, R. M. Everhart, Florentina, Nicole Folsom, Helena Š. George, Tiffany Goldman, Larissa Green, Nolalisse Han, Ilja, Ta-Keia Joi, Samantha Keil, K. Q. Kimler, Belinda Kroll, Jeanette L., Gabrielle Landi, Susan Laspe, Latisha, Ana Lewis, Liana, Christy M., J'aime M., Lexi M., Katherine Malloy, Jessica Manuel, Auntie Meow Meow, Jordan Michalik, Becca Mionis, Moni, Morgan, Dawn Morris, Monica L. Olsen, Polinchka, Emily Pruitt, Amy R. S., Melissa Schwarz, Jimmy Siegel, Madelyn Smith, Scarlett Luna Strange, Rebecca Taba, Tempest, Jason W., Victoria Wash, Ashley Willingham, Toria Wren, and Nicole Wright.

About the Author

Claire Kohler is a North Carolina author with a penchant for rich historical settings, heart-wrenching romance, and dazzling creatures. She writes clean historical romantasy that's immersive, meaningful, and compelling. She is also an editor and tutor. When she's not working, you'll find her chasing her two young children, bingeing Korean dramas with her husband, and leading Bible studies at her church.